Red Was the Midnight

A Novel

Portia Tewogbade

Dedication

Adeniran Akintunde II, Payton Omolewa, and Eliza Apinke, wishing you happiness and longevity. Be kind, be yourself and above all, have faith.

In memory of the 1906 Atlanta Race Riot victims.

A city lay in travail, God our Lord, and from her loins sprang twin Murder and Black Hate. Red was the midnight; clang, crack, and cry of death and fury filled the air...

—W. E. B. Du Bois, "A Litany of Atlanta"

Chapter One

Monday, September 3, 1906

Seventeen-year-old Ruby Norris bit into the towel that was tied across her mouth. "Ah, ah," she moaned as fire zigzagged through her hips. In the thicket of pain, she had no brain or heart, no breasts or buttocks, and no mind or memories. She had no God or soul. Instead of praying as her mother always did, in and out of bad situations, Ruby moaned, "It hurts, Mama. This hurts."

From behind a gauzy veil, her newborn's hazel eyes traveled across a skylight of missing shingles, a cupboard leaning to one side, a fat chair with fingers of stuffing poking out, and a table smeared with green paint. In a far corner of the one-room shack, teeth from a black iron stove glowed crimson with newspaper logs, even though the weather was as hot as the devil's birthday. Thinking her motionless baby was dead, Ruby howled with ferociousness that shook her cabin and scattered the brown thrashers that flittered in the dirt outside the window.

The baby gazed at the washed-out, hovering face of her grandmother, Queen Isabella Redmond, midwife and matriarch of the family. "Jesus," Isabella said breathily. Her pink lower lip, woven with black threads from years of dipping snuff, quivered as she stared at the ghostly baby. The lantern in her hand shook, and light skipped across the bed. When her mind settled, she placed the lantern on the seat of a ladder-back chair that served as a bedside table.

Grabbing the infant by her feet, as she had done with countless chickens down home, Isabella held her upside down and slapped her bottom. A sharp cry cut through air dense with the raw smell of blood. When she tapped the baby's upper lip, the tiny mouth opened into wide grin, displaying tender pink gums.

I'm alive.

Isabella cut and tied the cord and wiped the caul away with a clean cloth. She wrapped her granddaughter in a blanket sewn from flour sacks and, with dexterity developed from dozens of deliveries, deposited her on her mother's breasts.

As Ruby examined her baby's bonnet of light-brown curls and snowy skin, she fought off a shiver. The child's complexion was only newborn stuff, nothing to worry about. A colored baby's true skin tone would show on the tips of her ears and in dark crescents around her fingernails. Ruby had hoped for a child with a face like her husband's—smoky eyes, a nose with a slight hump to give it dignity, and skin like a soft summer evening—everything except his pampered black-and-white moustache. She pulled a lock of hair back from the baby's ear, sighed, and counted ten pale little fingers. When the baby latched on to her breast, Ruby winced. "Sweet flesh of my flesh, bone of my bone," she whispered. "You're lovely…Yes, Lovelee. That's what I'll call you. Your daddy won't care. He wanted a boy."

"And who might the daddy be?" Isabella diced her words into sharp little bits.

The question was insulting, and Ruby mentally waved it away.

Isabella continued to stand over the bed. She pushed back her straw hat with a hand that was missing a little finger, lost in a childhood accident. Puffs of cloudy hair fell to her shoulders, and sweat plastered a flowered dress to her broad back. She had been washing laundry in the back yard when she heard Ruby's screams and ran in thinking the baby wasn't due for two months. Now as her blood-stained hands gripped the chair, she declared, "Look like Beatrice was right. I didn't believe her when she said you was scandalizing yourself on Decatur Street. She told me—"

"Beatrice makes me sick."

"Don't talk that way bout your sister," Isabella said. "She's been trying to help you, with your hard-headed self, ever since we come to Atlanta. Now you gon tell me or not?"

"Ain't nothing to tell." Ruby was glad for once that the only window in the shack was a small, pitiful source of light that didn't show the confusion on her face.

"I taught you better 'n this." Isabella washed the baby and Ruby with clean rags and a bucket of water. "You know better." The harder she scrubbed, the more she badgered, as though the new mother was a small child, not a married woman. Ruby said not a word in reply. "I told you what happened to my mama," Isabella said. "I told you how that white man, my daddy, used her till he used her up. I did my best to learn you how life is. With three gals of my own, I knowed at least one of you would mess up. So when you married Lee with your belly showing, I said, 'OK, what's done is done. Better make the best of it,' now didn't I? This here, though…I didn't expect, and I can't accept.

"I don't blame you much, cause I know some low-down man forced you. Might even be the one who told me, the other day, to get my yellow hind parts off *his* sidewalk. There they was—a gang of them, laughing about hanging that poor colored boy in Norcross—pushing me around."

Ruby hadn't heard about the attack. "Did they hurt you?" she asked, rising for a clearer look at Isabella.

"They wanted that boy, not me." Desperate to believe the story she'd begun to weave, Isabella continued. "I've seen this before. Pretty colored girl like you comes along and some white man grabs her in the dark, just like he would a fat hog. Ain't that what happened? Nine times out of ten, she'll go with him, cause she don't have no choice. If she's married and her man understands these things—he don't agree, mind you, but his hands are tied—he'll at least let it be. And she don't tell nobody what happened, except her mama. Now I want to hear the truth."

Ruby's large eyes narrowed. "Like I said, ain't nothing to tell."

Frustrated by the girl's stubbornness, Isabella grabbed her Bible from the table. Opening it to First Corinthians, she read aloud: "The wife hath not power of her own body, but the husband; and likewise also the husband hath not power of his own body, but the wife. Defraud ye not one the other..." With sweat popping on her brow and palms, she laid the Bible on the bed.

"Take that away. I don't need no more preaching," Ruby said. Isabella had rubbed her down with castor oil that shone on her skin in subtle hues of brown, bronze, crimson, and purple. The girl twisted her plump lips, trying to understand how she had landed in such a mess. Lee was the father; he had to be. Although she had flirted at saloons for drinks, she wasn't like some women, whores, who would lay with anybody for two bits. She was Lee's woman for life.

The grandmother wiped her sweaty face with a rag. "I don't know why I'm asking. Even if I knowed who it was, I couldn't do nothing. But that don't mean it ain't a disgrace."

"My baby ain't no disgrace."

"So what about Lee? What you plan on telling him?"

"Nothing. Ain't nothing to tell."

"You know he ain't the type to look the other way. That man's got a hot temper."

Ruby sighed and kissed the throbbing soft spot on Lovelee's head. "Mama, listen to me. This is Lee's baby, and that's that. By the time he gets out, she'll be brown as a nut from the sun. You know how babies do."

"If they let him go."

"They got to when his time's up, don't they? He's served six months, so that leaves eighteen."

Isabella thought for a moment. "You can tell him she takes atta me," she said, despite the baby's long chin and light eyes that were nothing like hers. "You can say she's a throwback. Babies pop out all the time looking like they granny or gramps. I had a cousin once, that child had one brown eye and one gray. Don't nobody know how it happened." Of Isabella's four surviving children, Ruby was her youngest and favorite. For Ruby she would say anything and do anything. "And if Lee don't talk right bout this baby, I'll raise her down home myself."

Ruby's body curved protectively around Lovelee. "You can't take my baby to Soperton. That's where Rosetta died."

"Don't go dragging my poor dead baby into this." Isabella's voice cracked with anguish. Rosetta was not to be talked about—ever. Everybody knew that.

"I didn't mean no harm." Ruby pressed her lips into a thin line. If only her mother would let things be, if only she would shut her mouth.

Letting things be wasn't in her mother's nature. After a while, Isabella spoke in a choked voice. "This ain't fair. We came to Atlanta for a better life. God knows, it ain't fair."

Ruby stirred on the bed, wanting to reach out to her mother but hesitating, because shame, born with the baby, had become a living thing between them. Isabella was plucking at her nerves, making her remember things she didn't want to—twisting pain, the stink of motor oil, and her hair soaked with rain. Pieces she couldn't fit together, memories that had come right after her sickness.

The sickness showed up without warning last December. After a hard rain, she woke up late that afternoon on the ground outside the door of her shack, her legs and feet encased in stockings of red mud and her hair stuck in wet clumps. Unable to move and with a thumping headache, she couldn't remember how she got there in that condition. A neighbor saw her and banged on the door for Isabella, who ran outside, thinking her daughter was either drunk or crazy. She dragged Ruby inside, away from prying eyes.

It was soon clear that Ruby wasn't drunk. She complained about feeling split wide open. When it rained, headaches and crying fits tortured her. Someone in her head kept screaming, *"There's a tree out there with his name on it."* Her neighbors stayed away, fearing insanity more than "white hats" or the police.

Isabella washed the walls with potash and water, enough to rout demons from hades. Thinking that somebody had put a spell on her baby, she sent for a root worker, who rubbed sweet-smelling oil into Ruby's pores and mumbled with a slippery tongue over her body. Nothing shook the spell.

Beatrice stepped in and said anybody could see her sister was having a nervous breakdown, probably caused by illicit gin. The best thing was to admit Ruby to the state mental hospital. At least at night they would know where she was.

After ordering Beatrice to leave, Isabella fell to her knees beside Ruby's bed and remained there until daybreak, pleading for mercy from the Holy Ghost, the Blessed Savior, the One who can do and undo. The next day, Ruby astonished her by walking to the breakfast table. It rained and she walked outside, laughing with joy.

Isabella stood at the end of the birthing bed as if her feet were nailed to the floor. She cleared her throat to make room for some news. "Your baby had the veil on."

Ruby propped up on a shaky elbow. "She'll live, won't she?"

"Some say the veil is good luck; some say it ain't. But she's bound to know things beyond her years, cause she's got the gift. I knowed a woman whose people came from across the water, somewhere in Africa. She went by the name of Annie to folks, but her real African name, the one her daddy gave her, was Aminata, or so she told us. Old man Gaither owned her from when she was little, and when she was grown enough, she'd come from his place down the road to my mama's cabin, once a year at Christmas. Skinny...what you talking about? Legs like broom straws. Mama fed her yams to fatten her up. When we was freed, Aminata was fifty-eight, a whole year older than I am now, but she took off anyway, running with people going north. Back when I was little, I heard her say she was born with the veil, and it didn't bring her nothing but misery. I guess you can't know what a thing like that will do till you've lived awhile. The future is a secret the good Lord won't let us see, cause in His wisdom, He knows we can't handle it."

Unsettled by her mother's rambling, Ruby looked at her baby's clean face and sighed deeply. If the veil meant anything, it was gone now.

Sweat glistened on Ruby's smooth skin as flames leaped up in the stove. Her thick, coarse hair was matted, and yet there was natural prettiness in the high curve of her forehead and her large eyes. Her lovers—and she had had plenty since she was fourteen—said her eyes were dangerous and might lead to a man's death one day. As her hand searched for a cool spot on the sheet, she smelled onions in her armpits and between her thighs. Wanting to feel clean again, she asked for a real bath in the tin tub.

Isabella said a sponge bath was enough. "Don't let this heat fool you. Your pores still open from having that baby. You could catch pneumonia and be gone just like that," she said, snapping her fingers.

"It happens to plenty of women. Wait a week, let yourself heal."

Annoyed, Ruby shifted her eyes to the wall plastered with pictures of Jack Johnson, Lee's hero. The boxer's muscular build reminded her of Lee, except Johnson was taller and looked meaner. *September 3, 1906, Labor Day,* said a wall calendar from a funeral home. The bed felt crowded, and she put Isabella's Bible on the chair. Her mother would make a note of Lovelee's birth in it, as she had for her children, except for her last born, baby Rosetta.

"Ice!" growled a man in the alley. "Ice! Ten cents a block. Come and git it." Houses like theirs, one-room tar-paper shacks, lined a side of Lydell Alley that ran for blocks in southeastern Atlanta. On the other side of the alley were the back doors of larger shotgun duplexes, their front porches facing Jackson Row, which was unpaved like all thoroughfares in the area. Acrid smoke from chimneys and washtub fires hung in the air, punishing nostrils and burning eyes. Curtains across alley doorways shielded rooms but not secrets. It was as though conversations in one shack had legs that ran to the next and so on, down the line, spreading news. The alley's residents had already heard Ruby had a baby, and something was wrong.

"Mama, are you mad at me?" Ruby asked, fingering embroidered flowers on her gown that Isabella had sewn.

"I guess disappointed is more like it. I told Beatrice to look out for you, and she did her best. But you just had to mess up, didn't you?"

"Beatrice is ashamed of me. She don't want her big-shot friends to know we're related."

"That's not true. She lent y'all money and told Lee to take his time paying her back. She even tried to get you to go to college. Beatrice can be hard sometimes, but she loves family."

Ruby's skin burned with humiliation, which she tended to feel when talk turned to her successful, older sister. "I'm thinking about writing Lee," she said, hoping to change the subject.

"Wait till he comes home…if he ever comes home…then tell him the baby's a throwback, like I said. It's his own fault they locked him up. I told that boy, as plain as I could speak, to stay outta trouble."

"He didn't do nothing. They picked him up for so-called reckless eyeballing. Now you know Lee's got better sense than that. He's coming home, you'll see, and it'll be all right." Ruby spoke in a confident tone she didn't really feel. Lee had been sentenced to the chain gang, where there was a good chance he might perish.

Isabella ran a fingertip across a mole, a tiny drop of honey, on the baby's neck. "I'm happy bout my grandbaby but not your situation. No ma'am, I ain't happy bout it one bit. I'm only staying here, cause you ain't got nobody else."

Ruby squeezed her mother's rough hand.

"That don't mean I'm upholding you in your wrongdoing, missy."

If Ruby could say for sure, if she really knew that she hadn't had had relations with one of the white men who frequented the dives on Decatur Street, she would have argued with her mother, as she had many times about other things. But it was hard to dispute something that wouldn't come together in her head. If she had things straight, she might have told the old woman to mind her own business. Why couldn't she remember anything except *There's a tree out there with his name on it?*? The damn thing ran through her head like the bridge to a bad blues song.

Isabella went to the thumbnail space that served as their kitchen. A jar of bacon grease, a large, waxy rutabaga, and a small sack of cornmeal sat on the table. The pantry shelf above the table was bare. "Before I fix dinner," she said, "I'm a send word to Beatrice and your brother."

"Tell him when I'm stronger. Beatrice, too."

"Your brother might be a deacon, but he leaves passing judgment to the Father."

"Then tell the whole world if you want to." Ruby heard soft snoring and looked down. Lovelee had fallen asleep with her mouth open, and tiny pearls of milk adorned her lips. She then made a silent vow—*my daughter will have a better lifer*—without knowing that Isabella had wished the same for her when she was born.

Before dozing off, Ruby heard the rickety wooden doorsteps squeak under her mother's weight as she lugged the pail of afterbirth outside.

***

Patches of the yard were soupy with mud from a thunderstorm the night before. At the base of an oak tree a few feet from the cabin, Isabella knelt with the sun ironing her back and dug with a bent spoon, stabbing the soft ground into a grave to bury the placenta. She covered it with mud, rocks, and leafy branches to keep away the alley's mangy dogs. If caught in the jaws of a dog, she'd heard old folks say, the placenta would drive the new mother crazy. Then as supplicant as a woman before a cross, she prayed for her daughter, granddaughter, and the baby's father, only if he happened to be Lee Henry Norris. If the father was another man, she asked that open sores would run from his head to his toes and (because she believed in the New Testament as well as the Old) that God would have mercy on his sorry soul.

"Sweeeet peaches! Get em fore they's gone," called a blind woman, who sat on a stool, two doors down. She was stout and shielded her hair from the sun with a flowered headscarf.

Isabella straightened up and shouted, "Morning, Truth. You selling peaches, somebody else selling ice. This place is turning into a regular market."

Orbs of ripe fruit rested in a basket beside Truth. She could tell from the sugary smell that the best of them would make a delicious cobbler or run in juicy streams down the arms of greedy munchers. "That baby done come yet?" she said. "I heard a whole heap of screaming a while back."

"We got us another girl in the family." Isabella walked over, feeling proud all of a sudden.

Truth clapped her hands. "I'll be there directly, soon as my daughter comes from school."

"Be sho you do."

Truth was the first neighbor Isabella met when she arrived with her daughters. In the alley, with people going in and out of one another's shacks to gossip and borrow a little sugar, Isabella thought Truth was particularly friendly. At forty, her friend already had gray hair and wisdom that made up for sightless eyes.

A teenage boy posed on the steps of the house next to Truth, cigarette glowing between his fingers and a brown stingy-brim hat cocked back on his head.

"Hey, you, Charlie." Isabella said his name as everyone did—*Char-LEE*. "How come you not at work?"

"Barbershop's closed for the holiday, Miss Isabella."

"Then run tell Miss Freeman her sister done had a baby. Tell her to call her brother, too." Nobody in the alley could afford one of the new telephones, so messages had to be carried in notes or in the mouths of boys like Charlie.

"Yessum." Charlie dropped his cigarette and stomped it with his right foot. His left was twisted, shriveled from birth. He trudged over to the women. "Morning, Miss Truth," he said, grinning and taking off his hat.

"Humph," she responded, and the boy's face fell.

"Be careful, Charlie," Isabella said. "They talking about lynching.

Done lynched one already, ain't no telling who's next."

"Not me, Miss Isabella. I don't truck with no white ladies."

Isabella gave him a dime for the streetcar, and Charlie limped from the alley to Old Wheat Street, a muddy lane that sliced across it.

"Smoking those nasty cigarettes," Truth said and pushed her tongue against the wad of snuff in her lower lip. "If that shiftless thing don't stay away from my Carol, he'd better. Next thing you know, he'll give her something I don't want her to have." She worried that her fourteen-year-old daughter, a tall girl with a round, pretty face, might make the same mistake she had—pregnant and no husband.

Isabella followed Truth's hands sorting peaches. "Give the boy a chance. Charlie ain't bad, just mannish."

"They say they gon open a high school for colored one of these days, and I want my gal to be ready. This ain't like slavery. Better days are coming, sure as I'm sitting here. We got Mr. Booker T. Washington talking for us."

"Don't worry bout Carol. I bet she'll wind up teaching like my Beatrice."

"If she do, I'll be mighty happy." Truth sensed there was more on Isabella's mind. "You say everything at the house is all right?"

Isabella struggled to keep her voice steady. "Ruby disappointed me, Truth. I raised my daughters right. Ask anybody, and they'll tell you 'Isabella's gals are good.'"

"I recollect when y'all came here. Moved in in the middle of the night, just as quiet as can be and been that way ever since."

Remembering, Isabella snorted. "I bet they still looking for us down home, old man Callahan and them. After my husband ran away, we slipped off his place one by one, and the ones left behind worked twice as hard so Callahan wouldn't catch on. He trusted me cause I'd been on his place since I married, near about worked myself to death. His boys passed the bushes me and Ruby was hiding in the night we took off, coming to Atlanta. And if they'd seen us, they would've stopped us, for sure. That old man's probably still going to the cabin every day, just a calling my name like he's calling chickens." As she tried to laugh, her lower lip trembled, and she sobbed. "Truth, what did I do to make Ruby turn out so bad?"

"Well, she's always been a little grown for her age. Kinda womanish, if you don't mind my saying. But tell me what she did."

"The baby ain't Lee's."

"What? She said that?"

"She didn't have to. I got eyes." Isabella wanted to tell Truth the whole thing, and yet the words were too shameful even to share with her best friend. How could she say Ruby had soiled their family's reputation by lying with a white man? How could she say her beloved baby daughter had behaved like a tramp? Let Truth hear it from the alley's residents, who would be chattering soon enough, if they weren't already.

Truth swiped away buzzing flies. "I guess you know what you talking bout. She's your daughter. To me, all babies just bout the same. They eat, sleep, poop, and cry. It's funny, I could tell Carol's cry from anybody's, even if she was on the third floor of my daddy's rooming house, and I was on the front porch. Didn't you say mama and baby are well?"

"They fine, thank the Lord."

"Then what more can you ask for? I'm sick and tired of hearing bout women dying in childbirth. Having a baby these days is like going to court; you don't know how you gonna come out. Soon as I heard Ruby hollering, I thought about my sister's gal back home in Covington and got nervous. Now that was a wild one. I hate it, though, cause she bled to death having a boy. He died, too. Poor thing."

"If his children forsake my law, and walk not in my judgments…
then I will visit their transgression with the rod and their iniquity
with stripes."

"Whoa. Listen to you quoting scripture right off the top of your
head, like a preacher." Truth leaned forward. "So how do you know
the baby ain't Lee's? Don't it look like him?"

"I don't want to talk about it no more."

"Suit yourself. When it comes to other folk's business, I say let
every tub sit on its own bottom."

"That's the best way to be."

Isabella lumbered back to her shack with Truth's gift of a fat
peach. The iceman was gone, Truth had quit touting fruit, and the
alley was quiet. In a few hours, day laborers, porters, and maids would
return to their homes and exchange places with night workers,
stumbling out to jobs downtown.

Isabella opened the shack's door. Lovelee lay like a pink magnolia
flower in the bend of her sleeping mother's arms. At the sight of the
baby's rosy cheeks, she prayed aloud, "Oh, God, my Father, I leave
this mess in your hands. Cause you know I did the best I could with
this headstrong gal of mine."

Awakened by her grandmother's bitter prayer, Lovelee's face
darkened in a scowl.

Chapter Two

Anybody who had heard of Soperton, Georgia, a village south of Atlanta, but didn't really know much about the place, might think cotton and more cotton. They wouldn't have heard that in a tiny smudge on the map were: swaying pines and shotgun houses leaning way back on moldy brick pilings; a creek that slithered along, separating the shotguns from the expensive homes of wealthy white farmers; fields with collard greens as pretty as flowers; fat red-meat yams; and beans climbing trellises without end. They wouldn't believe that ignorance ran as deep and treacherous as a sinkhole or that poverty made stomachs talk to backbones and children stand naked in dirt yards on cool mornings. How would they know what drove hungry women to commit desperate acts with knock-kneed men and how come preachers in long black coats could lead whole congregations to pray for heaven or at least anywhere north of the living hell that was Soperton?

That was what happened to Isabella's husband, Elijah Redmond, on the evening of the last day in 1895. He took off, headed for Detroit, and wound up in Chattanooga when his money ran out. With his peripatetic history, nobody in his family—not even Isabella—missed him until he was long gone. Isabella knew the reason he left but wouldn't say. She sat in front of the fireplace, rocking in a chair and dodging frantic questions from her children. Old man Callahan, worried about cotton that would need tending, asked how long she expected Elijah to be away this time. "He'll be back directly, boss, and if not, you got me and the children," said Isabella, just up from childbirth. She had buried her infant under a tall tree—an old oak that stretched its heavy arms around the clearing that was their front yard.

None of it made sense to their only son, Elijah Jr., who was better known as Fat and for a good reason—he carried well over three hundred pounds on a medium frame. The extra weight caused him to walk leaning backward, so that his stomach came at you first. His sister, Beatrice, sometimes called him Red because of the natural tint of his hair, but Fat was the name that stuck. Sixteen when old Eli left home, Fat decided it was either find the old man and bring him back or watch his mama drown in a flood of grief. He left her at home weeping and talking to her dead baby.

Fat stopped first at the house of a Soperton conjure man, Big Chief, a father figure to Eli, who had not known his true father. Word in their hamlet was that Big Chief had murdered five men at five different times in his career as a hustler in Atlanta and had served a total of five years in prison. He left Atlanta for Soperton before the sheriff could arrest him for killing the fifth guy, a teenager with loose lips and slick gambling hands. The main reason for Big Chief's light sentences, everyone said, was he stuck to killing colored people.

"I ain't seen hide nor hair of your daddy, since I don't know when," Big Chief said.

"But he must've said something." Fat eyed the old man's shaggy teeth and the hoodoo scribbles on a brass bracelet he wore.

The conjurer shook his egg-shaped head and picked at a long hair growing from his nostril. "How long you say he's been gone?"

"Two months, give or take."

The conjurer's eyes stretched wide in surprise. "And you just now looking?"

"We thought he'd be back before now." Although it occurred to Fat that his father might have somehow crossed the conjurer and become his sixth victim, the old man's hooded eyes gave nothing away. "You think maybe somebody killed him?"

"Naw, he ain't dead. If he was, I'd know. Eli and me think the same, talk the same. Haw! I could tell when he was upset better 'n anybody. I do remember him saying he's got a cousin in Chattanooga, a woman named Florette. Now maybe she knows where he at." Big Chief pulled a white cloth, the size of a quilting piece, from a dresser drawer, sprinkled on drops of sickly sweet oil from a bottle, and passed it to Fat. "Here, boy. Put this in your pocket. It'll take you straight to your daddy, wherever he is."

The oil's scent made the boy's head swim with visions of his father in a city near mountains. "Must be Chattanooga," he thought when he returned to his senses. He left Big Chief and went home for the family's last two dollars to buy a train ticket.

Fat arrived in Chattanooga the next day, which was sunny and unusually warm for early March. His face and clothes had turned black from engine soot blowing on the colored car. He washed up in a cup of water given to him by an old lady standing in her yard. She told Fat she knew only one woman named Florette in Chattanooga and gave him the address of a rooming house near the train tracks. On his walk there, dread of what he might find drove his heart into a dreadful arrhythmia. His father liked to play with women, and this woman, Florette, might be Elijah's lover instead of his cousin.

When Fat walked up to the address, Elijah was in a chair on the front porch, a pipe of strong peach tobacco lolling between his lips. The old man was thinner, as weather-beaten looking as the house, and his face wore a scared look the boy had not seen before.

In the fields, Eli had been old man Callahan's "colored boy," but at home nothing happened without his father's say-so. One wrong move and the old man would beat Fat with a belt buckle, all the while daring him to "try me again." Afterward Isabella would bake fried sweet-potato pies for the boy to devour under her soft eyes.

Fat stopped at the bottom of the rooming-house steps. "Daddy?"

Elijah blinked like a man in handcuffs, as if he couldn't figure out, to save his life, how he had been found. "That you, Fat?" he said, peering down. "What you doing up here?"

"I ought to ask you the same thing."

Eli waved the boy to the porch, which was worn smooth from hundreds of footsteps. "Sit here awhile. You come by train? You must be thirsty." In a sudden fit of hospitality, Eli grinned and pulled the chewed-up pipe stem from his mouth. "I see that old engine dusted up your face and clothes pretty good. Florette," he hollered at the screen door, "bring some tea. We got company."

"Eli, you sho do like calling my name," said a husky female voice from inside the house. "Who is it now?"

"My boy. And don't put too much sugar in that tea. He's watching his weight."

Fat's face flamed with embarrassment. "I didn't come to Chattanooga to drink tea, Daddy. I came to bring you home. Mama's going crazy."

"Well, she got a whole lot to go crazy about if you ask me."

A large woman with coarse black hair that stood straight up appeared at the screen door. She poked her head out. "What's your name, boy? You the one they call Fat?"

"You know I ain't got but one son," Eli said, and Fat thought he heard a hint of the old querulousness in his voice. "Bring the tea, woman. My boy's thirsty."

She left, complaining that Eli had a lot of nerve ordering her around in her own house.

"It's going to take her a day and a half to make two cups of tea," Eli said. "You mark my words. That woman sho knows how to frustrate people."

"She ain't the only one," Fat thought, because he hadn't ridden in a filthy train and walked miles in Chattanooga for a load of horseshit. "Daddy, we want to know what you're doing up here. Is somebody with you? When you coming home? Mary Alice is running buck wild, acting like she's grown. She says she ain't, but I think she's doing it with this boy named Jonah. She won't listen to Mama or nobody. How could you just walk off like that from your family?"

"Look, boy. Stop whining like a gal." Eli stabbed the air with his pipe to punctuate his point. "Your sister's bullheaded, like your mama. Gonna do things her way like she's a man, which she ain't. Y'all don't need me no more. Your mama's done lost her mind, carrying on, making decisions like I'm not even in the house."

"What decisions? Mama's crying her head off."

Elijah didn't say what the decisions were. Instead, he presented reasons for leaving his family on a sharecropper's patch with only six dollars and forty-three cents. He claimed the plantation owner had run him off, because he spoke up and said the account book overcharged him for furnishings. He said sharecropping was just another name for slavery, if you wanted to know the truth. If they hadn't kilt Mr. Lincoln, it wouldn't be that way. Instead they got that rascal, President Johnson, and all the rest after him. Colored man didn't have a chance, going or coming. He had to leave if he was going to be free, and so forth and so on. Elijah even blamed the weather, because it had snowed two inches the week he left. As if it never snowed in Tennessee.

Elijah was spinning excuses. Fat could see it in the way he kept wiping his mouth with a rag. He couldn't understand why his daddy—who had been a force in their family and never took a whole lot from Callahan or anybody else—felt the need to lie. "When I get home," Fat said, "I have to tell Mama the truth, not a story, Daddy. You coming with me or not?"

"Did your crazy mama send you here?"

"No, suh. She just wants you to come home." *Why does he keep calling Mama crazy? He ain't said nothing to make a nickel's worth of sense.*

"She knows I ain't coming, and she knows why. What's between your mama and me is between us. It ain't none of your business. Now put that in your pipe and smoke it," Eli pulled hard on his pipe, snickered at his little witticism, and hollered, "Florette, where in the world is that tea?"

"It'll be there when it gets there," Florette yelled back.

Fat frowned at the small man in front of him and jammed his fists in his pockets. They hadn't fought since he grew tall enough to eat salt off the old man's head, but Elijah's arrogance and hints about dark secrets made him want to holler. "Forget the tea, Daddy," he said in a voice thick with anger. "I'm grown, Beatrice, too, so I ain't asking for us. But Mary Alice and Ruby still need training. If you don't come home and see bout them, if you don't care bout Mama no more, then I can't do nothing bout that. But every father's gonna be old one day, and guess what? He'll need his family. You mark my words."

"Boy, do you know who you talking to? I don't care how grown you get. I can still knock you in the middle of next week." Eli half rose from his chair.

Furious, Fat was already down the porch steps, on his way back to the train. He had heard Isabella say that Eli would come home when he could stand to look at her again and he wondered. What in the world did she mean?

20

When Fat was on the next block, Eli said, more to himself than to Florette, who returned with cups of tea on a tray, "Maybe I'll go home one day, God willing, but not while that evil woman is alive." Although he knew exactly why he left his family, nothing and nobody could make him say it out loud. Whenever he thought about it, which was too often, he felt like a man with his insides scooped out.

**

The Redmond cabin in Soperton was at the end of a narrow path that cut through lines of pine trees. When Fat opened the door, Isabella rushed forward and stopped. Her face turned ash white, as soon as she saw Elijah wasn't with him.

"You're better off without Daddy," Fat said. The old man was dead to him—finished—not even worth the salt in his bread.

He looked at a wedding picture of his parents on the mantel above the smoke-blackened stone fireplace. A thinly sculpted, brown man with sad eyes, Eli looked odd standing next to his chunky wife. Because he was not yet wise about the ways of people in love, Fat shook his head and wondered why his mother wanted a man, who didn't want her.

"Things just got too much for your daddy," Isabella said. "No money, no food. We didn't have no way out, and he couldn't stand it. He ain't evil—he's just a man, who has his pride."

"Stop making excuses for him," Beatrice said, pursing her lips in a chair on the other side of the room. "He's a low-down trifling nigger."

"Don't you use that nasty word in my house, missy. He's still your father," said Isabella. She sat in the family's only sturdy chair, an old rocker. The other chairs had wobbly legs, rag seats, and squeaked like mice in the walls.

"Let him go," Mary Alice said, looking up from a broken mirror propped against a jar on the dining table. "He didn't treat you the way a man's supposed to." She was straightening her curly hair with a hot iron, and the half that was finished lay like a red curtain next to her face. As the iron sizzled, the brown stench of burning hair permeated the two-room cabin.

"And what do you know about men, with your fast self?" Fat asked, still simmering because he had walked up on her kissing Jonah from the farm next door.

Beatrice turned up her nose. "She doesn't know a thing about men or anything else. She won't go to school and she won't work right in the fields, because she thinks all she needs is that light skin. I'm sorry to tell you, sister dear, you're as colored as the rest of us, and everybody knows it."

"Quit picking on me," Mary Alice said, putting down her straightening iron. "You think you're smart, a big-time teacher, just because you read books. They won't let you teach with that little bit of learning. Shoot, we already got us a teacher, and she graduated from Fisk University." Mary Alice stuck out her tongue at her sister.

Observing from a pallet on the floor, six-year-old Ruby stuck out her tongue, too.

"Soperton isn't my last stop," Beatrice said. "I'm going to Atlanta and leave y'all down here rolling in this mess. Just watch me."

Isabella pulled herself up from the chair. "Y'all driving me stone crazy. Mary Alice, put that hot iron away and plait your hair right back like I had it. Lord, I don't know what's to become of these womanish gals I got. Sometimes I wonder why I got a womb, cause it done brought me so much trouble." Tears flowed unabated down her cheeks that were already scarlet from weeping.

Although accustomed to their mother's anguish about Eli, the girls felt responsible this time and gathered around. Mary Alice kissed Isabella's forehead. "It'll be all right, Mama. He's coming back. You know how Daddy is when he gets hot about something. He'll cool off and come back."

Fat stomped outside to the field, which laid in wait for planting. Dried plants crunched under his feet, and leftover bits of cotton stuck to his clothes as he headed to the crimson dirt road that ran for miles before there was another house. He walked with his hands in his pockets under clouds of dust that turned his old, cracked brogans red. He was now the man of the family, and it was up to him to do something. Living as they did was like trying to escape from quicksand. The more they worked, the more they owed to Captain Callahan. They hadn't paid him for the last season's furnishings, and soon they would owe him for seeds, flour, salt, and sugar for the next planting. And the next. Fat didn't want to wind up like his father, spinning in circles and running away.

For years, the family had gotten letters from Aunt Viola, inviting them to stay with her in Atlanta until they could get on their feet. She was Isabella's half-sister, whose father left Georgia right after the war. "I'm on my way to the big time in New York *City* and real freedom," he bragged.

That night Fat wrote his aunt a letter, telling her Elijah was gone and they were having hard times. They had no money and very little food, other than canned vegetables, and their mother was acting funny. He didn't say crazy, which was what he feared, because Aunt Viola might withdraw her invitation, rather than have a nutty woman in her house. He mailed the letter the next day and received a reply in a week. He could come to Atlanta and stay as long as he needed to, Viola wrote. Once he was established, the rest of the family could follow, one by one. She knew people, big shots, who would help him get on his feet. With the letter in hand, he kissed his mother and slipped away under the tarp of a farmer's wagon to avoid night riders, who were paid to catch runaway sharecroppers. He rode to the county line and from there, made it the rest of the way on foot, sleeping in fields and eating raw sweet potatoes on the five-day journey.

When Fat reached Viola's house in an Atlanta slum called Buttermilk Bottom, a tall man in overalls, bald and about sixty, opened the door. "Who you?" he asked. His bleak eyes with brown sclera swept across the boy. Fat said he was from down home and asked for Viola. "She's in back," the man said and stepped aside to let him in. A girl of sixteen or so sat with an open book at a table near a potbellied stove. Her well-tended black hair was in two braids that hung down her back. She looked up with a flat expression when Fat walked in.

"I guess you're Isabella's boy Viola's been talking about," the man said. "I'm Blue, Viola's man, and this here's our daughter, Harriet. She's going to be a doctor."

Harriet's head, which was too large for her slender neck, bent again over the book.

Fat dropped the Croker sack holding his clothes, and Blue waved him to a green easy chair that looked new and matched the rug. It was Fat's first time in a room that did not have a dirt floor. He sat uneasily on the edge of the chair while Blue went for Viola.

"Vy, get out here," Blue yelled as he walked. "You got company."

The aroma of fried chicken and peach cobbler, his favorite foods, teased Fat's empty stomach and it growled.

Harriet looked up for a moment, frowned, and went back to reading and stroking her braids.

Fat shifted on the chair. It had not occurred to him that Viola might have a family who wouldn't welcome a country cousin. If he had known about her rough-talking husband and standoffish daughter, he wouldn't have come.

Viola appeared in the doorway, wiping her hands on an apron.

She was dark and taller than his mother—slimmer, too. Fat thought she was as plain as her faded housedress.

"Junior," she said, "I'm so glad to finally lay eyes on you."

Fat thought he heard Harriet snicker at that. "Uh, I'm Fat, Auntie, that's what they call me at home."

Blue walked in. "Vy, now you know we ain't got but one bedroom."

Viola scowled. "Ain't you late for work?"

"One bedroom, that's all." Blue slammed out the door.

With a nervous laugh, Viola walked over and patted Harriet's hair. "How's the homework coming, honey?"

"OK," Harriet said, turning a page.

"She's first in her class at the university."

"It's not a university yet, Mama. They just call it that."

"Well, it's more than I had." Viola turned to Fat. "So Eli finally ran off, huh?"

Fat hesitated, his eyes on Harriet. The girl looked smug with her little nose in the air. "Something like that," he said.

"Can you check on the chicken, Harriet, baby?" Viola said. "I think it's burning."

"No, it's not."

"I said check it—now."

Harriet stood on thin legs under narrow hips and sashayed out of the room.

Viola shook her head. "Just like her mama—smart, headstrong—but she don't get away with nothing round me."

"Oh, I thought she was yours."

"Blue's, but she might as well be mine. I raised her." Viola's sharp tone stopped further questioning. "Now, tell me what happened."

He told her about his mother's unraveling and how worried he was to leave her.

"Your mother and me, we were close growing up," Viola said.

"We slept in the same bed and shared clothes, what little we had." She said she wanted Isabella and the children to come up all at once but didn't have the space.

They decided Fat would work awhile and send for Beatrice. Mary Alice would follow, then Ruby and Isabella, if she would come. Fat said his mother had talked about staying in Soperton to wait for Eli.

"That's just like my sister—weak," Viola said. "And she's a fool for that man, always has been."

It stung Fat to hear his mother spoken of that way, but common sense told him to swallow the retort on the tip of his tongue. He needed a place to live and rebuking his aunt wouldn't help.

He soon found that Viola's harsh demeanor hid tender ways. She fed him that evening—crisp, moist fried chicken, greens cooked with fatback, thick cornbread, and cobbler—his first real meal since he left home. He ate with his fingers, country-style, ignoring the knife and fork next to his plate. Harriet and Viola exchanged amused glances but said nothing. After dinner, Viola put a plate in the oven for Blue and spread a pallet for Fat on the kitchen floor near the back door. "I thought Blue said..." began Fat.

"He always says that," Viola snapped. "He said it when Harriet came. Now he acts like she was his idea. I hope you don't mind sleeping on the floor. Harriet has the settee in the front room."

He glanced at Harriet, expecting more of her sardonic snickering, and was surprised to see a sly smile playing on her lips. *Hmm, there might be something more here than a pallet on the floor for me.* He covered his own smile with a quick nod to his aunt.

Fierce March winds on the other side of the door woke Fat during the night, and later he heard Blue taking food from the oven and sliding into a chair at the table. Listening to him smack and belch, Fat pretended to be asleep. Blue had struck him as a man who didn't much care for conversation.

Just after daylight, Fat stood on the back porch smoking a pipe, a habit picked up from Eli, and gazed at the yard that was fenced with cast-off pieces of wood. Large pines, oaks, and maples crowded out the sun and any chance of grass growing in the bare soil. The silence offered no early-morning field shouts, no mules fighting their harnesses. The quiet dumbfounded him, and he wondered where everybody was. It was already half past six, according to the kitchen clock, and back home, the chickens were fed and his family was working the fields before the midday sun could claw their backs. City folks had to be mighty lazy to stay in bed past sunup. He stretched and sat on the top step of the porch. He needed a job, but the only thing he knew was cotton and how to fix farm tools. Eli had taught him, and he had been a patient teacher. "You doing good, boy. Just one more time and you'll have it." Fat thought he'd find work, maybe with a blacksmith. Even a small job would be better than nothing.

He saw the kitchen light come on and killed the pipe ashes with his foot, thinking Viola was up and wouldn't approve of him smoking. He walked in as she was taking flour and lard from a shelf next to the stove. When he closed the door, she looked up. "I thought that was you out there," she said, smiling. "You must've got up with the chickens, like people do down home."

"Something like that."

Fat tensed against the door and followed her strong hands kneading dough, which she patted into cathead biscuits in a pan. Bent over the table with her bottom lip hanging down, she reminded him of his mother. He decided to plow right in. "Aunt Viola, I need a job. I got fifty cents in my pocket, which won't feed me, let alone Mama and the girls."

Viola straightened up and tied her head rag tighter, as she studied the large, earnest boy. "You think I don't know that? Blue and me done already talked. You got a job working for him, if you know how to handle yourself."

Fat's body relaxed. "Oh, I can handle myself all right," he said, keeping his voice confident. "What kind of work?"

Viola slammed the pan of biscuits into the oven and turned to lock eyes with him. "You're mighty young."

"I'm old enough. Be seventeen real soon."

"Some people got holes in their mouths, can't keep nothing. You that kind?"

"Heck no, Aunt Viola."

She put away the flour and lard and wiped the table. "I've been studying you, boy, and it seems to me you're in too big of a hurry. Slow down. I know you want a job and you need one. But don't try to rush things. These ain't no country folks you're dealing with up here. They as slick as greased lightning."

"Yes, ma'am." Fat could see she didn't trust him, and he didn't blame her, because he trusted no one except his mother. There was a girl back home, Sarah, whom he liked well enough and slept with when she let him, but he didn't confide in her. Although Viola and Blue were family, he didn't really know them, and they didn't know him.

Viola finally made up her mind. "Blue's in the rackets, mostly numbers, and a little whiskey, too. He needs a runner."

"Well, he's got one right here." Fat puffed up. This was the big time—no sweeping, toting, and fetching. He was going to do a man's job. The liquor side of the business wouldn't be a problem. He and Eli had helped another sharecropper, a white man from the mountains, run liquor into Soperton and other hamlets. Eli had made Fat swear to tell nobody, not even Isabella. The boy had heard about numbers, how people in Atlanta played them for pennies, a dime or two bits mostly, hoping to hit three random numbers in order or out of order in some cases. He wished he knew more.

Around one that afternoon, hours after Viola and Harriet left the house, Blue stumbled into the kitchen with sleep in his eyes. From the bit of dried slobber at the corner of his mouth, Fat saw the sleep witches had ridden him good that night, and he was nasty enough to leave it. He wore white long johns that showed where his thing was and no shoes. When he walked past Fat in the kitchen, he smelled slightly sour, and the boy turned up his nose.

Fat wanted Blue to know he preferred the whiskey side of the business. "I've been running whiskey since I was eleven," he lied. "That's six years of hauling some of the best stuff in the state." It had been only three years since his father took him on his first run.

"Well, experience counts in my business, like anything else. It's for men, not boys," Blue said, scratching his behind. He went to the stove for syrup and biscuits, which he slathered with gobs of butter, all the while keeping his back to Fat. "My business makes me independent in this town. People know old Blue's got money. They know I don't take shit from nobody, which is why I got money in the first place. Most of these colored boys, with they brooms and mops, don't have two cents to rub together. They ain't men—they's boys, who can't take care of they own self, let alone family. The average colored man is busy respecting the law, and it don't get him shit."

Fat liked what he heard and wanted Blue's kind of success.

Blue sucked syrup from his dried-twig fingers. The middle finger on one hand was bent as if it had been broken and never properly reset. "One thing—and remember this—I don't play around. If you mess up, I'll forget you're Vy's nephew and bust your head wide open. I don't like slick motherfuckers."

"You don't have to worry about me, Uncle Blue."

He put Fat to washing dishes and carrying out trash at his dive, called a lunchroom, on Decatur Street, a front for his main business of selling illegal liquor in jars from behind the counter. The place jumped from late afternoon until a cop rapped on the window with a nightstick around three in the morning and customers cleared out—fast. All night, women with ironed hair and lipstick-slick mouths and guys with big cigars poured into chairs at the tables. Mesmerized by glitter, profanity, and bragging, Fat kept his eyes open and his mouth shut. He watched how Blue quietly took liquor orders, slipping jars in brown paper bags across the counter and putting his hand over each customer's money before sliding it into his pocket.

After a month of standing up to his elbows in Octagon Soap and hot water, washing dried-on food from plates, Fat asked Viola, because he was afraid of Blue, "What happened to the money-making job?"

"It's coming," she said. "Rome wasn't built in a day."

Fat learned Blue was a cautious man, who studied a person the way gamblers study the roll of dice. He grunted when Fat talked, but all the time he was observing, seeing how the boy stacked up against other help in the lunchroom. Gradually, starting with an hour or two before midnight when the guitar player had his buzz on and the cop was dozing through his watch, Blue let the boy sell drinks and take numbers from a few trusted customers. From there, Fat went to unloading the liquor wagon and going on runs to a still deep in the Decatur woods. He kept his eyes on the action and thought hard about ways to make a few bucks for himself. Imagining himself as the boss of a similar operation and a big shot among the hustlers he met, he placed moonshine orders for his uncle and for himself, secret ones that he sold on the side and pocketed the money. Although Blue was good to him in his snarly way, a man had to do what he could to make it, and Fat intended to make it.

He soon saved enough to rent a room and send for Beatrice. In two years, he owned a lunchroom on Peters, between a Chinese laundry and a cathouse. Harriet, who had become his mistress, said it was just a start, nothing to get excited about. But to Fat, it was as grand as the finest establishment in the city because it was his.

Along the way he met Zenobia, a tall, redbone woman from Mississippi, who ran a catering business with her mother and understood that her customers sometimes needed "shine" to go with their pig-ear sandwiches and oxtails. Fascinated by her swaying hips and big, brown eyes begging him not to quote too high a price for his whiskey, Fat wanted her in his bed. He chased and she slowed down, because she was twenty, already on the cusp of being an old maid, and Fat was her type of man—a hustler, who knew the importance of making money. They married for love and business. Their wedding was featured on the society page of *The Independent*, the community newspaper.

"I'm a man," Fat said at their reception. "If anybody says different, you tell them Fat say they a lie." He was drunk and very happy. In spite of his prosperous appearance in a finely cut dark suit and soft leather boots, in spite of his thick moustache with curved wings and the business he owned, he knew nobody would assume he was a man. He had to tell them.

******

On the afternoon of Lovelee's birth, the phone rang in Fat's house as he was opening his eyes. He had had it installed only the week before and wasn't used to the harsh jangling. "Damn," he said and ran to grab it from the wall in the hall. "What?" he said into the receiver.

"It's me," the woman on the other end said. "What are you so mad about? Zenobia didn't cook last night?"

It was Beatrice, the last person Fat wanted to talk to before he had his head together. He had cleared a hundred dollars in profit the night before and drank too much whiskey to celebrate. "Don't worry about my wife. What's JC doing on your end, still talking about going back to Africa?" Fat chuckled. Beatrice's husband was obsessed with all things African. "And why you calling so early? Did somebody die?"

"It's one in the afternoon, sleepyhead. Mama said Ruby had a baby girl this morning."

"They doing all right, her and the baby?" He tried to sound concerned, even though to him having a baby wasn't anything to worry about. He had seen dogs do it, a few cows, too.

"As far as I know. I think Mama wants us to come over. I'm going now to get it out of the way. Can you pick me up?"

"You better hire a carriage."

"But you live right around the corner. Come on, Fat."

"I don't have time. Do you know how much money I can make tonight? Folks drinking and eating like it's the last holiday." He heard clicking on the party line that he shared with two neighbors. "Who's eavesdropping on this damn phone?" he said. The clicking stopped, and he figured Lena Walton down the street had hung up. "Zee has so many orders she's got to hire help. I don't have time to stand around grinning at no baby who don't know she's in the world. I've got to get to work or my crew will steal me blind. Tell Mama I'll be there as soon as I can. How's she doing, anyway?"

"Don't ask me. Ruby put me out the last time I was there."

Fat wasn't ready to take sides in the longstanding war between his sisters. He heard his wife singing a gospel song in the kitchen and smelled her smothered pork chops. It was time to get off the phone. "Look, Beatrice, I've gotta go." He put the receiver on the hook and peeped between the curtains that separated the front room from the kitchen. Zenobia was turning over chops on the stove. His young sons, Elijah III and Ethan, were at the table drawing with crayons on brown paper. He tiptoed back to the phone and asked the operator for a number.

"Who's this?" Harriet sounded as if the call had interrupted something important. She was working as a science teacher at Morris Brown College and would soon leave for medical school in Washington, DC.

Fat whispered, "It's me. I can't meet you. My sister just had a baby."

Harriet sucked air through her teeth, a habit she knew he disliked. "And so? Your sister had a baby, not you. Why do you have to cancel our date?"

"Listen, girl, I ain't got time to argue with you." He thought he heard something and, from the corner of his eye, checked the curtain, which wasn't moving. Zenobia was still in the kitchen with the children. "I gotta go."

"So when then?"

"This weekend. I'll let you know."

"Uh-huh. What about your wife? You bringing her, too?"

Fat held the receiver to his ear without speaking. He heard a click. If nosey Lena was eavesdropping again, she would spread news about his affair all over Brownsville.

"Eli, baby, are you still there?" Only Harriet called him Eli. "I was just playing."

"Yeah. Like I said, maybe this weekend."

Fat didn't know how the affair had lasted for so long. He had a devoted wife, children, and a good life, yet here he was—a replica of his two-timing father. Had Harriet seduced him, or was it the other way around? He couldn't remember much, except it started with innocent teasing while he lived with Viola. He discovered Harriet had a rich sense of humor hidden behind snappy comebacks. She was smart, not in a street sense, but in the way of a woman who read books, and his resentment of her turned to admiration for her intellect and ambition. By the time he moved out, they had been sleeping together for a while, and their affair didn't end when he married. It grew more intense, causing him to lie to Zenobia and be away from his sons too much. Both he and Harriet knew it wasn't going anywhere. He didn't want a wife with a sharp tongue, and she didn't want an uneducated husband, no matter how successful in business. He was in it for the best sex he'd ever had, and she wanted excitement, he figured, from involvement with a married man.

It was as sordid a situation as any and twice as dangerous as most. If Blue didn't find out Fat was shagging his daughter and bust him up, then Zenobia might. After meeting Zenobia at a family dinner, Harriet told Fat that, in her "estimation," his wife would be hell to deal with if she discovered their relationship. He'd tried to break it off dozens of times, but Harriet was like whiskey in his blood, spinning him out of control.

He had dinner later that afternoon with his family, and even helped Zenobia prepare an order of biscuits and ribs for a client. "How nice," she said and rewarded him with a deep kiss. Before leaving for work, he made love to his wife. Her birthday was coming in October, and he thought about buying a fox stole and something silky blue, her favorite color. Expensive gifts that she deserved, gifts he needed to control his conscience, which wouldn't leave him alone.

Chapter Three

After Beatrice talked to Fat, she returned to her kitchen where a sour-cream pound cake, her specialty, was baking.

Now that she had passed the message on to her brother, it was time to get busy. She washed flour from her hands and put the cake on a rack to cool. It was midafternoon, enough time for a visit to Ruby's before dark. She rushed about getting dressed, pausing to look out of the bedroom window as shirtless JC pushed a creaky mower across their front lawn. At forty, he was still lean with smooth, ebony skin that he liked to show off. She looked closer and spotted Lena Walton ogling from her front porch across the street. Beatrice ran down the stairs with a shirt for her husband.

"Satisfied?" JC asked, buttoning up.

"Somebody better tell Lena to keep her wall eyes on her side of the street."

JC's laughter roared as Beatrice strutted back inside.

She rented a carriage to Ruby's house, which was near the center of town, miles away from Brownsville. The journey took almost an hour over bumpy, unpaved roads bordered by hills of ripe garbage, dumped from affluent, white neighborhoods. She rode with a lacy handkerchief against her nose and urged the driver to hurry. He let her down at the Wheat Street entrance to Lydell Alley, which he wouldn't enter. "End of the line, lady. Too many cutthroats in there," he said. With bags of gifts on her arm, she waded through a torrent of familiar odors— mullet fish frying, hair smoking under hot irons, and outhouses—that reminded her of the depressing year she lived in the alley with her mother and sisters. She passed a leaning gazebo, which shaded two washerwomen and Truth.

"Cat got your tongue, Bea?" Truth called after she picked up the scent of Beatrice's jasmine soap. "I knowed the time when you used to speak."

Beatrice strutted on, as if she hadn't heard. Truth and her salty ways. It wasn't that Beatrice felt better than anyone, for she believed thinking yourself better was a sin; she just didn't mingle with each and everybody. And Truth apparently thought that being Isabella's best friend gave her the right to cast aspersions in front of washerwomen.

"I'm here," she announced at Ruby's shack, pushing open the door and kicking it closed. She emptied one of her bags on the table: a mother-of-pearl hairbrush, a dozen cotton diapers, safety pins, and cans of evaporated milk. "My goodness," she said when her eyes adjusted to the dim light and spotted the baby.

Isabella stood up from the chair, where she had been nodding off, and put a finger to her lips. "Shush. You'll wake the baby up."

"Who's that?" Ruby mumbled sleepily and opened her eyes. "Oh, it's you, Beatrice."

Beatrice walked to the bed for a better look at the baby. "What's her name?"

When Isabella told her, Beatrice laughed. "When will we stop giving children jazzy names? That's why everybody goes by a nickname. Lovelee—what sort of a name is that?"

"I can name my baby anything I want to," Ruby said, "and for the hundredth time, you can't tell me what to do. I'm grown."

Lovelee heard the stridency in her mother's voice and focused on the tall woman standing over the bed with hot coals in her eyes and thick, strong hair that stood out around a pushed-in face. *Who is she and why is she here?* The baby's narrowed eyes waited to see.

Beatrice leaned in closer and smelled milk on the baby's breath. The child was pretty, as pink as a piglet, altogether different from her daughter, Phillis, who was smart but would never be a beauty. "You're in deep trouble, girl," Beatrice said to her sister, "if I know Lee Norris."

Ruby grabbed her baby and held her like a shield against her breasts. "I ain't worried," she said.

"Really?"

"Really."

"Lee's a good man," Isabella said. "A little hotheaded, but as good as can be."

"I didn't say he wasn't," Beatrice said.

"Then help your sister, instead of fighting her all the time."

"I've trying, Mama." Beatrice sat on the edge of the bed. "JC's got this friend, you know, the one with the funeral home. He wrote to the new governor on Lee's behalf. Now, the governor hasn't answered yet, but JC's friend says another letter might get things going."

"The new governor? You mean Hoke Smith?" Ruby grunted. "He wouldn't pee on Lee if he was on fire. And who told you to meddle in my business?"

"Now wait a minute, Ruby. Your sister's trying to help. Talking like that, people might think you don't want your husband back," Isabella said.

"I ain't kissing Beatrice's ass."

"Watch your mouth, gal," Isabella said. "You ain't too grown to feel the back of my hand. That's what's wrong now. I spared you too much when you was growing up."

"She's always in my business, Mama," Ruby said, "Going to a man like Hoke Smith, who got people killed, just to be governor. Even a child has better sense than that."

Beatrice's cheeks swelled with indignation. "See, Mama," she said. "That's what I get every time I try to help your precious daughter."

"You ain't never done nothing for me," Ruby said.

"Well, if you call sending money to you and Mama in Soperton nothing, then I guess I haven't."

"And you ain't never let us forget it," Ruby said. "I'd pay back every crying dime this second if it would shut your mouth."

"The only payback I want is respect, which you haven't given anybody, including Mama and your husband. Besides it doesn't look like you have any dimes to spare." Beatrice's eyes roamed the lumpy mattress and the slop jar peeking from under the bed. The shack was in worse shape than she remembered.

"You a ugly heifer with ugly ways," Ruby said, turning away to hide her tears.

"I may not be as pretty as you, but at least I'm somebody," Beatrice said. "At least I've got a home of my own."

"Well, excuse me," Ruby said in a voice thick with sarcasm. "Not everybody can marry a rich man just before he dies from a so-called heart attack."

Beatrice looked as if she'd been slapped. "That's a terrible thing to say, even for you. It's not true and you know it. I didn't leave with a cent of Ben's money. Why do you always find a person's soft spot and dig in?" Beatrice had married forty-year-old Ben, a farmer in Soperton, when she was seventeen, and the marriage remained her shameful soft spot.

"Whoo, hoo. That's enough" their mother said. "Ruby, apologize to your sister." As Ruby stared ahead in stubborn silence, Isabella took her tin snuff box from the table. "I wish to God y'all would get along. You been fighting since Ruby was knee high to a duck. Over what, I don't know. Why don't you try loving each other for a change?" She opened the door and said over her shoulder, "I'm going to Truth's for some peace and quiet."

Beatrice waited until her heart stopped its furious staccato before she lifted Lovelee to her lap. She buried her face in the infant's hair and sniffed sweetness. The baby's fragile softness reminded her of a kitten her daughter brought home. She had found the little thing abandoned and starving, and Beatrice couldn't bear to turn it out. "Sweet little innocent girl," she said, nuzzling her niece's hair. She looked at Ruby balled into a knot on the bed and sensed that she was afraid. "Maybe you should go down home," she said, feeling rare sympathy for her sister.

"You know something I don't?"

"Well, think about what people will say. This is bound to get to Lee, you know. I mean, all people have to do is lay eyes on your…" Beatrice couldn't say the pernicious words—bastard, milk man's baby, nasty names people would hang around the child's neck—because Ruby was her sister, no matter what. She returned the baby to her.

"You're the one worried about people." Ruby put Lovelee to her breast. "Let them run they mouths and I'll run my business."

"Oh, you're impossible." Beatrice thought that Ruby was putting up her usual obstinate front. Inside, she had to be afraid.

After several minutes of listening to the baby's contented suckling and Ruby's silence, Beatrice stood, purse in hand, prepared to escape. Just then the door opened for Isabella and Truth.

. "Where's that baby?" the blind woman hollered, tapping her cane. "I've been trying to get over here all day."

Isabella guided her to the big chair, and Ruby put the baby in Truth's arms. Burying her head in Lovelee's blanket, Truth sniffed.

"Ain't nothing cleaner than new life. She ain't had time to mess up, and people ain't throwed they trash in her face. I sure hope she looks like her daddy. They say that's good luck, a girl child, who looks like her daddy."

Ruby and Isabella exchanged wary glances.

"She's got good hair, too," said Truth, running her fingers across Lovelee's head.

"It's baby hair," Isabella said in a rush.

"That's right. It'll turn," Ruby said, taking her baby from Truth's probing hands.

Truth shifted her body in the direction of Beatrice's jasmine scent. "That you, Bea? I understand you a big shot now, a professor married to a professor."

"I teach elementary school, Miss Truth," Beatrice said, frowning at Truth's signifying.

"Oh, that's right. It's your husband, who's a professor. Carol read me a story he wrote in the paper the other day, talking about the new governor. JC speaks up for us. Yessiree. I bet he speaks *to* his people, too, even if his wife don't."

Beatrice burned beneath a half-smile on her lips. She would not, no matter what Truth said, go down to the blind woman's uncouth level. She didn't see how her mother could stand being around the old busybody, who obviously thought blind eyes gave her the right to overwork her mouth.

"Now Truth, you know my daughter spoke to you. She ain't like that," Isabella said. "Bea, be sure to tell JC we like what he wrote about old Hoke Smith."

"He'll be glad to hear it," Beatrice said. "Things have been rough." The city's leaders had been riding the editor about the "tone" of JC's column in the colored newspaper, *The Independent*, and she was worried.

During the recent primary election campaign, Smith and his opponent had stirred up the state, including Atlanta, with newspaper accounts of colored men assaulting white women. In his column, JC wrote a response: *The average colored man does not assault, nor is he a criminal. When crimes are committed, criminals, whether colored or not, must be brought to justice. However, is it fair to smear a whole race with the actions of a few? So we ask the governor-elect to step forward, speak up, and ease tension in our fair city.*

"Down in the country, we had em like Smith and that other one, Clark Howell," Truth said. "But evil always goes too far and when it do, you mark my words, somebody'll turn things around. Who knows? Our new leader might be right here in this room, just born today."

"You got some imagination, Miss Truth," Ruby said with a grin. "A girl leader…"

Beatrice rolled her eyes at Truth, who sat beaming and unaware.

"You don't know, Beatrice; it might happen." Ruby glared at her sister.

Beatrice whipped a copy of *The Independent* from her purse. "Well, I do know what I read in paper this morning. They've got a story on the front page about Decatur Street—your second home, Ruby. It said they're going to clean it up so good colored women can leave their houses without being troubled by criminals, shake dancers, drunks, and other riffraff."

"The man who wrote that, I bet I seen him in a juke joint the other day," Ruby said.

"I bet you did," Truth said, laughing and slapping her thigh. "Well, I done stayed long enough. You know what they say, 'short visits make long friendships.'"

"Thanks for coming, Miss Truth," Ruby said.

Truth stood, grabbed her cane, and tapped her way out the door.

Beatrice gave the blind woman time to reach her cabin and out of her way before she flew up from her chair and pecked Isabella's forehead. "See you, Mama."

"Before you go, baby, let me see what you brought," Isabella said and unwrapped a newspaper bundle of coffee, sugar, beans, a slab of salt pork, cornmeal, and molasses. "This here's a lot of groceries. We appreciate everything, don't we, Ruby? I'm gonna make us a big dinner." She suddenly swayed but caught herself with the table edge.

"Ma?" Ruby yelled. "You having another spell? Help her, Beatrice."

As Beatrice grabbed her mother's arm, Isabella brushed her away. "It ain't nothing," Isabella said, "'cept too much excitement in one day."

"How long has this been going on?" Beatrice asked. "Why didn't somebody tell me?"

Isabella sat on an overturned carton to shell peas for dinner. "I said I'm all right, Beatrice Jean. It's just a little pressure; don't go making mountains outta molehills."

"For goodness sake, Mama, you're sleeping on this dusty floor and working yourself to death," Beatrice said. "You had your own room at my house with a nice rug and everything, but you left and for what—to live like this? Pack your things. Let's go. JC can get you an appointment tomorrow with his friend, Dr. Madison."

"I can't," Isabella said. "Ruby needs me."

Ruby dropped her eyes to the chair and a tiny spot of blood that Isabella's cleaning missed. When it came to making her feel small, there was no one better at it than Beatrice.

"I give up," Beatrice said and looked at her sister. No one seeing them for the first time would believe they had come from the same womb, fathered by the same man. When they were younger, she envied Ruby's good looks. But today she felt sorry for her—a husband in jail and a newborn of questionable parentage. Poor precious newborn baby; it wasn't her fault.

When Beatrice bent down to kiss Lovelee good-bye, an urgent voice in the baby's ear whispered, *"Days of blood and fire are on the way and you'll need family."* From the comfortable bend of her mother's arm, Lovelee pursed her lips and pressed them softly against Beatrice's cheek.

Outside, Beatrice leaned against the door to calm herself. It was hard not to cry after being whipped with spite in that shack. She had worked hard to raise herself up and wasn't about to apologize to Truth, Ruby, or anyone else. She wondered why she had foolishly returned to a house she had been banished from a few weeks earlier. She forgot what the argument then was about or even who started it, but she remembered wanting to break Ruby's neck. The girl lived life the way she wanted, carousing in dives and rolling in mud in the alley like a lunatic, dragging down the family's reputation, and now she had birthed a half-white baby. In spite of all that, Ruby remained the pretty one, always the first and last with Isabella, who wouldn't leave her side to save her own life.

As Beatrice plodded to Jackson Way to catch a carriage home, she felt depressed down to the last layer of her being.

Chapter Four

An hour later, Beatrice sat in her choked parlor of upholstered furniture and freed her aching feet from leather boots. JC had left a note. He and Phillis were visiting friends down the street. The house was too quiet, which worsened her mood as she stretched out on the divan.

Isabella said Lovelee was a throwback to white great-grandfather. Beatrice laughed out loud at that. If Lovelee was a throwback, then she was Queen Nefertiti. Nobody but a blind woman would believe Lee was the baby's father. As wild as she could be, Ruby had an affair with somebody on Decatur Street. No doubt about it. And unlucky for her, Lee was not a man to be cuckolded. There would be blood— lots of it. Beatrice shuddered at the thought.

Although Isabella hadn't said much, Beatrice figured she was unhappy about Lovelee. Maybe that was the real reason for her swooning spell. It was always Ruby first for Isabella, and it had been that way since baby Rosetta died. She poured the love she had for her dead child into Ruby, who became the baby again.

Rosetta's death happened quickly and mysteriously. Seventeen-year-old Beatrice awoke at midnight in their Soperton cabin to the sound of slaps and her mother's muffled sobs. Thinking that Elijah, who hadn't been around for days, had returned from bedding another woman and was beating Isabella, she sat upright on her pallet in the front room. The only one who could stop her father—Fat—wasn't home. The flames in the fireplace had petered out, and the cabin was freezing. Shivering, Beatrice left her sisters sleeping on the floor while she tiptoed and peeped through an opening in the curtain over the bedroom doorway. But she couldn't see her parents, whose bed was against a far wall. A candle on a table threw a silhouette on the wall of her father rearing back with a raised fist.

Beatrice quietly gasped but knew not to interfere. She had tried to one day, and her father left bruises on her neck and face. So she tiptoed to a dark corner of the front room and squatted with her hands over her ears, waiting for the beating to stop. She prayed that her sleeping sisters, who were exhausted from working in the fields, wouldn't wake up.

After minutes that seemed forever, Beatrice saw Elijah appear like a shadowy demon in the dark. In one hand he held a flickering candle and in the other, shoebox. Her mother stumbled behind him with the baby bundled in rags. As her father opened the door, cold air rushed in, killing the candle. But in the moonlight, she saw him walk out, pushing her mother ahead. She padded barefoot across the packed-earth floor to the window, and watched her father drive a shovel into their dirt yard, as her mother swayed in a billowing nightgown with Rosetta in her arms. Beatrice could hear Isabella crying, and she wanted to run to her, but Elijah would beat her raw for jumping in "grown folk's business". Even if that box contained little Rosetta, there wasn't anything she could do. She hadn't really known the baby, only five days old, but somehow she felt her family was worse off, because she was gone.

Satisfied at last with the size of the hole, Elijah pried the box away from Isabella, whose empty arms reached out as if she were pleading. He swore at her—"evil heifer"—and on his knees, with his bare hands, covered the box with earth. He then rose and shouted in the wind to his wife, "Stop your damn crying. I'm sick of it."

Beatrice pretended to be asleep when they came inside. The straw in their mattress rustled a bit as they settled down. She didn't hear any arguing or sobbing. They might have been coming home after a church supper, except they sighed and sighed as if they could not find a resting place. Beatrice glanced at the tangled limbs of her sisters, who had slept through everything. Poor Rosetta hadn't had a chance, crying day and night for food, until she starved to death. Beatrice held a hand against her mouth to muffle her sobs and fell into sleep filled with visions of winged cherubs pointing fingers at her parents before a large, flame-red bird with monstrous claws swept down and carried Elijah away.

The next morning, Elijah announced that the baby was gone. Too young to understand what he meant, Ruby asked, "Gone where?" Beatrice quietly watched her mother stare into a cup of watery coffee. There wouldn't be a funeral, gravestone, or death certificate. In those days, a person could come into the world and die without the state ever knowing about it. Although Elijah said crying wouldn't bring the baby back, Mary Alice and Ruby cried anyway. Trying to be manly like his father, Fat only sniffed and frowned.

In a couple of days, Isabella was well enough to help a neighbor give birth to a baby boy.

"How can you, of all people, be doing something like that at a time like this?" Elijah asked, during their supper of pot liquor and corn bread. "I think I'll have a talk with that midwife."

"Let it be, Eli. We need the money," Isabella said, and her trembling hands reached for a jar of water.

He slapped the jar to the floor and walked outside. His family continued to eat, as if nothing had happened. That night, he moved to a pallet on the bedroom floor, and Isabella tossed on the bed.

Listening to her mother's distress, Beatrice feared she might shake herself to death. In a few days, Elijah disappeared, leaving fat welts across his wife's back and stomach.

Little Phillis Wheatley banged open the front door, and Beatrice snapped out of her mental nightmare and set up on the divan. "What's wrong with you, Phillis, coming in here like a little heathen?" she said. "The cat must have your manners."

"Mama, we got company." Phillis giggled and looked back at her father. Named for the poet, Phillis had a flare for drama.

Beatrice saw that she was excited and craned her neck to see who was causing it.

JC stepped aside in the doorway. "Look who I found getting out of a carriage."

Beatrice turned on the lantern next to the divan to help the fading afternoon sun. She gawked as her younger sister walked in. "Oh, Lord, is that you, Mary Alice?"

"In the flesh," Mary Alice said. She had long pressed hair that shone like copper from under a floppy straw hat and stylish clothing—a red silk suit and matching pumps, a white purse tucked under her arm, and white gloves.

But under her hat's wide brim, her face looked as if it had been mauled.

Beatrice gasped and embraced her. She felt bones under the jacket. "Where in the world have you been? Were you in an accident? Girl, we've been worried about you."

"Oh, this," Mary Alice said, touching a gloved finger to her face, as if she had forgotten it was chewed up. "I fell down the steps at the train station in New York. You know how they rush up there and I tripped."

JC burst out laughing. "Sister-in-law, you sure can't lie, can you? If you got that falling down, I'm Ma Rainey."

"Ooh, Auntie, you've been fighting," said Phillis, staring up at Mary Alice with an open mouth.

Mary Alice's swollen strawberry lips tapped Phillis's forehead. "I've got something for you, little lady." She held out a piece of peppermint, which the child grabbed.

"What do you say?" Beatrice asked in a reproving voice.

Phillis thanked her aunt, curtsied as Beatrice had taught her, and put the candy in the pocket of her pinafore.

"That's my girl, smart like her daddy," JC said, as he dropped mail on a table behind the door. No one noticed him slide a thin brown envelope with foreign stamps into his pants pocket.

After Phillis skipped away to wash up for dinner, Beatrice wrapped her arms around Mary Alice and murmured into her ear, "Whoever did this was trying to kill you."

"I fell, OK?" Mary Alice turned her face away.

Beatrice's incredulous eyes flew to JC, who shrugged. "Don't look at me, babe," he said. "It's her story. Me—I'm hungry. What you got in that kitchen to eat?"

"In a minute, JC," Beatrice said. In her moody state, she had forgotten to prepare dinner. "First, we need to get to the bottom of this."

"We?" he said with amusement. "Who is we?"

"There's nothing to get to the bottom of." Mary Alice moved away from the light of the solitary lantern. She stepped out of her pumps and fanned out the pink toes of her narrow feet. "Aah, that's better. It's good to be with family again. When you don't have anything else, you've got family."

In amazement, Beatrice gaped at her sister. Still stubborn and secretive, just like when she was a child. But she couldn't hide those bruises, which had to be the work of a man. Heavy makeup didn't conceal black eyes and long, dark marks of strangulation around her neck. Only fear could have forced Mary Alice, who was vain to a fault about her looks, to travel in that condition. What had she been doing in New York? They didn't have relatives that far north. What kind of trouble was she in? Whatever it was, somebody had tried to kill her. "We've been worried sick," Beatrice said. "Not a word in seven years, and you show up like this. Mama's been crying her eyes out, worse than when Daddy left. Why didn't you write?"

"I wrote. Something must be wrong with the post office down here."

Chuckling, JC shook his head.

Beatrice noticed her sister's small leather traveling bag, hardly large enough to hold years of living. "How long are you staying?"

"I'm back for good. The weather up there is horrible—too much snow."

"And it took this long to figure that out? You sound like Daddy and his pitiful excuses," Beatrice said. "JC, please stop making fun and take her bag to Mama's room."

"Sure, babe," JC said, his fingers felt in his pocket for the letter before he picked up the bag and, chuckling, took it to the back bedroom.

"Come on, girl, take off those gloves and that hat. We can talk while I make dinner." Beatrice marched her sister to the kitchen. "I declare, if it's not one thing with this family, it's another." In her spotless kitchen with cast-iron pots, a red-and-white linoleum floor, and a shiny new icebox—a gift from JC on their seventh wedding anniversary—Beatrice's mood became sunnier. She did her best thinking there, while creating velvety pound cakes and tender roasts. No matter what happened, if she could turn it over in her kitchen, the rough edges would become smooth and everything dark would come to light. She made coffee and kept her back to Mary Alice to hide her face, which JC said was as easy to read as the funny paper.

Mary Alice removed her gloves, revealing square, blunt fingers with short, brittle nails. The ring finger on her left hand was wrapped in gauze and white surgical tape. Turning around, Beatrice noticed blood around the edges. "So what happened?" she asked.

Mary Alice covered her finger with her hand. "You wouldn't understand."

"Try me."

"You wouldn't, because you're not like me. You have a husband who loves you and a daughter. Your life's orderly, everything's in its place. Look at this kitchen. It belongs in a grand hotel—nothing like my life."

"Oh, Mary Alice, stop the foolishness. You can't expect to come home like this without some sort of explanation." Beatrice struck her forehead with the heel of her hand. "This family is so crazy."

"Maybe when I can think straight."

Beatrice gave up but only for a while. She figured the truth, no matter how terrible, had to come out. Sometimes you had to stop stirring a pot to let it boil.

After a few minutes during which neither sister spoke, Mary Alice muttered, "I'll tell you. Nobody else."

Beatrice nodded and rested her trembling hands in a bowl of snap peas.

"I'm not kidding. Nobody else, not even Mama." Mary Alice knew that confiding in Isabella, who despised her white father, would stir up trouble.

"OK." Beatrice waited across the table, scared of what was coming.

"I was engaged...to a white man in New York," Mary Alice said in a tremulous voice.

"A *white* man?" Beatrice's eyes opened wide. Over the years, she had imagined Mary Alice dead or in dozens of dangerous situations, but never this. What was wrong with her sisters and white men?

"Till he found out I was colored."

"*Found out* you were colored?"

"He…he didn't know in the beginning. We were together three years before he knew." Mary Alice spoke slowly, remembering the clacking sound her shoes had made on the parquet floor, the empty feeling of the apartment as she put away groceries and headed to their bedroom. She thought Reuben hadn't come home from work and stopped at the open door, surprised to see him in a chair beside the bed. He was quiet, although his face was fever red. Her eyes followed his to their bed, where a sepia photo of her family lay in the center.

"Well, that explains your face."

Mary Alice touched her bruised neck. and her eyes searched Beatrice's face. "Are you ashamed of me?" she asked. "I can't blame you if you are."

"Have mercy," Beatrice said. "Please tell me you don't love him."

"No, I don't think so, not now."

"Did you ever?"

"I wish I could say no, but the truth is yes, with all my heart." Mary Alice hung her head.

Beatrice came over and rocked Mary Alice in her arms, as she had when they were kids and her beloved but flighty little sister was in trouble. She understood. A woman had to do whatever she could to get through life, and Mary Alice had chosen a perilous path, available only to a few. People like her would disappear and be lost forever to their families, who did not speak about them because of fear. With skin and hair like her sister's, Beatrice thought she might have passed, too, for benefits such characteristics would bring. "My dear sister, let this be our secret," she said, relieved that JC wasn't around. "We'll act like it never happened. We don't want to give people anything to talk about."

"Yes. That's exactly how I want it."

Beatrice clenched her fists under the table. What a poor excuse for a human being the so-called fiancé must be. Only God could say why he hadn't killed her sister. Those marks on Mary Alice. Beatrice's hands ached to squeeze the bastard's throat.

Mary Alice asked about the rest of the family. Who was married? Who had children? Fat had two sons—how old? And so on. As Beatrice cooked dinner, she held back details about Ruby's baby. But as usual with secrets, the less said, the more questions generated, so Mary Alice kept probing.

"I just told you she had a girl," Beatrice said evenly. "There's not much more to tell. You'll see her—after you heal. If you go to Mama like that, she'll have a stroke."

Mary Alice put a hand to her tender neck. "I guess she would."

Chapter Five

The postmark on the letter in JC's pocket was from Freetown, Sierra Leone, and the return address a private mailbag number. He tore at the tissue-thin envelope and flattened it on the bedside table. The schoolboy script of his friend, Reverend Edward W. Blyden, covered two pages. "The moment a colored man from America lands in Liberia," Blyden wrote, "he finds the galling chains of caste falling from his soul, and he can stand erect and feel and realize that he is indeed a man." The words were like an elixir to JC. *What a wonderful place Africa must be. If only Beatrice would reconsider.*

He and Reverend Blyden had an unlikely friendship. A year earlier, JC had been rummaging through old religious tracts at Atlanta University's library and ran across a transcript of the 1861 speech Blyden gave at the Presbyterian Church in New York: "Liberia is a beautiful tropical country teeming with the rich fruits of a perpetual summer." Intrigued, JC read on. "No social disadvantage is felt by any descendent of Africa on account of color."

The place sounded like paradise. But JC had no love of preachers, those smooth-talking charlatans, and he suspected this one was lying. Such a place couldn't possibly exist. The pages had been copied and were probably fraudulent; still he couldn't put them down. When he finished reading, he went through them again and took notes.

He found an address for Reverend Blyden in Liberia and wrote to him. Blyden wrote back, inviting him to move to the country. JC asked for more information, and the reverend responded, "They are called Americo-Liberians, although some say they are 'Congo people.' Either way, they have prospered as preachers, university professors like you, lawyers, and political leaders. In their top hats and morning coats, strolling through places of power, they are something to see."

After a year of exchanging letters, JC wanted to accept Blyden's offer of a university position, but Beatrice mocked him for even considering a move to "the jungles of Africa." "But we'll be free, really free," he said, remembering that the name Liberia was rooted in the Latin word, liber or freedom.

"We're already free, been free for over forty years."

JC had given up until this latest letter rekindled hope. Maybe if he talked to Beatrice one last time.

At midnight Beatrice settled Mary Alice into the downstairs bedroom and went upstairs, carrying a cup of tea with mint from her garden. JC had complained about a headache and excused himself right after dinner. He was on their bed with a copy of the *Narrative of the Life of Frederick Douglass, an American Slave.*

"I brought you some tea," Beatrice said, pushing aside a stack of books to make room on the bedside table.

"Any whiskey in it?"

"You wish." Beatrice put the cup down next to the headache powder and glass of water she brought up earlier. They looked untouched.

"Mary Alice seems different," JC said. "I mean, apart from her face. She's sad and looks like a bag of bones."

"I guess that's how New York affects some people. They say it's fast, not like down here."

"What was she doing up there, if you don't mind my asking? Who beat her up? And don't tell me that crap about falling down steps. Even Phillis saw through that."

"She said she was a waitress. The rest is a long story, too long to tell tonight." Beatrice kissed his forehead. "Why are you reading with a headache, mister?"

He closed the book and set it atop the stack on the table. "How's Ruby? I forgot to ask, with Mary Alice showing up. She and the baby made it, right?"

"It's a girl, and they're OK." Beatrice spied the brown envelope exposed about an inch from the pages of the Douglass autobiography. Another letter. She sat on the edge of the bed and sighed. "Are you still writing to that African?"

"As a matter of fact, he wrote to me."

"Why? We're going to Ohio. What more do you want? "An official letter inviting JC to attend Ohio Wesleyan University for further studies came in the mail the previous week.

"That's another reason to accept Blyden's invitation. I'm going to Ohio because the state universities down here won't admit me. They'd rather pay to send me to Ohio. It's humiliating."

Beatrice rubbed a hand across her forehead. Sometimes JC was every bit the brilliant professor, but at times such as this, she wondered how sharp he really was. "I don't like it either, but you've got to go. Who knows when you'll have this chance again? It's a free education, JC."

"Did you know the upper classes in Liberia, the colored, who used to be American slaves and free people, are governing the country? We can't even vote, much less run something. Reverend Blyden will introduce us to the right people."

Although that idea brought a glimmer to Beatrice's eyes, she shook her head "Maybe it's a trick. You don't know this man. You've never laid eyes on him. He could be one of those African savages. He could get us over there and boil us in a pot."

"Don't be so damn ignorant. Reverend Blyden is an ordained minister."

"Says who? What do you really know about a place called Liberia? This guy could be lying."

"I know it was founded by people like us. Mr. Lincoln was even for resettlement. Henry McNeal Turner thinks it's a good idea, and you can't find a smarter, braver, or better man in this country." He grabbed Beatrice's hands and pulled her close. "Think about it, baby. Just think about the opportunities, the things we can do."

"Stop talking crazy" said Beatrice, pulling away. "If Bishop Turner thinks it's so great, why doesn't he go to Africa?"

"He did and came back. Nobody really knows why."

"And you want us to go off on the same misadventure. I love you, but I'm not a fool. We're Americans, born and bred, not Africans. This is our country. We've got good jobs, a nice house. I'm sorry, but it's too risky. I know things happen here —bad things—but not to respectable people like us. We're safe in Brownsville. Think about Phillis. Think about our family. Why can't you leave well enough alone?"

JC's response was a deep groan and he dropped the matter.

While working summers in an Alabama sawmill, he had graduated from Tuskegee and moved to Atlanta, only to become locked into Brownsville, a part of town that wasn't a slum but was inferior in infrastructure and opportunities. Impatient and furious with the caste system, he thought constantly about liberation. Liberia offered it but without Beatrice, who had his heart, it meant nothing.

Beatrice massaged his back, which was her way of apologizing. "You should be proud of going to Wesleyan," she said. "I'm going to announce it in church Sunday."

"I don't like calling undue attention, Bea."

"Undue attention? Plenty of people would be happy to take your place. Baby, this is a wonderful opportunity. When you come back, you'll be somebody big—maybe a dean."

"I'm already somebody, the baddest son of a gun in town." JC pointed his index finger at his heart and pretended to shoot. "Pow, pow."

Beatrice laughed nervously. "Will you stop making fun of everything? I don't understand what's so terrible about this. A tuition-free education, most people would kill for it."

"I'm going, I'm going. Just don't expect me to be happy about it." JC kissed her pouting lips. "Sweet Bea, I wish you didn't care so much about the wrappings on things."

"I'm talking about a better life for us, especially for Phillis, not just myself."

"Oh, is that what this is about? I thought it was about announcing it in church."

"Will you stop? I've been through enough already—first Ruby's mess and now Mary Alice." Although no one else was close enough to overhear, Beatrice told JC about Ruby's baby in a whispery voice.

JC said he wasn't surprised. "I hate to say it, because Ruby's a good kid, but she's not exactly a nun. And she's always acted a lot older, hanging out in juke joints. How do you know she wasn't balling some guy?"

"Balling?" Beatrice's eyes narrowed. "That's vulgar."

"Stop trucking with me, girl; you know what I mean. Now if I were Ruby, I'd get out of town—fast. Her husband acts like he's Nat Turner and Denmark Vesey all rolled into one. Do you know I had to stop him from going after a white man with a knife, just because the fool pushed him off the sidewalk? Scared me to death."

"We've got to help her."

"She can't stay here. I don't want trouble."

"You've never liked her. Be honest and admit it."

"Hey, since when did you start defending Ruby? Seems like I remember you used to give her hell."

"She's my sister, and I feel sorry for her." Beatrice rolled down her stockings in preparation for bed. She pressed her palms on shaking knees, a nervous habit since childhood. She did not like arguing with JC, especially about her family. It wasn't as large as most, but it was as complicated and foolish as any, and she loved them in spite of it, even Ruby.

As she washed in a large white enamel basin on a table, JC followed her movements from the bed. The dark patches in her armpits, exposed as she rolled her hair in paper curlers, put him in the mood. When she reached to the high chifforobe for her night bonnet, her nightdress rode up over long and shapely calves, and he wanted her. "Come over here," he said. She walked to the bed, slipped between the sheets, and they put aside their disagreement for love.

She awoke later that night, pressed against JC's back, and he turned to find her lips. Oh, she breathed, feeling full enough to burst. How lucky she was to have him. He was a good man, her JC, a thousand times better than her first husband, old Ben, a scoundrel from beginning to end.

Back in those days, Beatrice could feel her belly pressing against her backbone with hunger. Sometimes she ate dirt, gray, chalky stuff as dense as clay. It painted her lips white and constipated her, but she couldn't stop the habit, picked up from her mother. The women of Soperton ate dirt, because a stomach full of dirt was as satisfied as one full of bread.

She was seventeen when her trim waist and breasts poking against thin dresses stirred the blood of sixty-year-old Ben Grimes, a farmer in Soperton. It was the summer after her daddy ran off and Fat moved to Atlanta.

The day Ben stopped his mare in the yard, she rested under a pecan tree, reading her favorite novel. Her lips were chalky and her hair stuck up in several directions. If Ben had not spent months imagining his lips on her pointy breasts, he might not have stopped. As he climbed down from his horse, Beatrice frowned and shielded her eyes from the sun with her book. It took a moment for her to remember his name—Ben—one of the men her father went whoring with. She had seen the old farmer in the general store, supporting his sickly wife with a hand to her elbow. She heard his wife died not long afterward.

Ben's eyes ran over her as if he were looking at a sporting woman, not his friend's young daughter.

"Mama ain't home, Daddy neither," Beatrice said, speaking as if Elijah was in the field and hadn't run off like a hound dog in July. Isabella had sent her home to prepare a supper of boiled poke salad and hoecakes. After that was done, Beatrice grabbed her book, instead of returning to the fields. She expected Old Ben to leave, but he stood as if rooted in the spot. His thick limbs and wild branches of gray hair reminded her of a dead poplar tree her Daddy cut down.

"What you reading?" Ben said.

"Nothing."

"Looks like you're smart. What you studin to be?"

Although Beatrice had decided to be a teacher, she didn't reply.

"I didn't get much schooling as a boy. If I paid you, would you come by the house and read to me?"

"Naw."

"Well, it don't matter, cause I got to see the prettiest gal in Soperton today."

Standing in sullen silence, Beatrice waited for him to leave. Boys had called her "black, ugly thing" enough that she knew how she looked. They ran away when she smiled, showing blue gums. In their hamlet a bite from someone with blue gums was poisonous.

As soon as Ben climbed on his horse and rode off, leaving a peculiar metallic old-man smell, she returned to sighing over the doomed affairs of Emma Bovary. Even after she put the novel away, her head stayed in other places, where bored ladies in plumed hats and velvet cloaks rode in carriages through cobblestone streets to meet rich lovers.

After that, she stopped coming home to cook in the afternoon, but Ben would show up after church and bring peppermints for the children and a dime for her. He sat in the front room as though he had come to court Isabella, who stayed politely distant. Because Beatrice didn't want to explain the dimes to her mother, she hid them in her pillowcase. A dime could buy enough sugar to sweeten her tea for a month.

In the fall, she met Ben on the main road, where she was walking alone, and he persuaded her to come to his house and see his new parlor furniture. She rode to his forty acres in the woods, more land than any colored man had in the county. They rolled down a ruddy path, past a crystal stream with stones like huge gems, and into a verdant clearing dotted by a gray bungalow. Once at the house, she became stiff with fear and ran off, but not before a family friend saw her and relayed the news to Isabella.

Ben knocked at their cabin door the next day. "Miss Isabella," he said with an arthritic bow, "I want to do the right thing and marry your daughter."

Beatrice expected her mother to say she couldn't marry an old man, who would steal her strength. She wanted Isabella to tell him that she, the oldest child in the family but still a child, was going to college in Atlanta; she was going to be somebody.

"Well, ain't that something," Isabella said to Ben instead. Later she told Beatrice to marry him or starve. "I can't feed you no more. I ain't got no man to help me."

Feeling poor and trapped, Beatrice agreed to marry and rode with Ben to a justice of the peace. Afterwards, they went to his house. His penetration was over so fast she wouldn't have known if not for the pain. She remembered his wrinkled ass and breathing that sounded like he would die. A month later, he did die after saying he felt a little under the weather.

When his sister came from Savannah to claim his property, she pushed his young bride out of the house.

"Fine with me," said Beatrice, who had stopped caring about the wagon or the farm. With the dimes she saved and a letter from Fat in her purse, she grabbed a ride with a family going to Atlanta.

In the years that followed, she realized her first husband had to be, or she might not have given JC a chance. Without really knowing it, she had wanted to marry a big loving man like James Clarence Freeman all her life, and when he walked in to teach her evening history class at Morris Brown College, she was ready. Without Ben, she might have doubted that JC was the one. She might have thought the laughter that bubbled from his full lips was too loud or his unruly mane and moustache were uncouth. Without Ben, she might not have recognized the breadth and depth of JC's love, and she wouldn't have loved him back.

Her eyes followed a large vein down her sleeping husband's forearm before she pressed her wrist against his and felt the harmonious throbbing of their pulses. She loved him deeply. If, God forbid, he decided to chase windmills in Africa, she'd have to decide if love was enough.

Chapter Six

Saturday, September 8, 1906

The morning sun stretched across the living room, warming Beatrice while she worked on a lesson about Poe, mouthing: "It was many and many a year ago, / In a kingdom by the sea, / That a maiden there lived whom you may know / By the name of Annabel Lee." She loved the rhythm of his words. They made her feel like dancing, which she hadn't done since she could remember. JC wasn't a good dancer and it was disgraceful for a woman, who was not in the theater or a whore, to dance alone. So as she read, she merely tapped her feet to the poetic beat. "For the moon never beams, without bringing me dreams / Of the beautiful Annabel Lee." She thought about playing the part of Annabel for her students. She had once starred in a college's fall production of *Romeo and Juliet,* and people said she was a natural. No, she decided. It was more important to be dignified, a person her students would do well to emulate.

Beatrice walked around Phillis, who was sprawled on the floor with a book of fairy tales, and poked her head up the stairs. JC was sleeping longer than usual. He had been up during the night, roaming through the house like the ghosts her students liked to invoke in their writing. He couldn't enjoy life, no matter how good it was. Behind his joking and kidding lived a restless, edgy spirit. Up one minute and down the next. She had seen that flaw when they met and dismissed it, thinking he would settle down after they married, but over the years, it had become a source of disagreement between them.

It was noon before he came down with red eyes and uncombed hair. Beatrice stopped working and kissed his unyielding lips. "What's wrong now?" she asked.

He shrugged and walked to the kitchen, following the strong aroma of coffee.

"OK, sulk if you want to," Beatrice said as she popped in and started on a pan of dirty dishes. It was going to be another one of JC's days when everything was blacker than black. She could see it in the discontented downturn of his mouth. By evening, he would be distant and taciturn. This time she blamed that African preacher. She had searched and found old letters hidden under maps in his drawer. How could she compete with an obsession like that? Her husband wasn't in love with another woman, which she could understand, if not accept. His passion was for Africa, which he imagined as idyllic, a mecca for colored people, forgetting that the continent had sold their ancestors without even a backward glance. And now he wanted to go there? The very idea was too cockeyed for inmates at the state insane asylum in Milledgeville, and she wasn't buying it. She had struggled too hard to be somebody, and she wasn't going to throw it away.

JC opened *The Atlanta Evening News,* which carried stories about the new governor, and the latest attack on white women by colored men. Similar stories with inflammatory headlines had lit racial fires during the gubernatorial contest and they continued to burn. JC winced as he read an editorial aloud: "We are the superior race and do not intend to be ruled by our semi-barbaric inferiors." With a grim expression, he threw the paper on the floor.

Beatrice picked it up and glanced at the headline. "This doesn't scare me. It's all politics."

"What about that Walker boy they lynched?"

"He confessed didn't he? I mean he attacked that woman. They should've tried him legally but that doesn't mean he didn't do it. If you're innocent, you don't have to worry about things like that."

"Bea, you know better. Be honest."

"I said you're right didn't I? They shouldn't have killed him, but we can't bring the boy back or change those people. The best we can do is live our lives and try to be happy. There's nothing wrong with being happy, you know."

JC looked at her as if she had spoken Krahn, a Liberian language he wanted to learn. He opened *The Independent* to his final column, which somehow sounded vacuous and dishonest. But that was how he always thought about his column in *The Independent*. What he really wanted to publish was a call for resettlement in Liberia. "Let us rise up and be men," JC wrote in the copy he submitted. "Let's have the courage to strike against injustice, like Frederick Douglas and William Still." The editor struck through JC's "dangerous, fanciful writing" with a red pencil. Disgusted, JC made an appointment with the editor of a new periodical, *Voice of the Negro*, where he thought his writing would be appreciated. Beatrice didn't need to know about it until he had the job.

Phillis took a seat at the table with her father. "Morning, princess," he said, putting down his paper. "Look at you, as pretty as can be." Phillis soaked up his adoration, lifting her face for a kiss.

"Did you finish your lessons?" Beatrice asked.

"It's Saturday, Mommy."

"Only lazy girls procrastinate."

"She's not lazy," JC said.

"I know that. She's brilliant, ahead of her class, but she has to work twice as hard to get ahead. Everybody knows that. So finish your homework, honey, before our meeting."

"Yes, ma'am," Phillis said but her eyes brimmed with tears.

"She's only six, Bea. Lighten up," JC said.

"I'm just making sure our daughter has all the advantages we didn't have."

Beatrice served biscuits and eggs, which Phillis picked at. Before long, she asked her father's permission to leave the table.

"You know she doesn't like eggs," JC said after the child was gone.

"She's not old enough to have likes and dislikes. If she's hungry, she'll eat. I was raised to appreciate everything God sends, including eggs."

"When are you going to forget how you were raised?"

"How can a person do that? It's part and parcel of who you are. If you pretend it isn't, you're fooling yourself, because it's right there, for better or for worse. I try to make sure it's for better." Beatrice dried her hands and reminded him about the meeting. "Hurry up or we'll be late," she said as JC slurped coffee from a saucer. "Everybody who's anybody will be there." She was anxious to see their friends and savor their congratulations about his admission to Wesleyan, news she had spread by telephone.

"Is Mary Alice going?"

"Uh, no. She needs her rest."

JC looked at her knowingly.

"What? The girl's tired. She can meet our friends later."

"Did I say anything?"

******

They arrived late. The other guests, who wore white and pastels, had spread out like flowers across the backyard, fanning off bugs and sipping from sweaty glasses of lemonade. Phillis ran to join children playing games near the back fence. "Little Sally Walker, sitting in a saucer," they sang, and Beatrice smiled as her daughter blended in with children from good, respectable families.

Although their meetings began as officious business gatherings, they had morphed into social affairs and their homes became the restaurants, theaters, and downtown clubs that would not admit them. Beatrice and other members of the group—proud possessors of college degrees or small businesses—feigned a preference for segregation. "I don't want to force myself on anybody," she said.

Without the light skin and long hair of most of the women or a college degree, Beatrice used her high intellect and a certain haughtiness to assure acceptance. These were her kind of people, distinctly different from the "bad element" in Lydell Alley. It wasn't that she thought herself better than anyone, as she liked to say, because thinking yourself better was a sin. She just kept her distance from people who lacked ambition and manners. She had no desire to count bootleggers and uneducated washerwomen as friends. She said as much to JC, who reminded her that Isabella washed clothes for a living when she was not delivering babies. "That's different," Beatrice said. "Mama has inner dignity dirty clothes can't touch."

"What about Fat?"

"He's a deacon," Beatrice said, even though she knew her brother was in the rackets.

Their hosts that month, Ellen and Gilbert Gates, professors of home economics and chemistry, respectively, had planted large trees to shade the backyard of their brick bungalow. They had a smoking tub of pork and chicken set up near the screened porch, and every now and then Gil emerged from inside with a glass of spiked lemonade in time to turn over the meat. He had a loud, mocking laugh and a handsome face that attracted more women than he could handle. But he flirted anyway whenever Ellen's watchful little eyes didn't have him pinned down.

Beatrice left her pound cake on a picnic table up front, and followed JC to a circle of men and women under a spreading oak tree. They were in deep, hushed conversation about a recent lynching in Cleveland, Georgia. A Cleveland mob had cut off the boy's private parts, ears, fingers, and toes for souvenirs. The lynching, with pictures, had run on the interior pages of major Atlanta newspapers that reported it in the usual way—an "incident" perpetrated by "unknown persons." The papers then called for vigilante action, if need be, to control the city's "swarthy" population. *The Independent* published a cautious front-page account of it, without speculating about the identities of the terrorists.

"I see that boy's body in my dreams," JC said from a tight stance behind Beatrice's chair. "That could've been me back in Ocala when I was fifteen, and crackers chased me to my grandfather's house. As scared as Granddaddy was, he had sense enough to hide me in a barrel of sugarcane. They searched the house and slapped him around a little, but he wouldn't tell. I remember staying in that box all night and coming out half dead from red ant bites."

"Now you've got your big chance," said a prominent druggist in a white linen shirt and trousers. "Congratulations on the admission, big guy."

"They're paying me," JC quipped.

"Maybe, but at least you're getting away," the druggist said. "A colored man's life isn't worth a crying dime down here. Atlanta's getting worse and worse. They're talking about burning our homes down. I tell you what, if they come to my house, I'm taking one out with me."

"Be careful what you say, dear," said Fanny, his wife. Her straw hat shaded sunny brown eyes.

Feeling uneasy about the conversation, Beatrice excused herself and walked over to the grill, where skinny Ellen Gates had parked herself on a porch step.

Ellen was on her second glass of lemonade laced with white lightning, and her eyes glittered. "Hey, girl," she said. "What's going on? Is it the same old thing? We gon do this, we gon do that, and ain't nobody gon do a damn thing."

"Pretty much."

"What y'all need is some of this," Ellen said and lifted her glass. "Gil's in there fixing everybody up." She waved her hand toward the screen door. "It's coming."

"I think I'll go back with the others," Beatrice said, managing a dry smile. She liked Ellen, who was smart and made her laugh, but when drinking, she could be too much to take.

"Wish I could join you, but Gil's got me keeping an eye on his meat." Ellen yelled and laughed at her double entendre.

Beatrice kept walking. *Such an uncouth woman.*

"We need a constitutional amendment against lynching." Beatrice could hear JC's solemn voice above the others as she approached. "If we can't get it, then I say move to Africa. Y'all won't believe this, but I've got a personal invitation from a preacher over there. He's practically begging me to come home."

"Home?" Beatrice said, taking a chair next to his. "This is home."

JC's jaws tightened. Beatrice was really pushing him. He didn't understand her how she could be sexy and loving in bed and so unyielding when they disagreed. He decided to stay mum or risk having to put her in her place.

"I wouldn't hold my breath for that amendment if I were you, JC," the druggist said.

"President Roosevelt said he's considering it," said Solomon, a diminutive, mustachioed man, whose shyness usually kept him quiet.

"And that's all he's going to do—*consider* it," the druggist said.

"Fellows, please. You're depressing me," said Beatrice. "Atlanta welcomes, even celebrates, *responsible* colored people like us. Mayor Woodward, everybody, says so. Let's not stir things up."

"They're already stirred up," the druggist snapped.

"That Cleveland boy had no business messing with white women," Fanny interjected in a tiny voice.

The men looked at the druggist with an unspoken question: "Are you going to check your wife or what?" Since the druggist thought it would be easier to find new friends than another wife as beautiful as Fanny, he didn't say a word.

A solemn man in a beige suit and a goatee moved in from the group's periphery, where he had been listening. He had a black walking cane, carried lightly on his arm as if it were a wardrobe enhancer, and confident bearing.

Beatrice was the first to notice him. "Professor," she cooed, "what do you think? Isn't this a beautiful city?" In their social circle, "professor" was loosely used to address educators from primary school to university, but the way the group turned to him with admiring eyes showed that this particular professor was special.

"Well, I must be honest," the professor replied. "Something must be done. Our people are running from place to place, trying to survive and getting nowhere. When I taught in Alabama, it was heart-wrenching—terror, poverty, and disease had taken over—and there was no way out. It was like a heavy veil had dropped over our people. But it's not just Alabama. Violence rules from Texas to Florida. Despite brave efforts from sister Ida B. Wells, they won't stop lynching us. Atlanta has universities, churches, and black businesses, true enough, but that doesn't mean it's protected."

"That's why I want to move to Africa," said JC, who admired the professor. They had worked together after his appointment at the university. The learned man believed that higher education would be the salvation of their people, and JC agreed—but thought it could only come to fruition in Africa.

"Considering the current state of colonialism, this isn't the time to go," the professor said. "Oh yes, I know they say Liberia isn't a colony, but actually it's under the thumb of our government in many ways, not to mention the rubber company. What we need are political rights here. We can't cast down our buckets when we're standing in quicksand."

As they laughed nervously, the druggist jumped in. "So you're saying oppose the man from Tuskegee. You're saying fight our brother?"

The professor's gaze was fatherly. "No, no. I'm saying fight for our rights; there's no need to fight each other. We cannot have real progress without the right to vote. Who can vote in this city? Can you or you?" As he pointed an elegant finger around the circle, they shook their heads.

"But we're citizens," said Mrs. Deborah Robinson, a stout lady with heavy gold bracelets, testimonies to her family's success in the mortuary business. "We're as free as anybody, and we'll vote one day, men and *women*. Just mark my words. Why President Cleveland almost said as much when he was in our fair city."

The professor smiled thinly. "I remember another murdered boy. I saw his body after they finished, and I've never felt so powerless in my life. He must've been no more than sixteen. They cut the poor child open, burned him. We heard him screaming, smelled the smoke, and couldn't do anything, I'm ashamed to say. But I swear to God, if I ever see another thing like that, I'll take your suggestion, Professor Freeman, and move to Africa."

Beatrice's face burned. Despite the shade trees, hot air hung over the yard, and her temper had risen to match it. One more word about Africa and she would explode. A mosquito began to draw blood from her upper arm, and she slapped it away with greater force than necessary.

Deborah's husband, David, who had a mortician's taciturn tongue and usually left talking to his gregarious wife, said something he had been holding in for a while. "I know for a fact that a so-called colored body they gave me to dress right before the election was white. They shot him while he was breaking into a white woman's house. He had charcoal on his face and hands. I returned him to the authorities."

"What did you just say?" JC said.

"I saw it with my own eyes. The body was a white man."

"Now ain't that something?" JC's voice was hard. "The Boston Tea Party, southern style." He spotted his editor drinking with Gilbert on the porch. "Did you tell anyone at my paper?"

"They said leave it alone."

JC was more certain than ever that his journalism future, as part-time as it was, lay somewhere else, hopefully with *Voices of the Negro*.

"Unfortunately, I'm not surprised," the professor said, and his worried eyes stared over their heads, as if he saw distant danger. "Brother Freeman, I hope efforts to rouse the city's rabble are not successful, but they might be and they'll attack us. I'm sorry to say Mr. Washington's speech at the Exposition hasn't helped things. Not that I totally blame him, understand, but self-respect is worth far more than land and college buildings." He shook JC's hand. "We need thoughtful, educated young leaders like you at our next meeting. I'm not sure where it'll be. Maybe Niagara. Perhaps you'll join us. That is—if your university studies will allow it."

"I hope so, too." JC beamed, suddenly proud of his scholarship.

After the learned man moved on to a cluster of guests on the other side of the lawn, Beatrice gave her husband a congratulatory hug. "Darling, you hear that?" she murmured. "The professor admires you."

The druggist harrumphed. "The prof can afford to talk that off-the-wall stuff. It's easy to be brave when you can run off to a fancy meeting."

"Spoken like a jealous man," said a thirtyish fellow in rolled-up shirtsleeves, walking up from a few feet away. Dark and handsome with a reputation for fearlessness, the *Voices of the Negro* editor leaned against a tree, apart from the group, even though there was an empty chair next to the druggist.

"Who you calling jealous?" the druggist demanded.

The editor's response was a pointed stare.

"Come on, Fanny," the druggist said. "I need fresh air." He grabbed his wife's hand and half dragged her away.

"Misery starts in the stomach and flows out through the mouth," the editor said. "Jealousy. That's how we became slaves. It wasn't all about tribal wars. Those wars weren't more than small skirmishes, maybe a dozen casualties at a time. Jealousy, between tribes, relatives and neighbors, accounted for a larger number of captives. Right, Professor Freeman?"

JC nodded, and the editor's lips parted in a slow smile under the shade of his thick moustache.

"I heard what you said about the dead body, David. You should've brought your story to me," the editor said. "We're a free press, and you can bet your bottom dollar we would've published it. Still will, if you've got the details."

"Naw, naw. That's all right," David mumbled.

"I see," the editor said and turned again to JC. "Good luck with your fellowship, brother, but don't expect a lot. I'm from Chicago, and they're not exactly crazy about tan people up there."

"So I heard," said JC. "We still have our appointment. Right, chief?" He figured he could mail his column to Atlanta from Ohio.

"Of course," the editor said, "if things don't boil over before then and they don't run me out of town."

"Why is everybody so negative?" Beatrice blurted. "Let's enjoy the weekend."

"The truth is never negative, Mrs. Freeman. It's just the truth." The editor's eyes bore into hers.

Beatrice did not reply. She thought the editor was dangerously arrogant, the kind of man who looked for trouble. He was new to the city, not really a member of their group, and she wondered who had invited him.

The editor placed his hand on JC's shoulder. "Writers are a dime a dozen, but a brave man like you is worth ten of the other kind."

JC grinned and shook his hand.

Gil joined them with glasses of spiked lemonade on a tray. "Y'all come get some of this pig," Ellen hollered, waving the group to the grill. The roasted meat, dripping in a peppery sauce, and drinks soon loosened them up, and they laughed as they removed flesh from bone and emptied glasses.

Later that evening, after they had toasted JC and sang "For He's a Jolly Good Fellow" for the fourth time, Beatrice, giddy with pride, surprised her husband when she kissed him deeply in front of everyone. They were on their way to a famous university, where wonderful things would happen, and they would return to a new and better city. How lucky they were to be alive in such a glorious time.

Chapter Seven

Only after she heard Beatrice and her family leave the house did Mary Alice come out of her room. Clad in a slip, black with rich lace around the edges, a gift from Reuben, she drank what was left of the morning's coffee and ate cold toast in the kitchen. It was late afternoon. She imagined that in New York, Reuben would be having his first meal after the lunch crowd cleared out.

He had washed her scent from their bed that awful day, as if she were something foul. "A dirty nigger," he shouted, slapping the picture of her family from her hand.

Mary Alice blamed herself. Why hadn't she destroyed that picture? How could she have forgotten that it was in her bag under their bed?

The man bellowing was not her Reuben, who had touched her with such tenderness that she felt as precious as the Fabergé egg on his mother's mantel. This could not be the man, who said only she was good enough to bear his children. This wasn't the man who brought her pretty, sweet plums that she ate while he sucked her toes. This monster, who bounded up like a boxer and struck her with hard hands, was not her Reuben.

She didn't try to protect herself—not at first. Only when his fingers compressing her windpipe made her realize he meant to kill her did she struggle. In a panic she tore at his hands, injuring her ring finger. Her screams ignited their apartment before he clamped his hand across her mouth.

She would always be grateful to their friend, Joel, who ran in from his apartment next door and saved her. A giant man and owner of a butcher shop, he flung Reuben, who was shorter and slighter, against the wall as if he were the hind leg of a lamb.

"She's a goddamn liar," Reuben shouted. "I was about to marry a nigger."

Joel backed away and stared at Mary Alice, who had crumbled to the floor.

"I'll kill this lying bitch. She better get out of my sight." Reuben struck his palm with his fist and paced. "I don't want her in my apartment or this city. I don't want to run into her on the street. If I do, I'll kill her. I swear to God."

"You better leave before you get hurt," Joel said to Mary Alice.

She packed a few things while he stood guard near the bedroom door, and Reuben threw the bedsheets and spread into a kitchen tub filled with soap and bleach. She handed her bloody engagement ring to Joel and took the train to Penn Station, where she cleaned up in a restroom.

Weighed down by memories, She laid her head on the kitchen table and sobbed. Reuben hadn't killed her but he might as well have. No bright future in New York for her now; she had reached the end of her journey. Perhaps the future had not been hers from the beginning, but until Reuben found the picture, it felt right. She believed herself entitled to love whom she pleased. She had a right to live as she wanted, lie or no lie. Ahead of her lay hard work—a dollar a day, plus carfare if she could get it. No tips, and one day off— maybe Sunday. No fiancé to buy her expensive lingerie and suck her toes and show her off at parties. No place to be somebody. She had no choice, no say in life. She would do as her mother and Ruby had done and become a maid. Perhaps she would marry a laborer or porter and have children. Maureen McVey, the name she used in New York, was dead. Mary Alice Redmond, a country girl from Soperton, was alive, and she had to face up to that truth.

Feeling queasy, she spat out the last of her coffee in the sink.

After bathing and inspecting her bruises in the bathroom mirror, Mary Alice dressed in an old dress she found in the bedroom and bored, looked for chores to occupy her. The house was already as clean as a Monday wash. The beds were made, white and tight; starched doilies covered the backs and arms of chairs. She was not a savvy cook, so the thought of making dinner in Beatrice's spotless kitchen scared her.

Brownsville was too quiet. No vegetable hawking, fights, or loud music, nothing like Lydell Alley; no clacking trains or cacophony of languages, like New York. As she settled in a corner of the sofa, traveler's fatigue hit and she nodded off.

Pounding on the front door woke her. Mary Alice didn't know anybody who would visit. From behind the curtains, she saw a blond boy in a white jacket on the porch. *Who the hell is he and what does he want?* He pounded again, like he might break down the door. When she opened it, his pock-marked face didn't look so young. His hand gripped a wire basket with two bottles of milk.

"This here's your milk," he said.

She reached out, and he pulled back. "You colored?" he asked in an accent that sounded like an angry banjo.

She stopped, annoyed by his impertinence. *Even a delivery boy has the nerve to be rude to me, and I have to take it because I'm not Maureen anymore.* "Yes," she said and reached for the milk again.

"Whoa," he said with a grin. "What you gon' give me for this here milk?" He looked her up and down. "You mighty pretty for a colored girl, even if somebody did knock ya around a bit. Not like that other one. She's plain as dirt and black as a ace of spades. Right uppity, too."

Realizing he meant Beatrice, the expression on Mary Alice's face could have moved a mountain. "How much is the milk?" she asked, taking a quarter from a table near the door. "Will this cover it?"

"Will this cover it?" he mimicked. "Will this cover it...*what*?"

She realized her clear diction and choice of words were a problem. "Will this cover it, suh?" she drawled, suppressing an impulse to slam the door in his face. "I sho hope it do."

"That's better. Naw, it's plenty," he said and held his palm for the money.

She dropped the quarter in his palm the way custom demanded, without touching his flesh.

Watching him saunter out to the milk wagon with his round shoulders lost in the too-big jacket, she thought with sadness that she was finally home. *If Reuben were here, that boy wouldn't dare talk to me that way.* But there was no Reuben anymore.

She went back to bed for a proper nap. She flung out her left arm, which Reuben had tried to break, and pain shot from her elbow to the tips of her fingers. She touched her lumpy face. This was where he had tried to gouge out her eyes. Like a blind woman, she traced the puffy lines his fingers left on her neck. "You're choking me," she had gasped, and he wouldn't stop, not even when her eyes rolled back.

She had been wild for him when they first met. His dark curly hair was like silk between her fingers, and his smile melted her. She had opened her body freely and often to him, but in the end, none of that mattered.

She gave up trying to sleep, went to her bag under the bed, and took out the photo that had ended it all. Isabella sat on a bench, the girls and Fat lined up behind her, and behind them was the photographer's pastoral scene of a lamb and rolling hills. Covered in a sepia patina, the family smiled into the camera. Fat said the photo would bring her back to them. She turned it over. Beatrice had written, "From your family with love." Although Mary Alice looked to it for comfort many times during her first years in New York, after meeting Reuben, she hid it under the bed.

Isabella taught her children to be proud of themselves and their race. "No matter what you going through, keep your pride," she said. "Don't let nobody take that." She taught them that passing was shameful, done by weak-minded colored people. So when the idea came to Mary Alice, it was a brutal shock that she resisted—at first.

She had climbed on the trolley behind another maid, Janie, who paid her fare and rushed down the steps to the back door, the one for colored boarding. A driver Mary Alice hadn't seen before smiled as she stepped through the door. "Evening, ma'am," he said. She nodded and dropped a nickel in the fare box. Turning to follow Janie, she glanced at the front seats filled with men in dark suits and hats. They were there day after day like a line of defense.

"Hey, ma'am, where you going?" the driver said as she started out the door.

A man looked up from his newspaper and smirked. "Let er go, Jim. That's a nigger."

Jim's face turned crimson. "Well, I'll be damned," he said. "I wondered why she was so friendly with that other gal."

Mary Alice raced down the steps and to the back door. Colored passengers, who had overheard the exchange, stared and whispered as flames of shame spread through her body. Two women in white domestic uniforms tittered and smirked, as if she had gotten what she deserved. The men in front turned around and dirty eyeballed her. *Who are they to look at me like that? What gives them the right? I'm as good as anybody*. Deep down, though, she felt she wasn't. Her pride had always been vulnerable to public shaming, but that day was the worst she had experienced. An older woman seated next to her patted her hand. "Don't pay them no never mind," she whispered. "You know who you is." With those words propping her up, Mary Alice rode to her employer's home.

She began to wonder. Who was she really? In Soperton, she was Isabella's daughter and colored. During her early years in Atlanta, people often mistook her race and accorded her the courtesies of a white woman. She did nothing to set the record straight, because it was easier to let things be. Her nickel fare was as good as anybody's and if that nosy man had kept his mouth shut, she could've plopped down in a front seat to rest her feet.

In the following months, the woman's statement, "You know who you is", became a mantra in Mary Alice's mind. Who was she, exactly? *I can be whatever I want to be if they don't know I'm colored.* She struggled with the idea, turning it this way and that, imagining the dangers, as well as the benefits. She figured New York City was the place to go. Everything she had heard about the city's exploding population and ethnic groups migrating from every country with a port made it seem perfect for anonymity. She could wear her identity like a new coat and nobody would be wiser. Nobody would care.

And all that time, she told no one—not her boyfriend, Jonah, who would've laughed at her, and not Isabella, Fat, or her sisters, who wouldn't have understood.

Now she was back, beaten half to death, and living with Beatrice again.

"You're still up?" Beatrice poked her head in the bedroom door after her meeting.

"Oh. You're home," Mary Alice said, sitting on the white bedspread in red leather slippers, which she had forgotten to remove.

She saw Beatrice's disapproving glance and eased them off her feet. "How was your meeting?"

"The usual, nothing special. Hey, have you thought about work? Because I know a woman looking for a maid. She's been asking around."

It was typical of Beatrice, always trying to direct the lives of others. Mary Alice knew she needed to work; she just wasn't ready. "As soon as my face clears up," she said.

Beatrice patted her sister's shoulder. "Take your time, honey. We're family."

When somebody tells you to take your time, Mary Alice thought, what they really mean is giddy up. Later as she pulled herself into a ball on the bed and listened to sounds in the house—Phillis running upstairs, JC's heavy footsteps across the bedroom floor above her, and Beatrice starting the teakettle—she envied her sister's life. It was prosperous, if not rich, loving, if not exciting, and very normal. It was the life she'd planned with Reuben.

Chapter Eight

Monday, September 10, 1906

When Mary Alice was alone, which she often was during the day, she felt trapped in her sister's tidy house. But evenings were different as the house filled with people, friends of JC and Beatrice from the university, drinking and talking about race, politics, and money. Their talk made Mary Alice feel small, left out, as though she didn't belong. She thought they behaved as if their modest positions made them millionaires. Of course they weren't poor, like the people in Lydell Alley, but as she watched them take on the airs of the Roosevelts and Astors, she laughed to herself.

She had forgotten how much southern people liked to visit. They'd come to sit a spell and stay all evening, talking about poll taxes, unfair treatment, and what they almost told Miss So-and-So at a downtown store. JC sat in a broad-back chair like a borough president and presided over their charged conversations. One particular night, the topic was Booker T. Washington's Cotton Expo speech. More than ten years old, the speech was still controversial. They argued that Washington's ideas were a hindrance to progress. "Cast down my bucket where I'm at?" said English professor Geoffrey Butler, deliberately mangling his grammar. "What if I ain't got no bucket?" The men and women around the kitchen table laughed and lifted glasses of wine and bourbon.

To Mary Alice, the worst of it was their constant eating. Whole loaves of fresh bread, coconut cakes, fried chicken, and biscuits disappeared from Beatrice's kitchen. While her visitors relaxed, Beatrice showed off her considerable cooking skills and needlessly urged them to drink up. The smell of garlic, onions, vinegar, and peppers made Mary Alice sick to her stomach.

She'd watch Beatrice, sitting across from her husband and laughing, and think how happy her sister was in her skin, surrounded by Brownsville society. Mary Alice felt her spirit sink. Where was her place? It was as if she didn't belong anywhere.

Beatrice introduced her as "my sister from New York," and Mary Alice bent her lips into a stony smile. Two minutes later, she couldn't recall the new person's name or anything else about the introduction. The exception was JC's friend, Carlton Phillips—a teacher at the college and so black that Mary Alice thought he was Ethiopian when in fact he was from South Georgia. He appeared to have an opinion about everything. Speaking in a booming voice that carried to every room in the house, he interrupted others and threw his summer of studying political science at Harvard into every conversation.

Beatrice said he only talked that way when Mary Alice was around. "He definitely has his eye on you. He asked me about the marks on your neck, wanted to know if you're OK."

As Mary Alice tossed her head in dismissal, she became slightly dizzy, a regular sensation she had. "Tell him to mind his own business. I wouldn't have a man like that if he was presented to me on a silver platter."

"Is it because he's dark?"

"You know I'm not like that."

"Be honest now."

"I'm not color struck if that's what you mean."

It was maddening the way Beatrice wanted her to see Carlton as she saw him—a great catch. He was educated, she said, a society man, and she could do much worse. Mary Alice insisted that she liked the pleasure of her own company too much to bother with a loudmouth like Carlton Phillips.

In reality, there wasn't room in her heart for anyone but Reuben, even though their relationship was broken. Years with him wouldn't let her move on. To his coterie of restauranteurs, theater producers, writers, wealthy layabouts, and new-money boys on Park Avenue, she had been his mysterious "Black Irish" beauty from the hinterlands of Brooklyn. He entertained and showed her off in jazz clubs and his restaurant, where she had been a waitress. "Wear red," he'd say. "It makes your skin sparkle." Waiters she had worked with only a few months before fussed over her because she was with "Mr. Reuben." Who would treat her that well if she were with Carlton Phillips?

She smiled, remembering New York doormen bowing, "And how are you, madam?" Carlton Phillips couldn't give her that.

It was true that Reuben and his friends sometimes told nigger jokes. The vaudeville actors—their black faces, white eyes, and enormous red lips—weren't funny, but she laughed anyway—at least on the outside—which didn't matter because the real joke was on them for not knowing. How red their faces would've been if she had said, "You're eating dinner with a nigger."

And all the while she had been in a state of terror. If a bathroom attendant at a night club gave her a certain look, with an unmistakable sly smile, Mary Alice hurried her task in the toilet, so scared that she felt liquid inside. The attendant would quietly go about her business, amused at seeing one of her people getting away with something for a change. Worst of all were the too-friendly grins from colored men on the street. Were they flirting or mocking?

Should she hurry away or ignore them?

She wondered if she had truly loved Reuben. Maybe she had loved the *idea* of being his lover, and, deep in her heart, missed the lifestyle he provided. In any case, a man like Carlton Phillips definitely wouldn't do.

"I'm being as honest as I can about Carlton," she finally said to her sister. "He's too short. I'm five feet, five inches, and I need a taller man." Like Reuben, she could've added but didn't. "Besides, I'm not ready for another relationship this soon."

Fed up with life at Beatrice's, Mary Alice wanted her own place, and for that, she needed a job. It had been almost a week since she returned to Atlanta, and her face was healed enough to search for employment. She refused Beatrice's bossy offer to help her find something and began her hunt alone. On a day when the weather was like a thick stew, she picked her way down muddy streets and looked for window signs: "Help Wanted—Colored." Instead, she saw advertisements for Three Brothers Cough Drops and Carter's Little Liver Pills, and leftover posters from the governor's race.

The city had changed, and her search became a series of disoriented turns. Cain Street was now Magnolia, and Fortune Street had been renamed Nathan Bedford Forrest Avenue, after the Confederate slaver and racist. Something that looked like a flatiron had been erected near Five Points. Mary Alice stepped around ancient men in brown uniforms sweeping the sidewalk in the building's gray shadow. The old Rich's department store had been torn down, and a new building was going up in its place on Whitehall Street. Scaffolding skeletons towered over lots that were vacant when she left for New York. Beyond the city's limits, developers had marched into the peripheral areas of Decatur and Pittsburg like ants into sugar, wanting to become wealthy like the Allens, the Candlers, and the Rich brothers. Boosters hawked Atlanta— new, friendly, and ambitious. Young men no longer needed to go west. They could find their fortunes in the glittering jewel of the New South.

There was even a new train depot, Terminal Station, with gargoyles grinning down at passengers. Upon her arrival from New York, she had been amazed by the elegance of its marble floors and walnut benches. In new clothes and with straightened hair, she could have easily walked through the white waiting room but fearing recognition, she decided not to try it.

On Whitehall Street, she joined a line of maids in white uniforms with starched handkerchief flowers pinned to breast pockets. They queued up as cars and carriages slowed down, and women inside pointed with chalky fingers. "Hey, you. Yes, you. Over here." They hired for day work, a dollar and maybe carfare, far less than Mary Alice's tips in Manhattan. She waited in silence, head up, eyes scanning the street and smoldering with humiliation.

"My white lady think her pee don't stink," said a woman with lips painted like rose petals. Mary Alice laughed with the other women to be polite, even though she wasn't amused by such talk. Standing there, she felt like meat in a market in lower Manhattan, strung along the street with other maids like butchered carcasses. She wanted to cry, but somehow didn't. One by one they were hired until only Mary Alice and the woman with the rose petal lips were left.

A dumpy matron came up on foot, her driver following behind. "You ain't white, are you?" she asked Mary Alice.

Mary Alice ignored the smirking driver and replied, "No, ma'am."

"Just what I thought—a mulatto. Not in my house," the woman said and hired the other maid.

Standing alone as the sun burned off a fog that had settled over the city, Mary Alice fixed her attention on passersby—wealthy shoppers with their hands weighed down by bags from pricey Muse's and Regenstein's; nursemaids pushing carriages with rosy babies, their mistresses strolling in front and pausing at store windows; men in blue or black waistcoats, lugging leather satchels and searching for new angles; and laborers and country boys gawking at everything. Everybody had jobs or at least somewhere to go. And there she was—the last bit of soap in the dish, too thin to fool with. She couldn't go back to New York, nor could she bear going to Pennsylvania or Connecticut or anyplace to be found out again.

She looked in her change purse, which contained a dollar in coins, and snapped it shut. Her face burned as women looked her over and kept walking. *This is my last day of lining up. No more of this humiliation.* She'd rather take in washing, rough, heavy work but better than standing on a street corner like merchandise.

Hungry and tired, she shifted from one foot to the other. She'd skipped breakfast, because she woke up a bit nauseous. Coffee and a biscuit for lunch meant walking several blocks to a colored café on Auburn Avenue and spending a dime she couldn't spare. Besides, she doubted the food would stay down, because anxious about finding work, she'd thrown up her dinner. She smelled peanuts roasting in the Planter's store, and her stomach flipped. She'd just made up her mind to go for a snack when a new black automobile with wide white sidewalls pulled up. It was her last chance, and Mary Alice walked over to it.

A woman leaned out of the window. "You looking for work?"

"Yes, ma'am. I'm Mary Alice Redmond," she said and got in the back. The woman rode in the more comfortable front seat with her driver, a risky practice that invited assaults, newspaper editorials had warned.

The woman—who introduced herself as Gwyneth Forester—rattled on, as if she were talking to an old girlfriend. Her brother was in New Orleans—on business—and had been gone for a week. She didn't know what was taking so long but didn't mind being alone, because she was used to it. She had her knitting, club meetings, and friends who dropped by sometimes. Her last maid quit, because Mr. Forester docked a dollar from her pay for spoiling one of his shirts. The girl had put in too much starch and ironed "cat faces" into it. "Be very careful with his laundry. Mr. Forester prides his appearance," she said. "Are you looking for permanent position?"

Mary Alice had warmed to Gwyneth's friendly manner. "Yes, ma'am."

The work in the Forester house was enough for three maids—two days of dishes in the sink, dirty clothes and linens piled on the floor, dusty rugs, unmade beds in all five bedrooms. Just looking at the mess exhausted Mary Alice. She began with the beds and found a used condom under the sheets of a bedroom that faced the backyard. It was farthest away from Gwyneth's, and Mary Alice guessed that Mr. Forester brought women home. If that was his habit, she understood why his sister kept her bedroom door closed.

Mary Alice rolled her shoulder to loosen fatigue. Now that she had work, she thought she might stay in Atlanta. Beatrice and Fat were proof that there was opportunity if you were a striver. Her days as a maid would end when she opened a restaurant. So obvious was the idea that she wondered why it hadn't occurred to her before. A restaurant would be brutal work but satisfying—a white-tablecloth place like Reuben's, a niche establishment for high-class colored diners, such as Beatrice's friends. She was only a passable cook but could fry chicken and boil rice—the basics—and she knew the business side, having worked in New York restaurants.

When she was ready to leave at five, there was still work to do, and Gwyneth asked her to stay overnight.

"Sorry, Miss Gwyneth, I can't." That swimming in her head had returned.

"Oh, I don't mean to work. I need somebody else in this big house."

Like many lonely people, Gwyneth was garrulous, and she had talked and talked as Mary Alice cleaned. It was as though she'd saved up stories to tell. She said she was thirty-five and had always lived with her brother, "Mr. Forester," who was in real estate and really making a name for himself with city leaders. "Politics is a nasty business," she said. She didn't understand why Mr. Forester loved it. He was unmarried, which was all right for a man, but not a spinster, or so people said. Her last suitor had gone away—out to California to make his fortune—when she was nineteen, and since then, there had been no others. Not that she minded, it was just the way things were.

Mary Alice noticed that Gwyneth kept her hair, the color of fall leaves, in a tight bun, and bit her lower lip, which was too full for her narrow face, until it bled. It was certainly enough to discourage male attention.

"Will you think about a live-in arrangement?" Gwyneth asked. Good help was hard to find, and the girl was clean and well-spoken. "An extra quarter a day, meals included."

As a live-in, Mary Alice would be on duty around the clock, a situation that would leave no time for a personal life. Isabella had been a live-in, and during the times she was away, Mary Alice was lonely and felt motherless. She promised to think about it, although she intuitively dreaded living in that house with Gwyneth, who might try to talk her to death, and her domineering brother.

***

It was time to see her mother, who sent messages when she heard her prodigal daughter was back. After her first day of work, Mary Alice went to Lydell Alley and knelt beside Isabella's chair. "How fragile

Mama looks," she thought. Not fragile in a thin, wasting way of some elderly people, because Isabella was still stout. Instead there was a decided unsteadiness to her gait, and she used a cane.

Expecting rebuke—because she didn't know a loving mother's heart welcomes her child no matter what—Mary Alice was surprised when Isabella's arms opened wide. "My baby, my baby," she said, with tears rolling down her face.

Ruby, too, was tearful. "Shoot, girl, we just about thought you were dead, didn't we, Mama?"

"I knew God was taking care of my baby," Isabella said. "I didn't pay your foolish talk no never mind."

"Dead?" Mary Alice faked a smile, and remembering how close she had come to death, she felt a chill.

She gaped in surprise at Lovelee and then considered that she'd never met Ruby's husband. Maybe the baby looked like him. There wasn't enough African left in any of them to talk about, if you wanted to know the truth, she later said to Beatrice, who laughed and replied, "Speak for yourself."

In Mary Alice's arms, the baby hollered, arched her back, and didn't stop until Ruby took her.

"There's trouble in your auntie's heart," the voice murmured, as the baby lay quiet on her mother's chest. "That's why you can't find peace in her arms." And Lovelee understood.

Isabella peered hard at Mary Alice's neck and asked about the bruises, which were faint.

"I fell down some steps." Mary Alice's voice was barely audible, even though the room was quiet.

Isabella closed her eyes as if in prayer.

"Mama?" Mary Alice said.

Isabella's eyes opened. "Don't mess with those steps again, you hear me? Or next time they might kill you."

"You back for good?" Ruby sounded hopeful.

"I hope so." For now she would stay in Atlanta, maybe open that restaurant, but if another opportunity came, she would move on.

"Is it true nightclubs up there don't never close, and they got trains you hop on while they're moving?" Ruby asked.

Mary Alice chuckled, thinking there was no sense in trying to explain the subway to her sister. Even some New Yorkers had not yet gotten used to the new underground IRT.

Over bottomless glasses of sweet tea, she filled their ears with stories of glamorous parties and trips in new automobiles that gleamed like black diamonds against snowy banks on Fifth Avenue. She bragged about men with fat purses and theaters and shows with the "best people," although she didn't name names.

"How you figure?" Ruby asked. "I mean you colored."

"I swear it's the truth."

As Mary Alice talked and talked, Ruby listened with astonishment. *How could it be that she had seen and done all that? In what country? In what world?*

"Why'd you come back?" Ruby asked. "If things were that good, why not stay there?"

"Because I missed y'all," Mary Alice said, hugging Isabella.

She noticed Ruby and Isabella kept their distance from each other and thought it was unusual. She remembered how close they had been, how Isabella always gave Ruby the heart of the cabbage to munch, the best chicken parts, and forgiveness for misbehavior that would have gotten the other children a spanking. Whatever their disagreement was about, she left it to them to deal with; she had her own problems.

Like a small girl, she sat on the floor between Isabella's legs to have her hair brushed and braided. She relaxed as long brush strokes massaged her troubles away.

Isabella stopped brushing after a minute. "Pretty hair like this turns heads. I hope you didn't go buck-wild in New York."

"What do you mean?" Mary Alice asked.

"You know what I'm talking about, missy," Isabella said. "You were as fast as a buck rabbit with Jonah. Just remember, you can't hide from God. Confess and sin no more, and He'll forgive your iniquities. I know he forgave mine. That's why I stay on my knees in prayer."

"There she goes again with the iniquities," Ruby said. "To Mama, pleasure is a sin. Her religion don't allow no drinking, dancing, cussing or God forbid, sex, except if you don't enjoy it. What iniquities have you committed, Saint Isabella? Go head and tell us. What sins are you talking about?"

"Stop mocking Mama, Ruby. She doesn't have to explain anything to us." Mary Alice turned and studied her mother's face. In the lantern light, Isabella's eyes were luminous with tears and deep lines of sorrow pulled her mouth down. With the pads of her thumbs, Mary Alice wiped away her mother's tears.

Isabella pulled Mary Alice forward for a kiss. "You the one I worry bout the most. The whole time you was gone, I said to myself, I hope ain't nobody mistreating my gal. Beatrice, that proud child, wouldn't ask for help if she needed it. Fat, he's a man and can take care of hisself. Ruby, you're strong, too, except when it comes to that sorry behind Lee Norris. Mary Alice, did your sister tell you her husband's in jail?"

"Jail?" Mary Alice said. "What did he do?"

"Nothing," Ruby said. "Get off my husband's case, Mama."

"Anyway, it don't matter what he did. I done put your situation in God's hands," Isabella said. "He'll handle it better than you or me."

Mary Alice wondered what was going on. *What iniquities did*

Isabella mean? But she didn't pry. This was her mother, who had given birth to her, loved and fed her. A woman her age had the right to see life from lenses that suited her. And when she wanted to talk, she would.

"You know what?" Isabella said, taking Mary Alice's hand. "It's a shame your daddy's not here to see you. Maybe he'll come home, too…one day."

Mary Alice didn't say what she was thinking: Elijah wasn't coming home, and if he did, poor Isabella would be the only one glad to see him.

Chapter Nine

Fat went to Ruby's shack more from curiosity than anything else. Although Zenobia had seen the baby—went over there one morning with the boys and returned with a long face—she wouldn't say what the ruckus was about. Beatrice kept throwing hints but wouldn't say what either. *Isn't that just like women? Always trying to mess with a man's head.*

Even though Fat had figured Mary Alice would turn up again, he was surprised to find her propped against Ruby's bedpost, like she'd dropped by to gossip. In another setting, she could have passed for a Piedmont housewife in her neat blue dress and bone-straight red hair. And that strange accent—he didn't know if it was from up north or England. The way she spoke, as if she had marbles in her mouth, didn't sound like his sister.

"Fat, it's been a long, long time," Mary Alice said, throwing her arms around his neck.

"Whoa," he said, untying himself and standing back. "What wind blew you up after all these years? How come nobody told me?"

"I told them to wait. I knew you'd be mad and I was right. Look at you, huffing and puffing." She thought he looked bigger and more expansive, sure of himself in the way successful people were. His swagger reminded her of Reuben.

"Well, don't expect me to applaud just because you're back," Fat said. "I said you'd come crawling home one day."

"Who do you see crawling?" Mary Alice retorted.

Her bruises were slight, though he could tell she had taken a terrible beating and from a man. Women scratched and pulled hair, he had learned from Peters Street brawls, and men punched. Mary Alice wasn't as wild as Ruby or as headstrong, but she had run off, just disappeared, and he had long ago stopped worrying about her. He figured she was grown and could do as she liked. Whatever trouble she had gotten into was her business. Luckily the fellow who beat her hadn't killed her.

Fat listened, his head cocked to one side, as Mary Alice rambled on about Times Square, Broadway, and Harlem, trying to impress them. "I'm not a fool, girl. There's more to this than you're telling," he said. "But I didn't come to see you anyway. Where's that baby?"

Ruby pointed to a cardboard box, serving as a makeshift bassinet, on the chair.

"Why is she in that thing, Ruby?" Fat asked. "My children slept with their mother."

"Mama said no; it's dangerous. She said she don't want to hear another word about it."

Fat looked at Ruby with questioning eyes.

"Don't ask, cause I don't know."

"Where is Mama?" he asked.

"At Miss Truth's. It's her second home," Ruby said. "She took out over there to tell her Mary Alice is back."

Fat leaned over and peered at the sleeping baby. She definitely wasn't Lee's—a blind man could see that. "What did Beatrice say?" he asked, straightening up.

"About what?" Ruby's voice was sharp. "Why you so worried about Beatrice? You talk like she's the Queen of England, like she run everything. This is my house and my baby. Ain't nobody gon put me down in my own house. Look at the way she treated you after you helped her get on her feet. She said your money was dirty numbers money. She didn't even want you to live in her neighborhood. I hate so-called big-time, signifying folks like her."

"Hold it, girl," Fat said, putting up his hand. "Don't go cussing me out. I'm not Beatrice, far from it. As long as Lee's happy with things, I love it."

"Wow, Ruby, I knew you didn't get along with Beatrice," Mary Alice said, "but I didn't know it had gotten that bad."

Fat shrugged. "Those two? All they do is fight, and nobody knows what they fell out about. I don't think even *they* know. As for Miss Beatrice Freeman, I ain't forgot what she done—Zenobia still talks about it—I just don't hold it against her. Holding grudges ain't my style. I found a house, anyway, didn't I? Big enough for my boys to run around in and right down the street from her. Hell, she was there for our housewarming. Instead of low rating her, get a decent house yourself. And stop running the streets."

Ruby shot back. "I ain't doing that no more. How many times do I have to say it?"

"Thank God," Mary Alice said.

"Come on, Ruby, don't be mad," Fat said, taking a seat in the big chair. "You'll always be my baby sister, don't care what."

Ruby poked out her lips. "Uh, huh. That's why it took you this long to come see my baby. If it was Beatrice, you'd be over there before she could push it out."

"Ruby, shame on you," Mary Alice said.

"It's the truth, or my name ain't Ruby Norris."

"Look, y'all, I got a business to run," Fat said, slapping his knees and rising up from the chair. Sometimes he proudly assumed the role of family patriarch, and other times, when he was the only man around his quarrelsome sisters, he wanted to be a thousand miles away. "I can't make a crying dime unless I'm in that lunchroom, making cash-register music," he said, stepping to the door. "See y'all later."

Outside, he sat heavily on the seat of his wagon for a minute, thinking about Lovelee. *What a mess, what a helluva mess his sister was in.*

On his way downtown, he bought a sack of muscadines from a boy by the side of the road. The fruit was swollen to bursting with sweetness. He sucked the soft insides, spitting out seeds and tough skins as he drove.

Fat's restaurant, called Down Home Cooking, served the city's best potato salad, fried chicken, pigtails in greasy mustard and hot sauce, and sparkling moonshine fresh out of the mountains. It had the right location on Peters, a rough and tumble street of whore houses, gambling, coke dens, and illegal whiskey dives, where a man could find his soul from five in the afternoon until five in the morning and in between if he wanted. Naturally pleasant, Fat treated his clientele well and kept a pistol under the counter to deter trouble. A look from him was usually all it took, and the rowdiest of the rowdy would back off. To keep his place packed all night, he hired a musician—a rusty-throated guitar picker, who sang about hard times and cheating women—and took bets on the numbers, a business Fat picked up from his Uncle Blue. Trusting no one with his money—not even his wife—Fat watched the cash register, carefully counting the take from the two big-butt women who waited the tables.

He guided his horse through traffic that was slow with afternoon shoppers, newsboys darting in the street to hawk headlines—*Bold Negro Kisses White Girl's Hand*—and red soft drink wagons with slogans advertising: *A Delicious and Refreshing Drink, Relief for Headache and Exhaustion.* Fat pushed his horse, switching its backside and aggressively moving ahead of other vehicles. He was late and the first-shift girl, who opened up, had sticky fingers. He was at Marietta Street when a man—dark, sweaty, with eyes white with fear—ran in front of his horse. Fat pulled up fast, wondering what the hell was going on. "Help me, mister," the man begged. Before Fat could respond, a gang of five white boys appeared.

"Niggah, we gon' tear your hide off," screamed a lanky boy of about eighteen. The man ran across the street as if he were on fire, pursued by the boys, and Fat raced his carriage in the opposite direction. The encounter shook him, and although he wouldn't admit it to anyone, it showed a picture of him that he didn't like. He had run when a man would have stood his ground. He made excuses—he was outnumbered and they had weapons—but the truth kept returning. He had run.

******

Fat's children had been in bed for hours when he came home for a quick break that evening. He was tired from work and time in the backroom of his store with Harriet. Their affair would end when she moved to DC, and in the days they had left, she was pouring affection into him. In the bedroom at home, his hands massaged his knees, which hurt from hitting the hard floor while they made love.

He wasn't in love with her; she just made him feel good. When she came to the restaurant, strutting in right after it opened as though she owned the place, he made an excuse to his staff and followed her. He knew it was foolish to mess with that head-strong girl when he had good wife. Still, having more than one woman made him feel like twice the man. Zenobia loved him; Harriet *desired* him, and just the thought of her made him sweat. It was dangerous, the place he was in, particularly if her father, Blue, were to discover the affair. The last time he was with the old man, he acted funny, as if he suspected something. Fat prayed his Harriet fever would break after she was gone.

He cleaned up in a washbowl in the bedroom. Dressed in a clean shirt and pants, he joined his wife for dinner and shoved food into his mouth.

"I saw something today I hope I never see again," Fat said to Zenobia after they had eaten. "White boys chased a man on Marietta. He looked scared to death…."

"What do you think happened to him?"

Fat was quiet for a while, considering her question as if they both didn't already know the answer. "They tried to put their damn hands on me," he said, lying for her sake and his. "But I tore after them and they ran off. I remember when this city was peaceful. Everybody got along or at least claimed to. Then those politicians started turning people against each other. Something's gonna happen if they don't stop. I can feel it. Don't go downtown for nothing. You hear me?" His wife was more cloistered than most Brownsville women. She ran her business from their home and shopped only in local stores. He believed she hadn't heard the stuff about "white hats" straightening things out. But it was hard to tell with Zenobia, as quiet as she was. "And don't take my children out of Brownsville," he added.

"Mm, hmm," Zenobia said, because she didn't know how else to respond. Fat could be overbearing in the best of times, and she could see that the trouble with those boys had upset him. She brought a coffeepot and cups to the table and as she leaned over to pour him a cup, her eyes landed on a nickel-size bluish spot on his neck. "What's this?" she said, touching it.

Fat went rigid. "I'm caught, dead in the water," he thought. But to his wife, he said, "Now don't go getting riled up for nothing." Knowing that she had spotted a passion mark from Harriet, he thought fast. "That's from those boys who attacked me."

"Who says I'm riled up?" Zenobia said softly. The mark looked suspicious, but he was attacked and it could be from that. She decided to keep her eyes and ears open, just in case he was tipping around. "You tired?" she asked, noticing his slumped shoulders.

"Naw," he said, "just fed up." The man downtown begged. *"Help me, mister."* A real man would've jumped in, helped the guy out, and done some damage, even if it meant losing.

"Forget those racists," Zenobia said, massaging his shoulders. "You're my hero."

He relaxed under her soft fingers, feeling lucky to have an easy going wife. He felt sorry for JC, who had to cope with Beatrice, with her edgy self. And poor Lee. He hoped the guy wouldn't try to hurt his sister and force him to step in. They were friends, but blood meant more to him than water.

He returned to the lunchroom and worked until closing. On his way home at five in the morning, Fat stopped at Best Baptist Church—his spiritual home. As a deacon, he was immersed in church life. The Reverend H. E. Jackson, senior pastor, held his deacons to monthly meetings, funeral services, church dinners, Bible study, missionary gatherings, and front-row pews on Sunday mornings. Fat was an obedient servant, giving generously of his money and time when the lunchroom permitted, because there was nothing he liked better than to be called Deacon Redmond, a man of God. He turned his key in the brass lock, pushed open the heavy door, and felt the quiet sanctuary wrap its arms around him. Walking to the altar with his Sunday swagger, he dropped to his knees and prayed for courage if he should meet the Marietta thugs again. He prayed for fidelity to his wife and asked God to make him a better man than his daddy. As sunlight broke through the stained-glass windows, he raised his head and breathed in the calming, smoky scent of spent candles.

Chapter Ten

Thursday, September 13, 1906

Ruby's rent was overdue and her baby needed food. That was why less than two weeks after her daughter's birth, she went to work. Her white lady required a white uniform and a starched apron, which she donned in the dark, moving around on bare feet before quietly putting Lovelee to her breast for a feeding. With the thin pap on the table, it would have to last until she returned.

As Ruby eased the door open and stepped outside, she heard Lovelee sigh with a full stomach and Isabella turn over on her pallet at the foot of the bed. It was only six in the morning and already steamy hot. She walked down the unpaved alley, keeping an eye out for threatening shadows between houses. Hunger's heavy hand tugged at her as she smelled fatback frying and coffee brewing in neighboring shacks.

Ahead of her was a limping figure she was sure belonged to her neighbor, Charlie, on his way to the barbershop on Peachtree Street. He was a good fellow, hardworking and reliable. She had seen him sweeping the front of the shop, dragging his lame foot, and sympathy tugged at her heart. The roll of his buttocks as he hopped along was almost feminine. That idea would be funny to Truth, who said

Charlie "smelled his mannish self." Ruby slowed down behind the boy. She didn't want him to see her; it was too early for talking.

Charlie turned left on Old Wheat Street, and Ruby went right. Blackbirds, strung together in perfect formation created a winged arrow above her head. They looked more certain about the direction the day would take than she was. In minutes, the Buckhead-bound trolley clanged to a stop. The car was empty, except for the driver, who looked at her with bored, sleepy eyes as she climbed on and paid her nickel. She stepped back outside, entered the car again from the back door, and dropped into a seat.

Ruby couldn't stop worrying about Lovelee. It was awfully hard to leave her so soon. What if the pap wasn't enough and she cried for the breast? Her baby wasn't even old enough to hold her head up. "Though somebody like me, a mother without a husband," she thought, "got to do the best she can."

When Isabella read the note she left—*Gone to work, will return soon*—she'd be madder than usual. She and her mother had become like a married couple, who stayed together because they had no choice but didn't talk unless it was absolutely necessary, avoiding each other as much as they could in the tiny shack. Ruby believed she had lost her best friend. Sometimes in deep despair, she apologized to Isabella without really knowing what she had done. Instead of accepting her apology, her mother talked about bearing crosses and tedious journeys. It left Ruby scratching her head and wondering what more could she do. When would she forgive her?

She climbed down from the streetcar. The woman she worked for, Mrs. Oscar Louis Beale, was a slave driver. The only good thing about the job was it paid the rent. Ruby had sent a note that said she was returning to work. When she knocked at the back door, Mrs. Beale, a thin, pretty brunette, opened up with dark circles under her eyes. "Thank goodness you're here," she said, moving aside to let

Ruby in. "This has been the worst week. I had a girl in for a few days, but she was too slow to catch a cold. Mr. Beale said I had to get better help."

Ruby stepped inside, and her shoes stuck to something that looked like jelly. "Let me get started," she said, tying on an apron. "I have to leave on time—my baby."

Mrs. Beale glanced at Ruby's flat abdomen. "Boy or a girl?"

"A girl. I can't leave her long, cause I'm feeding her."

"Just make sure you polish the floors. Otherwise I'll cut your pay."

"Yessum." Ruby's face closed down as she cleared the table.

Mrs. Beale left the kitchen, and Ruby heard her going up the stairs to get ready for an "outing." Her outings began after Mr. Beale and the children were out of the house and lasted until just before he returned. She would rush in with her hair in damp ringlets and her lipstick gone. Ruby used to say to herself, "This woman is either a fool or she don't care if her husband catches her."

A couple of times during the day, Ruby stopped work to squeeze milk from her aching breasts. By the time the Beale brood barreled in from school, she was ironing clothes and lost in thoughts about Lovelee. Had she eaten the pap? Was she crying? The biting smell of burning cloth brought her back to her work. She tossed the ruined shirt in the garbage, as the youngest Beale child ran past. The girl was six and still had baby fat on her face; Ruby looked at her and ached for Lovelee.

Mrs. Beale returned an hour later and sent Ruby out the door with a dollar and carfare. The trolley's bell clanged in the distance. She reached the stop just as the doors opened. After paying her fare, Ruby took a back seat across from a hefty woman with a cheap purse and a cloth bag crowding her feet.

The woman saw Ruby's eyes on her bulging bag and leaned over.

"I'll tote her whole damn kitchen home," she said, "if the stingy heifer don't pay me right."

Ruby smiled. She earned five dollars a week and carfare. It wasn't enough, so she lifted food from Mrs. Beale's choked pantry. She placed her strong palms on the ends of fresh bread, slapped them together, and the loaves collapsed as thin as a fried egg sandwich into her big cloth purse. Thick slices of ham and beef, pieces of fried chicken, canned peas, hunks of butter, and sugar disappeared from the kitchen, and Mrs. Beale was too busy with her love affair to notice.

The large handbag resting on her lap held leftover ham, and a loaf of bread. That morning while she was in the house alone, she placed a ring from Mrs. Beale's jewelry case in an inner pocket of the bag and secured it with a safety pin. She wasn't proud of it, neither was she ashamed. Satisfied was how she felt. For once in her life of picking cotton and cleaning, she would have a few extra dollars. Some people might call it theft; she called it a chance.

"Times is hard, ain't they?" the woman on the trolley said, trying to be friendly.

Ruby gazed out the window and didn't reply. Her thoughts were on Lovelee and home.

At the next stop, Charlie boarded and paid his money. Ruby's heart went to him, as he hobbled to the back door and swung on. The back of the car had filled to standing room only, while there were two rows of empty seats in the whites-only section. The doors closed, the bell clanged as the car moved, and Charlie grabbed a pole. When Ruby saw his eyes on the empty front seats, she guessed what he was thinking and mentally begged him not to do it. Then in one quick move, he was on a bench across the aisle from a white man, who jumped up as though he had seen a rat. "What the hell's going on?" he said.

"Boy," Ruby hissed, thinking the boy had lost his mind, "get back here. You trying to give your mama something to cry about?"

"Ruby," Charlie said in surprise and scrambled to the back.

When he grabbed a strap hanging above her head, she looked up and saw his eyes burning and fixed on the passenger, who had jumped up. The man was back in his seat and turned away from them. She touched Charlie's knee to get his attention. "It's not worth it," she said.

He nodded and rode the rest of the way with his eyes closed.

She swung off the car at Jackson Way, hit the ground too hard, and staggered. An arm caught hers. When she turned around and saw Charlie's angular face, she mumbled "Thanks" and hurried on. She didn't see Carol, Truth's young daughter, fall in step with him and curl her hand into his. The two strolled behind, careful not to overtake Ruby and be discovered.

Truth was on a stool at her door. "Ruby, that you?" she called, hearing quick footsteps. "You see that gal of mine?"

"No, ma'am."

"She's probably with that mannish Charlie." Truth sucked the insides from a fat muscadine and spat away the skin.

As they approached, Carol pulled away from Charlie and walked ahead, slipping as quietly as a shadow behind her mother's stool.

Truth's head turned. "Carol?"

"Yessum."

"I thought so. I might be blind, but ain't nothing wrong with my hearing. You've been with that boy. I can smell his nasty cigarettes on you."

Carol's tearful eyes followed Charlie as he hobbled to his house.

"You could be a teacher like Beatrice," Truth continued. "Couldn't she, Ruby?"

Ruby thought that Truth needed to provide her daughter with a better example. Beatrice might be a teacher but she was hateful. Just once, she'd like to hear a kind word from her sister. "Miss Truth. I got to check on Lovelee."

"Isabella was out here most of the morning with her," Truth said. "Pretty little thing. People justa talking about the way she looks. Here, take your mama a sack of these muscadines."

Ruby took the fruit and stomped off to her shack, furious that the alley was spreading lying stories about her baby.

******

As Isabella was wagging a finger at Ruby for going to work too soon, a former inmate at a local brick factory, Calvin Brinkley, showed up in the alley. When Calvin asked for Ruby Norris, her neighbors shook their heads and walked away from the emaciated white man. At last he stopped in front of Truth, who wrinkled her nose at his unwashed body and pointed to Ruby's shack.

"You ain't got no business working in your condition," Isabella said as Ruby finished feeding her baby. "Just wait till you get my age and see what rheumatism gon—"

Brinkley pushed open the door and stepped inside.

"Oh, my goodness," said Isabella, peering at him from the far side of the bed. She wasn't wearing her hat, and a snowstorm of hair framed her startled face.

"Who you?" asked Ruby. "We ain't got no money for insurance."

"I ain't selling none neither." He held up a folded brown paper bag that was stained with grease and mud. "My name is Mr. Calvin R. Brinkley, and I got this here letter for a gal named Ruby. That you?"

"That's me," Ruby said. "Who the letter from?"

"Read it and see."

As he passed the letter to Ruby, she spotted crescents of dirt under his nails and was careful not to touch his hands. Lee's handwriting was on the folded, unsealed bag. She unfolded it and read.

> *My dearest darling wife, Mrs. Ruby Norris,*
>
> *I had to write, because being away from you is hell. I hope you git this leter and it finds you doing good. This ain't no place for human beings and I can't stand another minute here. We is being used worse than dogs. The mules get reel food, we get slop.*
>
> *The only thing keeping me alive is you. I wouldn't mind if I could see your face once more. I need to here your sweet voice and touch you.*

Ruby paused and looked at Brinkley, who was standing too close. "Mr. Calvin, can we get you something?" she asked, hoping he would leave. He had delivered the letter. What more did he want?

"That boy, Lee, told me he put word about some money in there."

"I'll see." It made her feel better that Brinkley couldn't read and didn't know her husband's intimate thoughts. She returned to the letter.

> *Do you have enuff to eat, my darling? I worry, because you is eating for to. I promise to buy you a whole hog when I get out. I'll salt it down and we'll have meet to last a while. The center cuts go to you.*

Ruby glanced at Brinkley, who said, "Go on, it's in there, what he promised me." Continuing to read, she felt her face turn warm.

> *I love you more than birds love to sing. I love your thies, breasts, the way your brown hips roll when you walk. Don't laff at your man, it's true.*

Hope I'll last till the end of my sentence and come home. But rite now, the only thing in my cards is misery. This hell hole ain't fit for the lowest animal, let alone a man. These guards ain't nothing but devils with they whips and cussing. I seen men sick and dying in the mud, and I seen bodies caried out in the midle of the night. I don't meen to scare you, that's how it is. Maybe I ain't strong enuff, that's why I'm here, caged up worse than a animal.

When you git this, give the man who brought it a quarter. They let him go at the end of his time. I don't think I gon be that lucky. He said he'd sneak my leter out if I paid him.

Pray for me, my darling, like I pray for you and our unborn child.

Ruby finished reading through a curtain of tears. *Men sick and dying.* The man she loved could die in that miserable brickyard. She wanted him home, but then she didn't because of Lovelee. Her head spun with confusion. "You think they gon let him come home soon?" she asked.

"Naw, he's got to serve his time like everybody else. I was in for six months, honest time. Boys like him try to play sick to get outta things, but it don't help none."

"When did you see him, Mr. Calvin?" She glanced behind at Lovelee asleep in a box on the chair and hoped Brinkley couldn't see her.

"Near bout three days ago."

"How...how was he?"

"He looked good, bout like me."

Ruby blinked in amazement, thinking Brinkley hadn't looked in a mirror in a long time. In all her years in the alley, she hadn't seen a worse-looking human being.

"They had him stretched out on a cot in what they call the infirmary, where I worked," Brinkley said, "He said he was sick, vomiting and all. I think he just wanted a chance to give me the letter. They kinda slack in that sick tent, if you ask me, and you can sneak things out. Took them a whole hour to figure he was faking and throw him back in the yard. Now what about my fifty cents? The boy said he wrote you strict instructions."

Ruby pursed her lips, opened her coin purse, and paid him two quarters. He grinned, showing broken top teeth. Hoping that he would leave, she turned and laid the purse on her bed.

As he started for the door, Isabella came closer and studied his face as if she were going to draw it from memory.

"What do you want, auntie?" Brinkley said, pulling the brim of his old hat down over his eyes.

"Suh, look to me like I know you," she said. "I knowed you when you was a lot younger." Isabella reached up to push his hat back for a better look.

"Touch me, and I'll kill you on the spot," Brinkley said, stepping back with his hand on a knife in the front pocket of his grimy pants.

Ruby brushed Isabella hand away and held it down. "You crazy, Mama? That's a white man," she whispered and felt a sudden lightheadedness. The odor of motor oil fumes nauseated her. *There's a tree out there with his name on it.* An image of a man larger than Brinkley flashed in her mind, and then it was gone.

"Humph. You used to be something, now you ain't," Isabella said to Brinkley. "You ain't nothing no more."

"Why I oughta slap the fire outta you, old hag, for giving me big talk," the old man shouted.

"It's OK, Mama. You don't know Mr. Calvin," Ruby said. "She's been sick, Mr. Calvin. She real sorry. She don't mean no harm." She led Isabella to a chair, nailed her to it with her eyes, and pressed the old lady's shoulders against the back cushion until she stopped resisting.

When she turned around a minute later, Brinkley had disappeared and so had her coin purse. She looked at the empty space on the bed where it had been, and tears swelled in her eyes. Fifty cents gone, all she had in the world. Then she remembered the ring in her bag. "Saved," she thought.

Isabella sat in the chair with her eyes closed, as if sleeping.

It didn't fool Ruby. "Mama, what did you do that for?" she said, putting Lovelee to her breast. The baby's frantic suckling tore her heart apart. Her poor baby hadn't had a proper feeding all day.

Isabella opened her eyes. "I thought I recollected him from way back before you was born."

"He could've killed us."

Isabella said Calvin looked very much like a boy who used to come to her mother's cabin with his father, a white man. "The man I told y'all was my daddy."

Ruby's eyes flew wide open, and she stared at her mother in astonishment. "You mean Calvin is your half-brother? That's crazy. He didn't even know who you was."

"I didn't say he was. I said looked like. He got the same name. His eyes and mouth look like…I mean, they put me in the mind of that boy I used to play with. That rascal gave me a piece of chocolate fudge on day, and poor greedy me, I ate it in one bite. I never tasted such a delicious thing in my life. Then he told me he put a bug in the fudge and I threw up. I can't stand the stuff till this day. He was mean but better looking than his daddy back then. I ain't seen him since we was young. Now he look like the devil had a fit with him."

"Jesus, Mama. After all this time, you just now telling me you have a half-brother." Ruby had suspected there were things too terrible to share in her mother's head, so she wasn't as surprised as she pretended.

"Didn't you hear me say he *might be* my half-brother?" Isabella said. "I was ashamed, though everybody back then mixed and mingled." Her eyes lowered to the baby. "Still do, I guess. And Beatrice, well, you know how she is. You can't tell her nothing she won't get on her high horse about. Fat's the same way sometimes, and ain't no telling about Mary Alice. I can't keep up with her long enough to know. You're my baby, the heart of my heart. You understand me better'n the others."

Ruby's heartbeat sped up with happiness. They were finally back on good terms. "Where this man, you *think* is your half-brother, been?"

"Don't know. When he disappeared after the war, I didn't try to find him. What for? He probably didn't know we was kin. That's just the way it was. If he was my brother, didn't nobody but me and Mama know about it. Talking about things like that brought trouble. And like I said, the boy was downright mean."

Settling back in her chair, Isabella kept talking, as if she couldn't stop. "I heard his daddy was killed in the war. I say 'his,' because he never acted like no daddy to me. After the war, me and Mama and Viola moved to a house in the middle of cotton that almost grew up to our front door. You could run through it near bout a hour fore you got out." Isabella chuckled. "At night, you couldn't see nothing but haints, ghosts jumping in that cotton like they real people. They probably was, cause some of that cotton grew over graves. Mr. Callahan said he couldn't waste the land on them. The soil was red, though, burned that way by the sun, cause God wasn't happy with the people on it. They say red soil is a sure sign that next time, like the Bible says, there's gonna be fire." Isabella said she used to cry at night from loneliness. "Vy was long gone. That bullheaded girl moved to Atlanta after Mama said she was too womanish to stay under her roof. When Mama died, I married your daddy and set up housekeeping in Soperton."

"Seem like ain't no peace in this world, no matter what you do," Ruby thought. Lovelee stopped feeding for a moment and licked Ruby's salty tears raining on her lips. Her tiny hand tapped her mother's chin as if to say, "There, there."

"I ain't worried about seeing Calvin again. He too scared somebody might find out we related and think he's colored. I seen it on his triflin face."

"Plus, he stole my damn money."

Later that night after Ruby had put her baby down to sleep, she kissed Isabella's cheek. . "Mama, you got any more shockers before I go to bed?" she teased.

"Just one, but it ain't time yet. My heart's too full to talk now."

Ruby looked at her in wonder. *What else could there be?* She was afraid to press Isabella, no telling what she might reveal. Ruby didn't know what was real anymore. The things she knew about her mother, she didn't. What other shock might come from the woman snoring at the foot of her bed? It scared her to think about it.

The alley was quiet, very different from its usual din of: blues singing; fighting men and women, too drunk to know what they were doing; crying children; mean, howling dogs; and broken-down horses clopping on packed earth. Ruby smelled wet air seeping through the boards of the shack and heard a thunderclap far away. She lay in bed with Lovelee and listened to the weather. For safety, they had closed the shutters, preferring a stifling room to a break-in. A mosquito hummed, too drunk with blood to bite, and staggered into the slop jar under the bed, as Ruby fell asleep. After a couple hours, she awoke to the heavy beat of rain on the roof and lightning crackling. She hoped Lee wasn't sleeping in mud at the work camp.

Chapter Eleven

When the grocery bills came, Gwyneth Forester handed them to her brother, who handled their money. "Who the hell are we feeding—an army?" he asked one afternoon, slamming his fist down on the pile of unpaid bills. "That gal in the kitchen," he said, "she's stealing."

Later that afternoon when she told the "gal" what he'd said, Mary Alice opened the pantry and pointed to shelves crowded with sacks of flour and sugar, jugs of syrup and molasses, jars of pickles, and flat tins of sardines. As the sweet and sour smells turned her stomach, which had been delicate all week, she snapped, "What's missing?" She didn't dare use that sharp tone with Mr. Forester.

"Nothing that I can see," Gwyneth said, which meant nothing, because she didn't have a habit of counting their supplies.

"I am not a thief."

"Just be careful," Gwyneth said. Like most women with housemaids, she accepted a certain amount of petty theft as the price to pay for help. "Brother hates to spend money, even for food."

As Mary Alice finished cleaning the kitchen, she swelled up, angry that Mr. Forester had accused her of stealing. That little bit of coffee and sugar she had at breakfast was hers—she'd worked for it. Mr. Forester was rich and could afford to pay her more but wouldn't. Besides she'd had a queasy stomach for days and had hardly eaten anything, not even at the Foresters. She slammed the last pot away, and instead of hanging her apron on a nail in the pantry, she threw it across a chair. "Miss Gwyneth, I'm leaving. OK?" she yelled up the stairs. Gwyneth was napping behind her closed bedroom door and didn't respond, so Mary Alice went on her way.

At the trolley stop, an older maid she knew watched her approach and said, "You doing kinda poorly, ain't you, Mary Alice?"

"Just tired, Miss Nollie, that's all."

"I know how you feel," Nollie said and sighed. "My white lady made a song out of my name today—*Nollie do this, Nollie do that, Nollie, Nollie*—like I run by electricity."

Mary Alice didn't know what it was. Maybe the cheese and crackers she forced down for lunch or the sight of Miss Nollie's bad teeth, but her stomach flipped, her skin turned sweaty, and somehow she knew what she should have known for days. *I'm pregnant.* Even as the words entered her mind, she couldn't believe it. She needed to sit down—fast—and was relieved to see the trolley making its way down the avenue of trees.

She cried in secret and tossed in her bed, wishing she were dead. Maybe if she phoned Reuben, he would help. He had money from his restaurant and as the only son, he had a large inheritance from his father's estate. He wouldn't marry her, she knew that, but he might send money for the baby. Despite everything, he was a good man and had every right to be angry. She had lied and lies hurt. But if she could talk to him and let him know a baby was coming, he might choose their child over anger.

In the morning, she awoke with her face swollen from crying. She stayed in her room until Beatrice and her family were out of the house. Reuben would be dressing for work and if she talked to him before his mind was cluttered with restaurant problems, if she could simply tell him about her condition and not demand anything, he might listen. He might offer to help. After all, she was carrying his child; that should count for something, no matter how he felt about her. Dreading the call, she walked on legs of lead to the phone in the living room and dialed. Since Reuben probably wouldn't accept a collect call her, she charged it to Beatrice's phone.

When he answered, his voice was gruff, typical of Reuben before having his morning coffee.

Even so, the sound of his voice brought back loving memories, and Mary Alice almost said, "Darling, it's me," because that was the way it had been between them. But those days were history, so she said, "Reuben, please listen."

"What the hell do you want?"

She drew in a deep breath. "I'm expecting your child." The words tumbled out in a cascade that didn't sound like her voice. She gripped the receiver and waited. *What will he say, Lord, what? Please help me.*

Seconds that seemed like hours passed before he said, "You're a damn lie."

"Please Reuben, listen and don't get mad. I am really pregnant. I wouldn't make this up."

He laughed, as if mocking her. "You'd make up anything if you thought you could pull it off. If you are pregnant, it's not mine. What did you do—shack up with some spook down there? Now you want to blame it on stupid Reuben."

"No, no. It's the truth. I'm carrying your child."

"The truth is you want to get your hands in my pockets. If you phone me again, you lying whore, I'll have you arrested for fraud." He hung up.

She felt dizzy and had to sit. Crying, she pressed a hand against her pounding chest. All things considered, Reuben had a right to believe she was lying again, yet he didn't have to be so brutal, accusing her of being with someone else. She hadn't been in Atlanta long enough for that and he knew it. The truth was—he didn't want their baby.

Mary Alice went to work and returned to Beatrice's house well after dark, rushing to make the bathroom in time. When she finished being sick over the sink, she looked in the mirror at her blanched face, her bony clavicle, and thought it couldn't be true. She was too skinny, yet she knew it was. She was pregnant and Reuben hated her. She lay in bed running her fingers along an abdomen that was as flat as a plank of wood. She tapped her belly and the sound was hollow, which didn't reassure her. She was three weeks late and she was never late, so it had to be true. Oh, she sighed. Oh, what was she going to do? Beatrice would be outraged, of that she was certain. What would her mother say? Where could she go? How would she care for a child when she could barely take care of herself?

In her despair, she saw Reuben with new eyes. She believed, in spite of his rejection, that he knew she was carrying his baby. So he lied, too. Brutal and unforgiving, he was a man she didn't hate but couldn't love any longer.

Beatrice stuck her head in the door. JC and Phillis were upstairs with lessons, and she had volunteer work to do. Would Mary Alice like to join her?

"Tonight? I'm tired." Mary Alice turned away. She couldn't sit through another night with Beatrice's chattering friends.

Left alone for several minutes, Mary Alice thought the matter was settled. She was startled when her sister returned, hat in hand, and told her it was time to go. "I'll wait for you in the front room," she said. "The meeting's just down the street."

When Beatrice wanted something, there was no resisting her. Only JC could say no, and he didn't do it often. Mary Alice tried again. "I'm tired, Beatrice."

Beatrice lectured her about helping others. "We can't sit back and say, 'I got mine; you get yours. I started the Willing Workers to raise money for the primary school and an orphanage. If you live in this house, you have to help the children in our community. That's just the way it is."

With a sigh, Mary Alice put on her shoes.

On their way there, Beatrice said, "These are the most responsible women you'll meet anywhere. They're kind and loving. They're going to make you feel at home. You'll see."

Although Mary Alice trudged beside her, she wasn't listening. How could she tell her upright, social climbing sister that she was pregnant and the father, her ex-fiancé, wouldn't marry her if you held a shotgun to his head? Her mind went in and out of focus as they covered several blocks. They passed lighted windows of families sitting down to supper, and Mary Alice worried that their perfect lives—loving parents and obedient children—were beyond the reach of someone like her, pregnant and unmarried.

The sisters walked into a meeting that had already begun. Four prosperous-looking women in their thirties worked at a dining-room table spread with pencils, pens, writing tablets, crayons, primary schoolbooks, and small bottles of golden glue. A pine hutch of china crowded the room. Wall light sconces gave everything a tranquil, warm feeling.

As Beatrice predicted, the club threw its arms around Mary Alice. Mrs. Moses Hampton, a sylph of a woman with skin like polished onyx, admired her lily complexion and pressed hair. She joked that Mary Alice could get away with sitting on a streetcar's front seat, maybe even in the driver's lap. The other women laughed, as Mary Alice bit the inside of her lower lip and tried not to burst into tears.

"Smile." Beatrice nudged her. "Why are you so glum?"

Mary Alice shrugged and didn't reply. Nothing was going to make her confide in Beatrice until she had to.

"Our gain is New York's loss. Welcome, my dear," said Mrs. Leon Simpson, the wife of a postal clerk. She had three children and was expecting twins in a couple of months. Her hands were swollen, and so were her feet, which were propped on a stool.

"Where did you live in New York—Harlem?" asked Mrs. Hampton.

Beatrice jumped in before Mary Alice could reply. "Uh, in an apartment with another young lady, a nurse."

Mary Alice listened with a forced smile, and her mood darkened. *How can I tell this woman, so full of airs and pretense, that I'm pregnant?*

"One hundred and twenty-fifth? Up that way?" asked the hostess, a pretty woman with a longish chin and glossy black hair piled high on her head.

Because it was clear Beatrice was showing off and she didn't want to make her look foolish, Mary Alice, who knew nothing about Harlem, said, "Not quite that far but close."

The woman smiled and nodded, though she, too, knew nothing about Harlem.

Beatrice took a seat that was reserved for her at the head of the table, and Mary Alice sat on her left. For two hours, they sorted books and filled two large boxes. The pencils and tablets went into smaller boxes that they labeled with the names of primary schoolteachers. Mary Alice was impressed by their efficiency. Unlike Carlton and his crowd, they neither ate nor drank.

"How many boxes so far?" Beatrice asked, pausing as she counted pencils.

"Ten," somebody replied.

Mary Alice felt sick. *How exactly can I put it? I'm pregnant...no, that's too blunt. I'm in the family way...softer but the message is just as bad. What about I done broke my leg, the way old folks talk about girls in my condition?* She laughed inside at how stupid her announcement would sound.

"OK, let's do five more. If we don't take care of our children, nobody else will," Beatrice said. "You know Phillis attends that school, and I can't imagine her not having what she needs."

Listen to her—so proud. She'll throw me out of her house. I can't go to Ruby's crowded one-room shack and disappoint Isabella. Forget about Fat. He still treats me like a kid sister. I don't have options, not a single one.

At ten o'clock the boxes were filled and stacked along the wall. Mary Alice and Beatrice walked home on pitch-black streets. It had rained while they were inside and the air was dense enough to slice. A cat in heat moaned somewhere. Otherwise it was quiet as could be.

Beatrice said JC and other men would deliver the supplies to the school, which had opened with bare shelves. She worried aloud about what would happen after they moved to Ohio. A few children would bring books and paper from home, of course, but most could not afford them. "Somebody has to do something," she said. "They're our future."

"I'll do what I can," Mary Alice said.

Beatrice cleared her throat. "What about your baby?"

"You know?" Mary Alice's steps slowed to a stop.

"The way you've been throwing up—who wouldn't know?" Beatrice grabbed her hand. "Come on. We'll talk about it at home."

Mary Alice stumbled along beside her, dreading the talk.

Beatrice's rosebushes had bloomed in bursts of red that appeared black along the dark path to the house. Mary Alice breathed in their perfume as her sister broke off mint leaves growing near the roses and they went inside.

"What if you're just late?" Beatrice said, adding sugar to hot water and mint leaves. "You could be wrong."

Mary Alice said she was sure. "Oh, Beatrice, what am I going to do?"

"It's Reuben's, right? He was going to marry you."

"He wants to kill me."

"That's what he said, but this is his baby. When he knows, he'll step up. Most men do." Beatrice set down her cup and probed Mary Alice's face with anxious eyes. "What are you thinking? Talk to him. Tell him about the baby."

"I called him today from your phone—I'll pay for the call—and he hung up on me."

"That dirty dog. So what are you going to do? Raise it yourself?"

"I can't have this baby."

Beatrice put down her cup. "That's evil, a sin before God."

"Beatrice, you're my sister."

"I'm a Christian, first and foremost."

"Then you won't help me?"

"Listen to me. You can have this child. I'll rent a place for you and the baby in Lydell Alley. Houses are available over there all the time, what with the riffraff that…" Beatrice stopped, realizing that her argument was headed in the wrong direction. "We'll say you married in New York, and your husband died. That'll keep people from talking. See. It's settled."

Mary Alice didn't want to return to the alley, a place for riff raff, as her sister almost said, and she didn't want to lie about being married. Lies were at the root of her trouble. "Why can't I stay with you?" she asked. "Just until I get on my feet."

"I can't expose Phillis," she said. "She's at an impressionable age."

Her refusal cut Mary Alice to her core and solidified her decision. "Don't you think I'm ashamed, too?" she said, near tears. "I don't want to have this baby and ruin what's left of my life. If I hadn't left Atlanta, a room in an alley would be fine, but it's not, because I did leave and I want more."

"I said I'm a Christian…"

"Maybe I'll jump up and down." She placed her palms over her flat abdomen. At a few weeks, it wasn't a real baby, only morning sickness.

"That's a sin, and it's the silliest thing I ever heard of," Beatrice said. "If a baby could fall out over some stupid jumping, wouldn't be so many people in the world."

"There are other things I can try."

"Until you kill yourself." Beatrice grabbed her sister's hands across the table. "What you're thinking is against the Bible. I don't believe in it and I won't have anything to do with the devil's work. I remember when you were sweet and loving, but New York changed you. It's made you hard. The problem is you want too much. Have your child, settle down like everybody else."

But I'm not like everybody else. Mary Alice left her cup of tea untouched and went to bed. In the days that followed she shook her head whenever Beatrice asked, "You ready to rent that house?" She asked to borrow five dollars, wouldn't say for what, and Beatrice refused. Mary Alice asked Fat, and he handed her a ten. A woman she'd heard about charged five for an abortion, leaving enough to rent a furnished room until she recovered—if she survived. She had heard the risks were grave, but desperation gave her courage.

Chapter Twelve

Saturday, September 15, 1906

On the morning of Mary Alice's "appointment" (her euphemism for abortion), she boarded a wagon in Brownsville. The driver, a sour-looking old man named Adam who had plied the route to the inner city many times, took her down dirt tracks only wide enough for one vehicle. A sickening odor of outdoor fires and horse dung hung in the air, and as her breakfast rose in her throat, she pressed a hand on her stomach. They rumbled past colored women washing clothes under a sign, "We Wash for White People Only," outdoor barbershops, bars belching the stench of beer, pool halls, and a theater sign touting Black Patti's Troubadours. A man in a cloth cap and red suspenders touted hot sweet potatoes from a metal drum on a corner, and Mary Alice's stomach turned over again at the sugary smell.

The wagon descended into a gigantic hole in the city called Buttermilk Bottom, a slum that went on for blocks. Tar paper shacks covered the ground like mushrooms. Rain had begun to pour, slick paths slowed them down, and big, sloppy drops slapped Mary Alice's body. Miserable but determined, she looked this way and that for the house. When they stopped, it was just as she had imagined: an unpainted shotgun on stilts, like the deserted cabin back home, where she used to meet her boyfriend Jonah. It was as ugly and dismal as she felt. She jumped from the wagon, and it struggled away to find a hitching post. "Make sho you keep quiet," old Adam said over his shoulder. "She won't tolerate no screaming."

Mary Alice's heart flipped over. Suddenly she was petrified and had to command her feet to move twice before they complied. She ran through the downpour to the covered porch.

A woman opened the door. She was about fifty and had hefty breasts that pushed up almost to her chin. "Miss Irene," Mary Alice said in a shaky voice, "My name is—"

"I know who you is." Miss Irene grabbed her arm and yanked her inside. "I can see why you're in trouble. You ain't got sense enough to come in outta the rain. Get in here fore folks see you." She stuck out her hand. "You got my money?"

Mary Alice gave her the five-dollar bill that had turned soft in her sweaty palm. Now that she was there, second thoughts hit her. It was possible to have the child and raise it alone. Women did it all the time. The thought was fleeting, erased by memories of Reuben's rage and her mother struggling to care for them after Elijah left. No, she didn't want the child. She didn't want to live and die in Lydell Alley either. This was the only way.

Miss Irene stuck the money in her blouse. Mumbling about fast-ass gals, she pulled Mary Alice through a parlor with wooden folding chairs lined up like church to a narrow back bedroom. A thick rope hung low like a noose over a bed of white sheets and pillows. Light came from two large lanterns on a bedside table. There were no windows and only one chair. Mary Alice felt as if she had fallen to the bottom of the earth.

"Take your clothes off," Irene ordered and wobbled out of the room.

Mary Alice undressed and sat with folded arms on the edge of the mattress that was as hard as a block of wood. Pots banged in the kitchen, and she jumped. The sound of rain on the roof started a nervous twitching in her cheek, and she prayed that Irene would hurry. If she survived this, she vowed, she would find the right road and travel it alone if she had to. She would forget the restaurant and leave Atlanta, because nothing good had ever happened to her in the "Gateway to the South," so they called it. She felt a flutter in her stomach and sighed. *It had to be gas. It couldn't be the baby this early. No way.*

Irene returned in an hour with a metal pan cradled in her arm. "Lay down," she said. "I ain't got all day."

Mary Alice peeked in the pan and saw a frightening jumble of shiny, metal objects. She fell back on the bed, arms stiff at her side. "Lord," she silently prayed, "if you help me through this, I'll be good."

Irene moved to the end of the bed. "This ain't nothing. It's like going to the bathroom if you know what you're doing."

Like going to the bathroom. Mary Alice grabbed the hanging noose. She felt something cold and a pinch between her legs. Fire followed. The cracked ceiling spun around as Irene worked and sang, "We are climbing Jacob's ladder…soldiers of the cross." More pain. Mary Alice groaned and raised her hips.

"Don't move. It ain't safe," Irene said and continued singing, "Every rung goes higher and higher…"

Mary Alice screamed before passing out.

She opened her eyes as Irene shook her shoulder. "Sit up. Can you stand?"

Something salty was in her mouth. Running her tongue across her lip, she realized she had bitten it bloody. A wad of cloth, like raw meat, was between her legs. As she shifted from her back to her side on the bed, her bottom throbbed.

"You gon be all right," Irene said but looked worried as she helped her dress. "You just need some rest. I done hundreds of these and ain't lost a gal yet. It's raining, which ain't good, but if you get home fast and keep warm and dry, you'll be all right." She walked Mary Alice to a straight-backed chair next to the front door and pressed her down. "Let me find your driver. He supposed to be here directly." Cold, damp air blew in when she opened the front door. "Lord," she said, "it sho is nasty out there, more like December than September."

Mary Alice hugged her body, which shook in the storm breaking inside. She heard the driver's crusty voice and that of another man close by on the porch. "Another one done got herself in trouble, man," the driver said. "That's what women do. They trap men."

The other man snickered.

"Well, one thing I know, she didn't get that way all by herself," Irene said, stepping onto the porch. "Hey, you, Adam, she ready to go."

Mary Alice could hear the driver's low grumbling.

Miss Irene sucked air through her teeth in derision. "You better get this gal outta my house quick."

"I'll bring the wagon," he said and stomped away.

Mary Alice shriveled up in the chair. "I raised you better than this," Isabella would say if she knew. The disappointment in her voice would whip Mary Alice worse than an actual lashing. She hadn't told Beatrice where she was going. She would have tried—again—to talk her out of it and Mary Alice's mind was made up. To Beatrice, she was a fool, who had gotten in the family way by a man who despised her. The bud of dislike for Reuben the phone call planted had grown into full-blown hatred. If she never saw him again, it would be too soon. A gush of warm blood left her weak, and she worried about being able to climb up to the wagon seat. She wondered what was keeping her trifling driver.

Irene sang in the kitchen, "There is a fountain filled with blood, drawn from Emanuel's veins." Mary Alice thought the woman had the voice of a crow in pain. "And sinners plunged beneath that flood lose all their guilty stains…"

When Adam walked in a few minutes later, the singing stopped, and Irene appeared in the doorway to the kitchen. "My children be back from school directly," she said, standing with her hands on ham hips. "I don't allow no clients when they's home." She pushed damp hair away from Mary Alice's face. "Look at how you sweating. How old is you, honey?"

"Twenty-five."

"Old enough to know better," Irene said, "but I guess we don't never stop making mistakes no matter how old we get. Don't let me see you round here no more, because this here ain't nothing to play with, unless you know what you doing. And you don't."

Mary Alice grunted as she climbed to the wagon seat and the driver's hand steadied her. The rain came in gales, blowing furiously, and she shivered under an old jacket borrowed from the driver. Looking back as they rumbled away, she was startled to see Irene's porcine arms outstretched in the rain.

At the rooming house, Mary Ann dropped down from the wagon and struggled to a back room she had rented for a week. The room was bare except for a chair and a mattress that she fell upon and surrendered to sleep. She woke up to rain pouring in the open window, which she closed and fell asleep again. After napping until late afternoon, she gave a boy from a room up front a quarter to take Gwyneth Forester a note saying she was sick. The boy returned with a reply: "Mr. Forester say either come in tomorrow or they won't need you no more." Mary Alice figured that slave driver, Forester, wasn't kidding. She had to go in, because the hired wagon, the room, and the abortion had taken her last dollar.

Waking up from a deep sleep before dawn, she heard boarders shuffling out. The sound of rain beating the roof had stopped. Mary Alice cleaned up for work, an arduous, painful ordeal that required frequent stopping to catch her breath.

"Oh, dear, look at you," Gwyneth Forester said in one breath when she opened her back door and saw Mary Alice.

"Morning, ma'am." Mary Alice scurried to a closet for her bucket of cleaning supplies. She was shaking with fever, weak, and in no mood to answer questions. At the bottom of the staircase, she sank to the floor, scattering containers of bleach, ammonia, and scrubbing powder. She woke up on a cot in a room under the stairwell.

Gwyneth's eyes, as wide as the mouth of a grave, stared down at her. "It's not consumption, is it?" she asked. "Because my friend's in the TB hospital—caught it from her maid."

Mary Alice shook her head.

"Thank goodness." Gwyneth's face relaxed.

Mary Alice swung to a seated position and saw two Gwyneth Foresters weaving before her. She rested her head against the wall.

"You've soiled your dress," Gwyneth said.

Mary Alice pulled her dress around and saw the wide stain. Blood rushed to her face. "It's my monthly," she explained.

"You're burning up with fever, you just fainted, and you say it's your monthly? Don't take me for a fool, Mary Alice. If you insist on lying, I'll call the Grady Hospital ambulance, and they'll have you locked up for what you did."

"Please, I—"

"Uh-huh. It's what I thought. Well, why did you come here instead of to your mama? Don't you have one?"

"Yes, ma'am. Mr. Forester said he'd fire me, so I had to come," said Mary Alice, realizing the woman only knew her as a maid, not a real person with a life but as a mechanical thing that cleaned, cooked, and washed.

"Mr. Forester might fire you indeed. One lucky day I expect he's going to fire me. Stay in bed until I get back."

After Gwyneth left, Mary Alice thought about what she said. She didn't know anything about her family. Mary Alice closed her weak eyes, and a tiny, ironic smile slipped across her lips. She knew *everything* about Gwyneth Ann Forester—who didn't have a beau, probably because she was too shy around the men her brother brought home to look her over; who had blanched skin because she stayed in her room crocheting ugly little scarves and crying over novels instead of getting out in the sun; who hated dogs but loved cats, although she was allergic to them; who had her time of the month around the tenth; who had seen *The Klansman* twice but said the play was overdone because "things aren't that bad"; who, for some reason, wrote a generous monthly check to the Florence Crittenton Mission for "wayward girls"; who had wanted to be a teacher but quit college all of a sudden; and who liked the song "Dixie" and the color beige because it went with everything.

Gwyneth returned with a cold cloth, which she applied to Mary Alice's forehead. "With a thing like this, infection can set in, even death. I don't want anything to happen in this house. If my brother finds out what you did—I know him—he'll go straight to the police."

Mary Alice covered her face with her hands and bawled. Caught in a deep river with rough currents, she was drowning with nobody to rescue her.

"Stop it,"—Gwyneth's voice suddenly broke—"before I start crying, too."

"I can't go to Mama. She…she said it's a sin, girls like me will burn in hell. I couldn't—"

"Be glad you have a mama. My dear mother died giving birth to me, and Daddy passed when I was fifteen. My brother's all I have, and he's part devil. He says he's protecting my reputation. He says a woman isn't like a man—she only has her reputation, and if it isn't good, she won't get married. Even if she's as rich as the Vanderbilts, he says, she'll wind up an old maid. But of course, the rules aren't the same for him. The way he hangs out in brothels is a sin and a shame." Gwyneth sniffed. "Don't worry, though. Someday you'll stop crying, but that doesn't mean you won't imagine holding your child in your arms. Sometimes when you're alone, when the house is quiet, you'll mark the calendar for a birthday or graduation that never was. You'll do it in secret. Maybe it'll be different for you, though, because you're colored and don't have a reputation to worry about, but you have a heart, like everybody, and it'll always be broken."

Mary Alice stopped crying and let the meaning of Gwyneth's words sink in. She tried to figure how old Gwyneth had been when she had the abortion. She looked at her pasted against the wall, all sharp angles except for softness in her amber eyes, and remembered her talking about a serious suitor when she was in college. But the suitor left for California A story made up by a lonely spinster, Mary Alice thought at the time.

Gwyneth left and returned with a stack of white cloths, safety pins, a washcloth, rose-scented soap, and a faded black dress. She went back for a basin of water. "You don't look as flushed now, which means your fever's down," she said. "Clean up and rest, and I'll check on you from time to time. By morning, you'll be all right."

"Miss Gwyneth, I—I really appreciate—" Mary Alice reached for her hand, which moved away so subtly she would have thought it was her imagination, had she not known that touching Gwyneth was taboo. She flushed with embarrassment, realizing she had forgotten her place.

Gwyneth turned in the doorway. "As for the black-hearted boy who's responsible for this, I expect he's run off like they do. You thought you were in love, didn't you? Bless your heart. Well, pretty soon, you'll wonder what you ever saw in him. Sorry, my dear. That's the way it always is."

Mary Alice finished cleaning herself and lay on the cot in the dark. Gwyneth Forester understood her pain and heartache and was helping her. God bless her. As for Reuben, who had been like a fever in her blood, he could rot in New York. She had lied to be who she wanted. "When all doors are closed and a lie is all you have," she thought," then who's to say you can't use it?" It was then, sick and lying on a narrow bed, in that closet-like room, that she stopped loving him. She promised herself that she wouldn't speak his name again.

When she recovered in a couple of days, and Gwyneth asked her again to live in, Mary Alice agreed. The room under the stairs was clean and free, better than the rooming house or living under her Beatrice's judging eyes. Better than Lydell Alley.

Chapter Thirteen

Ruby came to work a half day at the Beale house. She was supposed to be at Mrs. Donahue's, but the pay there was only a dollar, no carfare, and the Beales paid carfare. The family liked to sleep late on Saturdays, so at seven in the morning, she let herself in with a key they kept under a flowerpot.

She bent over a soapy tub of tablecloths and napkins in the backyard. Water from every pore ran in gullies between her breasts and thighs, and her dress clung to her round backside. She looked up and the sky had turned dark. Another rainstorm was on the way. They'd had so many unusual storms in September that people carried umbrellas everywhere. With the rain came humidity that could collapse a mule. Ruby stopped scrubbing on a washboard and gulped in air.

She didn't mind the work because it kept her from dwelling on her trouble. Since the letter, she hadn't heard another word from Lee. He wrote that the camp was horrible—abusive, humiliating, and brutal—and she felt guilty about not wanting him to come home soon. If he could stand it for another year, she would know how to handle things. She needed time to think and remember. Then she could talk to him the right way. They were in love and he would understand. She just had to tell him the right way.

She straightened up, and a pain hit her pelvis like a giant scissor, cutting off her breath. She thought about her mother's warning about going back to work too soon. After the pain subsided, she finished scrubbing and carried water in a bucket from a pump in the yard, enough to start another tub. Done with the clothes, she stretched and sniffed the air, which was aromatic with the smell of bacon and coffee she prepared for the Beales.

On Saturday afternoons, they liked to picnic in Piedmont Park, where she could accompany them if she wore her uniform. Ruby didn't understand why people with a dining table that seated eight wanted to eat on the ground with swarms of blue flies and ants. Some people didn't have the sense they were born with. She glanced at the clouds. They wouldn't be going to a picnic today. No ma'am, because it was going to rain on that foolishness. As soon as she finished washing the breakfast dishes, she was going home to her baby. As the first rain drops hit her back, Ruby looked up from pouring out the rinse water and saw Mrs. Beale's ghostly face in the window. Was she keeping an eye on her again, trying to get two times the work for every penny of pay? The look on her face was hard, though, more like hatred than spying. Ruby thought about the ring, which she had taken in a moment of recklessness. *What was I thinking, stealing that ring?* Fear, hotter than blood, raced through her veins.

"Ruby, is that you?" Mrs. Beale was in a far corner of the large kitchen when Ruby opened the screen door.

"Yes, ma'am. It's getting ready to pour down raining out there." She walked in with a tub of clean but wet clothes and set it down. "I'll hang these tomorrow if it's sunny." Her eyes scanned the mess the family left on the table. Mr. Beale's cigar soaked in his coffee cup. Half-eaten biscuits, spilled juice, and milk littered the children's places. Blueberry jam stains on the tablecloth would have to be soaked and scrubbed twice.

Mrs. Beale looked at her, lips pursed, as if she had caught a mouse.

She knows. This has to be about the ring. The pawnshop owner had offered her twenty-five dollars. "Take it," he said, "or see what that cop on the corner will give you." Although she knew the ring was worth much more—coming from a wealthy woman like Mattie Beale— Ruby accepted the money. "Imagine," the elderly pawnbroker said as she left his shop, "a gal like you with a ring like this."

"Do you need something, ma'am?" Ruby asked Mrs. Beale. "I'll clean the table up right now." Self-conscious under the woman's gaze, she stacked plates with shaking hands.

"Go ahead. I want to talk to you, but it can wait."

Ruby hated when people put off saying what they had to say. If it was important, they should say it and get it over with. But maybe Mrs. Beale *didn't* know. If she did, she would be screaming as she did in arguments with Mr. Beale.

For the rest of the morning, Ruby had a feeling she was being watched, but when she spun around, nobody was there. After Mr. Beale left to run an errand, Mrs. Beale's nasal voice hollered from their bedroom, "Ruby, come up here."

She knows. She knows.

Ruby trudged upstairs. She heard the children screaming at one another in a bedroom at the opposite end of the hallway. The door to Mrs. Beale's room was open, and she stood in a slash of light from a slender opening between maroon draperies. A circle of cigarette smoke rose from an ashtray on the table beside her. Mrs. Beale smoked, though never in public.

"Have you seen my sapphire ring?" she asked. Sharp elbows jutted out from her hips.

Ruby opened her wordless mouth and closed it.

"Does the cat have your tongue? Answer me."

"Your ring?" *She don't need the damn ring. She's got about twenty in that jewelry box, and I only took one.*

"It's missing."

"A ring Mr. Beale gave you?"

Mrs. Beale's eyes turned mean. Her face went from ash white to pink to scarlet. "Never mind who gave it to me. I want to know where it is. I keep it right here." She marched to a jewelry box on the dresser and snatched open an empty drawer in the back.

"Miss Mattie, I didn't even know that drawer was there. I don't bother what ain't mine. I'm not a thief." Ruby wiped her hands on her apron and tried to look innocent. She had seen Mrs. Beale hide the ring after coming from a Friday "outing." A round sapphire surrounded by diamond chips mounted on a narrow band of gold— it was too impractical to be from Mr. Beale, who gave linen and china gifts. Ruby spotted it before Lovelee was born, and long before she took it, she had the ring on her mind.

"I want my ring right this minute or I'm calling the law."

"I didn't take your ring. Did you ask your *husband*? Maybe he's got it. You want me to ask him?"

"You little bitch. Who the *hell* do you think you are? If you so much as part your lips to my husband, I'll have you thrown *under* the jail. And when you come out—*if* you come out—you'll be too old to dream."

Ruby wished she hadn't taken the ring, which wasn't worth the chain gang. A gift from a backdoor lover to his married mistress, the ring was an under-the-table thing. Ruby had slipped it into her apron pocket without even a twinge of conscience. Now she had gone too far, as Beatrice predicted she would one day, and she could go to jail.

"I have a newborn baby, Miss Mattie. Please." Ruby glued her scared eyes to spittle in the corner of Mrs. Beale's pink lips and didn't see the open hand coming. The slap felt like a punch from a steel driver. Pins of light flashed behind her eyes, and her head snapped back. "You hit me. Why did you hit me?" Ruby moaned as she held her cheek.

Mrs. Beale's hand hovered in the air. "I'll hit you again if you don't give me my ring."

Ruby shook her head, staggered to the door and down the stairs.

"That's right! Get out of my house," Mrs. Beale screamed as she leaned over the banister, her children running into the hallway to see what was going on. "You little thief. You better bring my ring or I'm calling the law."

The sound of the front door slamming behind her back buoyed Ruby. She was free and certain Mrs. Beale, for all her threats, wasn't going to tell her husband or the police. What would she say? "My maid stole my ring, a gift from my lover"? Mr. Beale would have something to say if he heard about it. By the time Ruby reached home, she wasn't afraid anymore.

That afternoon she bathed in a tin tub at home and had a cup of coffee rich with sugar and milk, the only luxuries she could afford. Drinking it with a biscuit made her feel highly favored and energetic. So while Isabella was at a church meeting, she cleaned the house. Although it was only one room with a dirt floor, she hummed as she worked, happy to take care of her things instead of someone else's. She fixed a wobbly leg on the table, emptied the slop jar, and brought in wood from the yard—things Lee used to do for her.

She was stacking wood beside the stove when Isabella came in with her Bible. Her mother looked at the pile of wood. "I believe you trying to work yourself to death. Charlie would've carried that wood in here. You better slow down." She sat in the big chair, opened her Bible, and before long, she was dozing.

Lee's older sister, Laura, showed up while Ruby was telling her baby a story—"Now old Bro Fox, he spied dat tar baby on the side of the road." Ruby hadn't seen Laura since Lee's arrest, and she thought, too late because Laura was already inside, "I should've locked the door."

She and Laura had been close friends, but their friendship dissolved after the girl made it plain that she didn't want her brother to marry Ruby. "She's too fast," Ruby had overheard her say.

Laura was with Ruby in a juke joint when she first saw Lee. Ruby was deep into a cakewalk contest, kicking her legs high and leaning back, rocking her hips to a guitar. She glanced at him as he walked in and thought he looked like those Africans in the magazines she never tired of fanning through. His gait was straight, almost military. She later found out he had not served and was fresh out of Alabama, where things "had not gone well." That was the most he ever said about home. She won the cake and afterwards when he kissed her, he said her tongue tasted like sugar and cream.

"Let me see her. Let me see that pretty little thing. I bet she took after her daddy, or from me, which is even better." Laura gushed, rushing straight for the baby. At the sight of Lovelee, she stopped as though her feet had brakes.

Ruby spread a thin cloth over her daughter, and her eyes flashed a warning to Isabella, who woke up at the sound of Laura's shrill prattle. "Who told you?" she asked her sister-in-law. "I ain't even had time to write Lee."

"A little bird," Laura said.

Ruby suspected the "little bird" was Calvin Brinkley, the type of shiftless, down-in-his-cups man Laura liked to dance with in the clubs.

"Can I hold her?" Laura asked. "What's her name?"

Ruby told her and handed the baby over.

"What a big baby," Laura said, "She sure don't favor my family."

Thank God for that, because this woman is as ugly as they come, with her bug eyes and loud clothes," said the voice to Lovelee. *"I bet a fly could ride to town on that big rump of hers. Watch out for this Laura, baby. She's Lucifer's handmaiden, a carrier of his footstool. Look at her smiling, Miss Nice Nasty. Don't let her deceive you. Follow your mother's lead, and keep your wits, because you'll need them with this one."*

Lovelee burped and shot a warm volcano of sour milk on to the front of Laura's new yellow dress.

"Oh, damn. Here, take this child," Laura shrieked and wiped at the mess with a handkerchief. "I wouldn't mind, but this dress cost a lot of money."

After her sister-in-law was gone, long after the sun set, Ruby went outside to get away from the hundred and one what ifs about Lee that Isabella was throwing around. Laura knew, so Lee would soon know about the baby if he hadn't already heard from Calvin Brinkley. If only she could talk to her husband and tell him her side, but work camps didn't allow visitors. She tried to see him while she was pregnant, and a guard with an iron pipe turned her back. Mean gossip had brought Laura to her door, and gossip would turn Lee against her. Maybe Beatrice was right when she said a person's reputation, especially if it's bad, gets talked about sooner or later.

Truth stepped out and sat on her stool. Ruby kept still and hoped the blind woman wouldn't know she was there.

The alley boiled with the sounds of people living too close together. Charlie's mother, Mamie, stopped singing a spiritual in her loud contralto and shouted, "You ain't never too grown to mind me, Charlie Anderson!" Guitar Johnny, tall with a back unusually stooped for a young man, played a few chords, getting ready for his nightly jam on Peters Street. Miss Sukie's brood of four boys, playing a half dozen doors down, shouted curses like their alcoholic father. Ruby shifted on her wooden crate as she heard Frank Brown's wife scream. She figured he was roughing her up again.

"You're evil, Annie Mae, just like that ho, Ruby, with the white baby," Frank thundered, while lights came on the houses that backed up to the alley.

Ruby jumped up and clumsily overturned her crate.

"That you, Isabella?" Truth called.

"It's me—Ruby—fixing to go in."

"Don't worry, honey. Frank ain't got no business scandalizing your name like that, none at all. That's what's wrong with people." Truth's voice rose for Frank to hear. "They leave they business alone to tend to everybody else's." She said this without realizing the irony of her own words. "Frank's got a good wife and don't appreciate it. Big old bully. I wish he'd hit me, and I swear to God, I'll cut him everywhere but on the bottom of his feet. You hear me, Frank Brown? I'm talking bout you. Now come out here and slap me if you want to."

Laughing softly, Ruby closed her door. *Poor Truth, blind and yelling at a drunk who's probably passed out.* It wouldn't be hard to leave loud, gossipy Lydell Alley. The sooner the better.

Chapter Fourteen

Lee worked on a chain gang, hired out by Atlanta's police chief to a private brickyard. The brickyard, run by one of Atlanta's wealthiest families and headed by a former mayor, was on the western edge of the city and had only a handful of white prisoners. The others were colored men arrested for such trivial violations as unemployment, littering, or "reckless eyeballing." A few were in for assault or other felonies. The prisoners suffered from beatings, starvation, harsh living conditions, and brutal labor details that worked them naked or nearly so. Their sentences were long and renewable on a whim. Death was often their only escape.

Shortly after Calvin Brinkley left Ruby's shack, he sneaked back to the brickyard to bring Lee's uppity hide down a peg. From behind thorny holly bushes that grew along the yard's wood fence, Brinkley whispered loudly enough for his voice to carry to the mud pit where Lee and other convicts were shaping bricks. "Sssh," he hissed. "Hey Lee, over here, boy. I saw your daughter."

What daughter? Lee was suspicious. The two were not friends; he had only paid Brinkley to deliver a letter. So why was he back, risking arrest again for loitering too close to prisoners? The old man was a snake with a sly way of distancing himself from colored convicts by cozying up to overseers, for which he'd received a few privileges and early release.

"What did you say?" Lee gritted through his teeth, staring at the bushes. Either Calvin was lying or Ruby was two months early.

"Yeah, and the baby's whiter than me. Somebody's been plowing your field, boy, that's for sure."

Half crazed with anger, Lee tried climbing out of the slippery pit but slid backward. "You a lying dog," he said, struggling to stand, "and I'm a turn you every which way but loose."

The guard, who did not see or hear Brinkley but saw Lee trying to climb out, came running and pointed his rifle at him. "Boy, git back to work. Git, I said, or I'll blow your damn brains out."

Lee went back to his shovel as Brinkley scampered away. By the time the guard returned to his stand and finished his dinner, Lee had decided to escape. There was no way he could stay in the brickyard another day without seeing Ruby. Then he would prove Brinkley was a bald-faced liar. An hour later, he deliberately struck his leg with the sharp end of a shovel. Blood gushed out, and he was put down for the night with a wound that wasn't deep, although it bled convincingly for the unlicensed doctor, who examined it.

To make his move, Lee waited until the overseer and trustees were dozing after their nightly whiskey orgy and the other prisoners were asleep. On his hands and knees, he crawled out of the ratty bunkhouse and ran to a wagon that had just delivered bales of straw. The burlap that had protected the bales was still there, waiting for the driver to leave for a second load. In inky darkness, where a man couldn't see his feet on the ground, Lee covered himself with burlap and waited for the wagon to roll. The driver returned in minutes and drove away. Lee lay on the wagon bed, listening to the sound of horses clopping and his heart thundering in fear.

When the wagon stopped at a straw merchant's shed close to the city, he slipped out into dark woods, and the driver, busy talking to a sleepy merchant, didn't notice. Lee turned around blindly in the woods for a few minutes, looking for a way out. He was a wanted man, a prison escapee, who, if caught, would be returned to the brickyard, probably for life. After several minutes, he discovered a slender footpath and followed it to the opposite edge of the woods. There, he saw the orange lights of the city in the distance and ran in that direction. On his way, he passed a figure dressed in rags, young, with a face like fresh milk. *Surely he'll try to stop me. The law says he has a right to, but I won't surrender unless he has a gun. If he don't have a gun, I'll knock the hell out of him, kill him if I have to.* He came face to face with the man and hesitated. Blank eyes stared from dark circles, and the man, probably thinking Lee was only a harmless bum, let him pass. Relieved beyond measure, Lee rushed on.

He had trouble finding his way, because had somebody rearranged the city and, in a fit of expansion madness, stretched it out to the woods. For an hour, Lee ran on, and then he saw a familiar landmark, a store that sold roasted nuts. He doubled back between buildings as a clock on Peachtree Street struck five, two hours before dawn.

He sprinted past the statue of Henry Grady, a champion of southern pride and progress, and the shadows of buildings until he was on Peters Street. He stopped there, a bum in raggedy clothing, barely noticed by crowds of good-time men and women, weary at the end of a raucous night. They smelled of stale perfume, cigars, and cheap liquor. Paved streets in the northern part of town had meandered south and turned into dirt roads, obstructed by gigantic boils of garbage, horse droppings, and everything else foul. The city's development stopped at the edge of the forbidden "dark district" on the south side.

First he wanted to clean up. Ruby always said that she liked the scent of soap on his skin, and he didn't want her to see his filthy condition. He stopped at the lunchroom, arriving just before Fat locked up.

The big man cracked the door and pulled it wide open when he saw Lee. "Man, what you doing here?"

"They gave me the key to the prison," Lee said with a fake laugh. He grabbed Fat's broad shoulders in a quick hug. "I heard Ruby had a girl."

"Yeah, born some days ago. Congratulations."

"Wonder why she didn't send word?"

Fat, a man who didn't scare easily, wouldn't look Lee in his eyes. It shook Lee a little. *Naw, he ain't scared. Not Fat. Not my fearless brother-in-law.*

Fat shuffled to the counter and washed glasses with his back to Lee. Friends as well as in-laws, the two had enjoyed many glasses of shine and hours of street philosophy at that counter.

The lunchroom was as quiet as rainfall on a field of cotton. Its sporting crowd of customers had gone home to their beds. Chairs lay upside down on tables. No music; no dancers shaking to hoochie-koochie songs. Lee had never seen the place so dead, but then he always left well before closing to go home to Ruby. "Hey, Fat," he said, "I got to get clean before I see Ruby."

"You can wash up in a basin in the back room, but my stuff won't fit you. You see how big I am." Fat pushed a glass of clear moonshine across the counter to Lee.

Lee swallowed half of its contents. "Man, that's good. What about your guitar player? He's about my size. Got stuff of his laying around?"

"Not a thing. Try Reinbeck's." With two fingers Fat offered him a ten.

Lee, who hadn't a dime to his name, took it. "Thanks, but Reinbeck's ain't open this early. Even if it was, I can't go to his store dressed like this. He might call the law."

Fat glanced at his pocket watch. "Look, man, I'm beat. Zenobia's got some ham steaks and biscuits waiting for my knife and fork. I'm surprised she ain't been calling to see where I am. Take the ten and find a place that's open, get yourself something to eat. You can wash up real quick in back."

"What's going on, Fat? You know me. You don't rush home when Harriet's around."

Fat's jaw tightened. "Like I said, move on."

"Aw man," Lee said, "I didn't mean nothing—just tired of running, that's all."

"What I do with Harriet is my business. You don't mess in my business, and I'll stay outta yours."

"Damn, man, don't get mad. I didn't mean nothing." Lee walked to the back room, rubbing his beard and wondering what was eating his brother-in-law. He washed his face and hands with cold water and returned to the lunchroom.

Fat was waiting. "One more thing, whatever you do, don't disrespect my sister's house. I know you got a temper, just don't forget I love my sister, and I ain't letting nobody mistreat her. Nobody." He was at the door with a hand on the knob, signaling that the visit was over.

Lee thought Fat was acting funny. Fat, who said family should stick together, was pushing him away. Queasiness that had brewed in his belly as soon as he escaped the brickyard grew worse. "It's OK, man. I don't have to be hit upside my head. I get your message," he said, walking out the door.

For the first time, he thought Calvin Brinkley's dirty insinuation might have been right on the money. Well, if it was true, he wasn't the only one who had a surprise coming.

******

Ruby had put Lovelee down for a nap when she heard the door to her shack crawl open. She heard Isabella's loud intake of breath as

Lee jumped inside. "Lee, oh goodness, it's you," she screamed, rising from the bed.

Lee walked to the bed for a better look at the baby. "I'll be damn. Brinkley was right," he said and shoved Ruby down.

"They let you out?" Ruby said. Her heart sank at the sight of him in filthy rags with sticks and dried grass studded in his hair.

"I let my own damn self out." Lee's hands curved into fists.

"Touch her again," Isabella said, advancing on her cane toward them with a knife that had ripped open hog bellies, "and I'll kill you."

Lee backed off, although his body remained coiled and his eyes bit into Ruby.

"I named her after you—Lovelee," Ruby talked fast. Lee looked as if he wanted to kill her. "She makes funny faces like you. And she looks like my mother's side of the family; she's a throwback. You know they got a lot of light-skinned people."

"Don't try to play me for no fool," Lee said. "Brinkley told me and laughed in my face. Do you know how that felt? He laughed because he knew something about my wife I didn't. I've been thinking about it ever since. I couldn't sleep or eat, cause I didn't want to believe it. There I was in hell, and Brinkley threw hot coals on my head. I couldn't stay put. I said, 'Lee, you gotta go see for yourself. You gotta know for sure if the only woman you ever loved wronged you.' I had to get outta that brickyard. If I'd a stayed, I would've killed me somebody and died and gone to hell for it.

"Just look at you and me, black as the ace of spades, and this is supposed to my baby? Ain't no way. Ain't no eyes like that in my family. I'm a full-blood African." He slapped his chest. "My daddy was African and his people before him was African. My grandma said she came from the Fulani people." He pointed at the baby. "You ever seen a Fulani look like that?"

Looking up at him, Ruby's tongue tied up in her dry mouth. She was sure he could hear her heart knock against her chest.

"You better answer me," Lee said.

Ruby shook her head. How could she explain something she herself didn't understand? Her mind was mixed up, seeing him so suddenly before she had time to get herself together. She looked at Isabella, who wouldn't meet her eyes.

"You better tell the truth, before I knock you in the middle of next week. I ain't scared of no old woman's knife." Lee said.

"Well, you better be," Isabella said.

Ruby found her voice. "It ain't like that, Lee. You know I wouldn't do nothing like that. I love you from the bottom of my heart."

"Stop talking horseshit, woman." He remembered Brinkley's mocking laughter. "Is this Brinkley's baby?"

"I ain't never seen him before. Tell him, Mama."

"I know Brinkley, but she don't."

"Now baby, you know I wouldn't let that nasty thing touch me if he was the last man on earth. I love you," Ruby said, reaching out to him.

Lee knocked her hands aside.

"Watch it," Isabella warned, holding the knife as her other hand rested on her cane. "I took beatings from my husband, and maybe you heard about it, reason why you think you can put your hands on my daughter. Touch her again and draw back a nub."

Lee slumped down in the straight-backed chair, hands dangling between his knees. "Why, Ruby? Why?"

The smell of wet earth, sweat, and fear filled Ruby's nostrils. In her mind flashed a screaming mouth, a body as big as a bear, and a smothering feeling. She shook her head, gulped air and heard the steady, soft drip of rain. Somebody was crying—a woman. Her mind deceived her as she struggled to stay focused. She needed a clear head to deal with Lee, but everything was fuzzy, except his eyes which seemed to cut deep inside of her. How could she convince him that she still loved him, that they belonged together as much as sun and flowers? She dropped her shoulders and gazed straight at him. Lee wasn't wife-beating Frank Brown of Lydell Alley, he wouldn't really hit her. But she had to know at least that much for sure, because there were too many things she didn't know.

Lovelee turned her head for a better view of Lee, and the familiar voice said: "*Pretty mean and dirty looking, isn't he? But looks don't define a person,* any *more than the color of a peach tells you how sweet it is. He's the man who loved and married your mama, making you his by law and custom. He's your father, don't forget that, and never mind what people say. Those who say don't know. Never mind what he's saying, either, because a man might say anything when he's hurting.*"

Lovelee cooed.

"See. She's trying to say da-da," Ruby said.

Lee jumped up. "I ain't that thing's daddy."

The hateful way he looked at Lovelee was hard for Ruby, and it changed her heart. She couldn't really love a man who despised her baby. He had to love her child or she couldn't love him. Maybe if she explained what little she knew.... Most of it was hazy, but maybe. "Wait, Lee, don't go yet. I got something to say."

"Careful, Ruby. Don't talk too much," Isabella said. "I know men, and they better off not knowing most things. Even when they think they the captain, women have to steer the ship or it'll run aground."

"I gotta say this," Ruby insisted.

"There ain't nothing you can say to change my mind," Lee said but stayed where he was.

Ruby drew in a deep breath and collected the disjointed thoughts that had haunted her for months. The truth, which had been there all along, though murky, was now plain. She believed Lee would understand if she told it the proper way. "Let me tell you what happened. I've been shutting it out of my mind because it hurts to think, but I remember now, and I gotta tell you."

"Wait, baby," Isabella said. "Don't say another word. He want you to make him whole again, because that chain gang done broke him, and you can't do that. He don't want to take care of his own child. He's denying his flesh and blood, just because she's a throwback. That's what she is, a throwback, and one hundred percent his."

Ruby held up an index finger to stop Isabella. "I was assaulted, Lee, right before we married."

Isabella dropped the knife and picked it up. "No, please, baby, not another word…"

"And you didn't say nothing? You came to my bed with a thing like that in your belly? When were you going to tell me—never?" Lee's eyes narrowed. "Give me a name so I know you ain't lying." His eyes, fierce and red-rimmed, demanded blood.

Haunting words popped into Ruby's mind: *There's a tree out there with his name on it.* "I—I can't," she murmured. "I don't know who it was."

"Then you're lying." Lee's generous moustache, with its tiny patch of white hair, followed the curl of his lips. "I should've known not to marry a woman I met in a juke joint. I should've done like my sister said and left you where you was, hot-tailing it in the streets. The truth is, you had a lover right under my nose, and he left you something to remember him by. You one of those low-down gals that brings another man's leavings home. But I ain't nobody's fool. I ought to kill you *and* him. What's his damn name?"

Ruby pressed her lips together. If she said the man's name, Lee would go Jack Johnson crazy on him, and in the end, her poor, hurt husband would be lynched. *There's a tree out there with his name on it.*

Lee took Ruby's silence for defiance and slapped her. Her head snapped back, and when she pulled it forward, he slapped her again, yet the pain in her head was less than the pain in her heart.

Isabella shuffled forward, knife in one hand and cane in her other.

Ruby grabbed her. "Don't, Mama." She put the knife on a shelf above their heads, too high for Isabella's short arms.

"I would kill you, Ruby, but you ain't worth killing," Lee said. "You ain't nothing to me no more. I can't stay in this house with that thing. When I look at it, I see police running me down in Alabama. I see the judge sentencing me to that brickyard. I see that sheriff, too, and every white man that's done me wrong. Maybe it was rape, maybe not, but you can't prove it by me. Miss Isabella, you don't need no knife, cause I'm through with your daughter. I won't never touch her again."

"We can work this out," Ruby said. "Plenty people do."

"Not me." Lee remembered the sneer on Calvin Brinkley's face and his mocking words. He would go to Canada—New York wasn't far enough—where he might have a chance. Nobody would look for him way up there.

As Lee opened the door, Ruby lunged forward and he dodged. When she fell, he stepped over her and stomped out.

"Ruby Redmond Norris," Isabella hollered, "now I taught you better 'n that. Ain't no child of mine begging nobody. Get up off this floor and let that man go. You can't *make* nobody love you. Have some pride about yourself, baby. Gird your loins with the truth, and put on the breastplate of righteousness," she said, wiping tears from her daughter's face. "And God will set your feet on solid ground."

"I don't want to hear nothing else about your God. What's he ever done for a colored woman?"

Isabella pulled back. "What did you say?"

"Nothing. Just don't go telling me about God, cause I ain't listening."

"I give up on you, gal. I tried to help you, but now I gotta leave this blaspheming house. As much as I love you, I can't stay here. You're a devil if I ever saw one. I give you till the end of this month to make other rangements for your baby. Then I'm going back to Beatrice, the only daughter I got who fears the Lord." Without another word, Isabella spread her pallet and laid down.

For a while Ruby tried in vain to sleep in spite of her torn emotions. After a while, she gave up and left Isabella and Lovelee snoring, She went to Decatur Street, where she danced from one after-hours club to the next. Dancing, rollicking music, good-timing people, and gin kept her from thinking terrible things.

"Girl, you lucky you ain't dead," said her friend, Hattie.

They were in a blind pig, not far from Fat's place, where Ruby didn't dare go, because her brother, the deacon and family man, wouldn't allow his little sister on the street.

"I know plenty of men, rough gents from Buttermilk Bottom," Hattie said. "They'd put a razor to your throat."

"Lee would've if Mama hadn't stopped him."

"Bless Miss Isabella's heart."

"I said some awful things to Mama, but she drives me crazy, Hattie. It's like I want to break her because she's too perfect. And then the next minute, I want to be like her. She ain't even had a boyfriend since Daddy left. It's been ten years and no man. I would've dried up if it was me. Not that I've cheated on Lee. I couldn't."

"I know what you mean." Hattie's eyes were unbelieving as she tapped her foot to the bluesy piano in the corner. "Girl, let's dance."

Ruby continued talking. "Ain't nothing in the papers about Lee's escape from that chain gang, not that I want to see something. Even if they had him again, the papers wouldn't say. They too busy carrying on about assaulting white women. The law ain't never used assault and a colored woman in the same sentence. I wonder what it's like for people to write about you in the papers like you're something special. You know…like the world would end if a man laid his hands on you. I bet ain't nobody touched them women…well…most of them. They're just being…what you call it, Hattie? You're good with big words."

"Hysterical."

"That's it. They scared of us. Just like you'd be scared of a dog that got loose after you beat him. It's hopeless, unless you're nearly white like Mary Alice. I don't blame her for what she done. I'd do it, too, if I could."

"What'd she do?"

"Nothing. I'm just running my mouth. Ain't nobody said nothing." Gin swam in Ruby's head, slurring her words. *There's a tree out there with his name on it.*

"Girl, let's dance. I don't feel like being sad all the time," Hattie said in her loud, rough voice.

Two men, both in overalls, walked over from the bar and asked the women to dance on a floor that was only a narrow split between tables. Ruby and Hattie stumbled up. With closed eyes, Ruby laid her head on her partner's shoulder and followed him in a slow grind. She imagined the man, whose name she had not asked, was Lee. As she held him, he pushed into her, and she sighed. After the dance, she opened her eyes, and Hattie and her dance partner were gone. Ruby let the man buy her another drink, which he took as an invitation and whispered his desire in her ear.

"I ain't that kind of woman," she said.

"Well, you could've fooled me, ho." He went back to his seat at the counter. Pretty soon, he was with another woman—a regular at the club.

When Ruby came home before dawn, the alley was still and her baby and mother were asleep. She sprawled on the bed with her clothes on and dreamed a dream she frequently had. She saw Lee with a long knife tussling with a bulky man dressed in dark clothes. As they fought, they didn't see her standing in the shadows. The man was winning the fight, and Lee fell on his back. "There's a tree out there…" the man said, and Lee screamed, spewing black liquid from his mouth. The nightmare kept her tossing, and before falling into a deep sleep, she remembered everything.

Chapter Fifteen

Sunday, September 16, 1906

Ruby awoke to the lush smell of fresh coffee Isabella was having at the table. Ruby watched her pour the hot liquid in a saucer and dip a cold biscuit in it before taking a bite. Her mother looked as though she hadn't slept; dark circles ringed her eyes and her face was puffy. A bevy of birds sang in the tree near their shack, the tree where the placenta was buried. Instead of cheering Ruby, the birds put her in a sour mood with their singing, which sounded to her like a funeral dirge. In an hour she was supposed to be at her new day job, working for a retired woman doctor, the first one in the city. The old woman, who needed companionship as much as she needed a maid, talked in a disconnected way, as though her mind had gone bad. Ruby decided the doctor would have to get along without her that day, because she wasn't leaving the house.

She placed her hand on Isabella's shoulder. "Mama, I didn't have no business saying that about God. I was just mad and had the devil in me. I know, as good as anybody, God is with us."

"I hope you believe that." Isabella put down the biscuit she was holding and patted her daughter's hand.

"I do, and I'll tell you something else. The assault I was talking about was real. I can't tell Lee. If I did, it would cost somebody's life, probably his. I don't want him killed. I love him."

"Then you was right to keep your mouth shut. Don't stir up trouble. I always say let sleeping dogs lie, because when you talk too much—"

"Mama, please. Just listen. I've got to tell somebody or I'll bust wide open. People have been saying awful things, calling me a slut and all. Maybe I've made mistakes, but I remember now, and I want you to know the truth more than anybody." Her saintly mother's approval meant that much to her. "That's what you said the day Lovelee was born, remember? You said tell the truth."

There's a tree out there with his name on it. Ruby now understood the words were a warning. Isabella could handle the story. After nearly sixty years of living, her mother understood better than most what it was like to be female in their hostile world.

***

Ruby told Isabella her story.

On a cloudy afternoon in December of the previous year, a sharp wind cut Ruby's skin as she hung wash in the backyard at the Greenleaf house. She glanced now and then at angry clouds that threatened a storm. She was supposed to be the family's cook, but domestic job descriptions were fluid, and she had been washing and ironing since morning. Ruby had learned a bitter lesson in Atlanta— housework could be just as backbreaking as picking cotton.

One of her fingernails broke down to the quick. "Shoot," Ruby said and sucked on it until the bleeding stopped. With a dry limb from an old pine tree, she jabbed at a heavy yellow chenille bedspread, pushing it into a tub of water as big as a small pond. Vapors from the hot water mingled with cold air, creating a spirited mist that floated around her. She hung the spread on a line that stretched from the back porch to a pecan tree near a wood fence.

A pain ripped through her back, and she thought, "That's it; time to go home." There was a Christmas tree in her house in Lydell Alley, small but pretty, to decorate with strings of popcorn and cranberries. Her new man, Lee Norris, was coming over the next day, so she wanted things to be nice. Their affair was moving fast, and she expected to become Mrs. Norris before spring.

She walked into the kitchen as Nancy Greenleaf examined a cracked china cup. Mrs. Greenleaf had threatened to deduct twenty-five cents from her pay as a lesson about the evils of tardiness—twenty-five cents from a dollar a day. Ruby couldn't believe how mean that was. Could she help it if the streetcar driver had hell in him that morning and wouldn't stop for her, even though she yelled like crazy? A law unto himself on that streetcar, the driver did whatever he wanted.

Mrs. Greenleaf set the cup down and glared at Ruby from amethyst-colored eyes. Dark hair frizzed around her face. "This was Mama's china." She wagged a finger that was mostly bone with skin wrapped around it. "Didn't I tell you not to touch it unless I'm in the kitchen?"

"Maybe one of the children—" Ruby said in a whiny voice she used when dealing with her employer.

"My boys wouldn't touch Mama's china."

"Well, it wasn't me, Miss Nancy."

Mrs. Greenleaf gave her the evil eye. "If it happens again, I'll fire you on the spot."

"Yessum," Ruby said, though she was not intimidated. Mrs. Greenleaf was a nervous person, afraid to be alone in her own house and given to making threats she didn't carry out. She hated scenes, which her husband knew and went about philandering with much carelessness. Ruby leaned sideways with a hand on her hip. "I'm sick, it's my back."

"What about dinner?"

"You got leftovers in the icebox."

"I can't feed my husband leftovers."

Then feed him air sandwiches.

"You're just lazy," Mrs. Greenleaf said. "Even Mr. Greenleaf asked where I find so many trifling gals. The last one sassed him while the boys and I were at my sister's house, so he fired her—let her go on the spot. He fired two more before that…also on the spot for sassing him. Don't let yourself be the next one."

"Yessum, I'll be here tomorrow if my back lets me."

In a few minutes, she was on the street, her purse tucked under her arm and a large brown shopping bag in her hand. In the bag was meat she took from the shiny new icebox, and in her purse was a packet of BC Headache Powder Mrs. Greenleaf offered with a warning, "Make sure you're here tomorrow…and on time."

Ruby looked at the sky, which was dismal with clouds, and smiled as she pictured Nancy Greenleaf taking down the bulky chenille bedspread in pouring rain.

That wealthy section of town was on high ground, out of reach of floods that plagued the city after heavy rains. She hurried past two-story houses sat far back from the street. For socializing on hot nights, the owners had spacious front porches shaded by tall magnolias, poplars, and crepe myrtles that dripped bloody blooms in summer. In her gray uniform and brown oxfords, Ruby was mostly invisible, even to the family she served. When the neighbors happened to glance her way, the expressions on their faces were hard.

A block from the house, quarter-size raindrops hit her back, and she heard thunder. Afraid of thunderstorms because lightning split her mother's bedroom trunk when she was a child, Ruby ran with her head down.

"Ruby, over here. Get in," said a voice from a brand-new black touring car.

She looked over her shoulder and saw the driver was Irving Greenleaf, smiling behind glasses. He wore his usual three-piece suit, watch chain, and silk tie—a lawyer's uniform—and his big belly pushed against the steering wheel. Ruby peered down the street. The streetcar with its cranky driver was nowhere in sight. Rain pounded her back and soaked her hair, and instead of preparing for Lee's visit, she'd have to spend hours with a hot iron to straighten it. Still, she hesitated because she had heard plenty of warnings from other maids. "Some won't let you work in peace, less you give them a piece." Lee was against her working in private homes. "You're pretty, just the kind they like," he said. But Ruby wasn't afraid of Mr. Greenleaf—a cold customer, who was remote and forbidding when he was home.

Suddenly, lightning cracked and snapped a gaslight pole that fell and just missed her. Ruby ran to Greenleaf's car and reached for the door.

"Get in before you get fried," he said, talking around a cigar.

Ruby jumped into the rear. "It sure is raining a lot. Feels more like April, don't it?"

"There's a towel on the floor," he said and steered the car south on Peachtree Street.

She picked up the towel, smelled nauseating motor oil, and dropped it. Bending forward to pat her hair dry with the edge of her uniform, she said, "I stay on Jackson Row," Jackson was an unpaved, garbage-dump street, but more a presentable address than Lydell for a man like Mr. Greenleaf. It was her first ride in an automobile, and she smiled to herself, surrounded by the rich, comforting smell of new leather.

"I know the area." Greenleaf's large head bobbed up and down. "I bet Mrs. Greenleaf made you wash that old chenille spread, didn't she?" He chuckled. "She likes you, you know...at least better than most gals we get. The rest, soon as they had a little money in their pockets, they ran off. You're different, mighty pretty, too."

Ruby cut her eyes at his watermelon head and finished drying her hair with a handkerchief from her purse.

They passed Five Points and the Flatiron Building, coming closer to the turn for Jackson, where she would be rid of him. The car crawled through the center of the city. The showers, though heavy before, had turned to sprinkles. A man sold stalks of sugarcane from a crate on a corner. "I bet that cane is some kinda sweet," Ruby thought, remembering the cane in Soperton. They stopped behind a streetcar at Five Points.

White boys knotted together on the opposite corner, a couple of them waving newspapers over their heads. In their center, a greasy-haired boy stood on a milk crate. "Them damn niggers is taking over," the boy shouted. "They're assaulting our innocent white women. Are we men or what? If we're men, we'll do something about it. Let's send em back where they came from. Let's burn em till ain't none left in this town." The crowd then moved as one, hooting, hollering, and pumping their fists in the air. Ruby looked at Greenleaf for a reaction, but his back was as still as a wall. Ashamed of the things the boys were saying about her people, she slumped in the seat. As they neared Jackson, she said, "Mr. Greenleaf, turn left here, please."

"I'll take the back way, make it safer," Greenleaf said. "Those boys sounded pretty riled up."

So he *had* heard the gang. Ruby felt stupid for thinking otherwise.

"Down on Decatur," Greenleaf said, "isn't that where I saw you shaking your ass?"

"No, suh." Ruby straightened up. *How did he know?* She had gone to Decatur when she was lonely or bored, which was most of the time. Ruby liked to dance, drink, and chat with men. There seemed to be hundreds of them, new to the city and as lonely as she was. She had slept with some, all colored, but no one special until Lee, who was now her only lover. Ruby bit her lower lip. She thought back to the men she'd seen going into the white-only front rooms of clubs and didn't recall Greenleaf.

The car bumped down a log-pressed road in the middle of fields of naked cotton plants. The noisy bustle of downtown was gone, and they were in an unfamiliar place, far from her neighborhood. *What shortcut was old man Greenleaf taking?*

"Is this the way?" she said, trying to control her anxiety. "I can get out and ask for directions." There wasn't anybody in sight, but once out, she would run as if her life depended on it, because she was sure it would.

"I told you—it's a shortcut. You sassing me?"

The friendliness in Mr. Greenleaf's voice was gone. She considered jumping out, but the rumble seat did not have a door. She didn't want to climb to the front, where he sat with wide shoulders and heavy arms. If he knocked her out or killed her, no one would find her in that part of town for days, maybe never. Colored people disappeared that way all the time. Ruby knew Greenleaf wasn't just above the law. He was the law when it came to people like her. Nobody would believe her if she accused him. Screaming wouldn't help on the lonely road.

"Mr. Irving?" It was best to remain calm. If he saw she was calm, he might reconsider and turn the car around. "Mr. Irving, what we doing way out here?" The automobile bumped over logs, and her heart jumped with each jolt.

"You're sassing me, and I don't like sassy gals. A pretty gal like you should have better manners. Mrs. Greenleaf said you were polite."

As Greenleaf swung onto a dirt road that cut through a grove of pecan trees, Ruby sobbed, hoping to stop what was about to happen.

He pulled over. His bulky body heaved over the seat with the agility of a man a hundred pounds lighter. Ruby screamed. A thick hand slapped her and covered her mouth. Another hand tore off her cotton drawers. She felt him stab into her. He pounded and pounded and finally grunted before collapsing like a mountainous pile of dirt. Ruby hawked up a slimy glob and spat into his face.

"Black whore," he said and punched her in the nose, which spewed blood over her uniform.

Helpless tears rolled down Ruby's face, and thick saliva streamed from her lips.

Greenleaf tossed the soiled towel on her lap. "Clean up. Your face is disgusting."

In a daze and sobbing, Ruby held her torn uniform together and didn't touch the towel.

Minutes later, Greenleaf had arranged his clothes and was back in the front seat. The engine groaned as he backed the car onto the road. "You can stop your crying," he said. "Everybody knows you colored gals got hot tails. It's not like you never tasted it before with that tar-black coon I saw you with on Decatur. Looks like he used to swing through trees in the jungle. I bet you don't cry with him."

"My husband will get you for this," Ruby said, even though Lee wasn't her husband—yet.

Greenleaf laughed. "You've got a lot of nerve for a colored gal. Yessiree. If you've got any sense, you'll tell that boyfriend you walked into a door. I've got friends, and there's a tree out there with his name on it."

Ruby covered her face with her hands. She had gotten into his automobile because of a little rain and rode out to this field knowing what could happen. She knew violent things happened to women like her, and she accepted the ride anyway. If she said anything, it would be his word against hers, and her word didn't count under the law. She was lucky to be alive. Although he could have killed her and left her body in the field, he hadn't, so maybe he was taking her home.

Colored men trekking home with empty lunch pails stared at the automobile when it rolled close to Jackson. Everybody in the neighborhood drove wagons or carriages, so a car like that drew their attention. Ruby saw them and slumped down in the backseat. "Stop at the candy store on the corner," she whispered.

Greenleaf didn't answer. He was back to being aloof, steering the car as though his backseat was empty. Ruby looked at the floor for a forgotten bottle or something heavy to bash in his head, but the floor was clean.

Greenleaf whistled a familiar tune: "Camptown Races."

The old monster was happy, which was more than Ruby could stand, and she hollered, "Stop your stupid whistling."

He pivoted and bashed her head with a heavy book. Lights and bees swam in her head. Even though Ruby didn't pass out, she was close to it when he stopped at a shed that was the neighborhood candy store. "Get out, and don't forget what I said about that tree," he said. "Don't bothering coming back to work. I'll tell Mrs. Greenleaf I fired you for sassing me."

Ruby dragged herself out from the backseat. As soon as her feet left the runner, the car sped away, churning up clumps of wet earth. She threw her head back, and screamed unintelligible words as passersby, mistaking her for drunk or crazy, scampered away. She finally quieted down and stood for a moment before pain, knifing through her head, knocked her to her knees. Crying, she crawled and stumbled to her shack. That was where Isabella found her, lying stunned on the ground at the front door.

Ruby recalled her muddy feet and legs and bloodlike streaks in the sky. Her body felt as if she had ridden home on wild horses. She shivered in the cold air and mumbled nonsense as Isabella dragged her inside. She remembered her mother's ear close to her mouth, trying to understand, as she complained about a headache and pain between her legs.

"You recollect it, Mama. Don't you?" Ruby asked at the end of her story.

Isabella could only weep.

Knocked senseless by Greenleaf's book, Ruby—herself—remembered nothing for months, except: *"There's a tree out there with his name on it."*

***

Ruby kept her eyes shut while telling Isabella about the rape, and it played under her eyelids like a horror show. Describing how Greenleaf violated her, she groaned, because the pain felt real again. As the last of the story burst from her lips, she sighed and opened her eyes.

Isabella's face looked as if it had been dusted with talcum powder. "Why didn't you tell me?" she murmured. "I'm your mama. I would've petted you. I love you."

"I didn't remember till now," Ruby said. "It's been shut up inside me, like somebody locked the door to a dirty room. I couldn't remember much after he smashed me in the head. And even if I did remember, how could I tell you a man used me like I'm a ho? You was always praying and everything, and I was always wrong. I thought you'd blame me."

A sledgehammer slammed into the back of Isabella's head, as she opened her mouth to reassure her daughter. In the seconds before her legs buckled under a second stroke, she thought Lee had sneaked back in and attacked her.

Ruby's wailing ran through the narrow alley and brought people running to her front door. They streamed in and choked the room—Truth, Carol, Charlie, his mother, and the Browns from next door. On her knees beside Isabella, Ruby hugged herself and rocked from side to side. When Charlie said it looked like Miss Isabella was dead, the blind woman ordered everyone to clear the shack. She sent Charlie for an ambulance and Isabella's family. She put her hand near Isabella's open mouth and felt warm breath, so she sat beside Ruby and tried to calm her, even though she didn't think there was much hope. Two strokes in less than a month, a small one and now a big one. Truth hadn't heard of anybody living long after something like that.

When the family arrived—the ambulance never did—they saw that Isabella was paralyzed.

"What happened?" asked Mary Alice, who had run in and fallen on the floor near Isabella.

"Did you do something, Ruby? I bet you did." Beatrice dropped to her knees and cradled Isabella's head in her arms. "Mama, say something."

"Please, God, please. Ruby said, rocking and weeping. She felt an arm around her shoulder and sank her head into Mary Alice's soft bosom.

"Now you're praying? You hypocrite," Beatrice said.

Fat stood in front of them. "Y'all must be crazy, carrying on with Mama as sick as she is. Help me get her in the wagon."

"Your brother's right," Truth said. "Calm down for your mama's sake."

They wrapped Isabella's body in a sheet like a shroud, and Fat carried her to the bed of his wagon. Beatrice and Mary Alice jumped on the seat beside him, and they took off, leaving Ruby pasted in the front door with a lost look on her face. "Send word when you get to the doctor," she hollered. "Mama, please," she begged, even though

Isabella couldn't hear her. "Me and Lovelee ain't got nobody but you."

Truth had returned to her shack to keep an eye on Carol. "No telling what she might do when ain't nobody looking."

Ruby wished she had kept her secret. Once she knew for sure, though, the truth had fallen helplessly out of her mouth, because it wasn't the type of thing a woman could keep to herself and not lose her mind. She wanted comforting and hadn't considered her mother's fragile state. She should've known Isabella would take it hard.

From their days in Soperton, Ruby knew that her mother despised the ways of planters, grocers, and other men with power over colored women. Isabella had vowed that her daughters wouldn't be used that way, not as long as she had breath in her body. Even other sharecroppers said she was a "haint," a ghost with eyes in the back of her head when it came to protecting her bowlegged gals. Isabella taught them to carry themselves tall. This was post-emancipation, the time of the rising sun, and she spoke with hope, "Act like you got some pride about yourself. Act like you free and you will be." It was an axiom she drilled into their heads. *Act like you free.* After Greenleaf, Ruby scoffed. Did her mother really think the way a woman carried herself mattered? Didn't she know that legally a colored woman couldn't be raped? That she had no rights whatsoever when it came to her own body? That she didn't own herself? Isabella surely knew those things; Ruby had heard her say that she did. She knew what her daughters were facing, the same terror as she and their grandmother had endured, and yet she persisted in dropping that weight on them. What, Ruby wondered, was fair about it?

She remembered hearing the old conjure man, Big Chief, say to Elijah one day while she was playing within earshot, "Be careful with

Ruby." The sound of her name pricked the little girl's ears, and she listened. "This world ain't safe for her. She too pretty." Ruby didn't understand. Pretty got her hugs from Isabella and the biggest piece of cake. What was wrong with pretty? Ruby now believed it meant the assault had been inevitable. It could have happened anywhere with a certain type of man, who thought he owned her body. If not in Greenleaf's car, it would've been in a club on Decatur or a dark street.

She took Isabella's Bible from the floor, where it had fallen during the struggle to put her in the wagon. The Book felt awkward and heavy in her hands, though the pages were silky soft from Isabella's fingering. It had serendipitously opened to "God is my refuge, a very present help in trouble," words Ruby had heard her mother say after rainstorms drowned crops and the boss man refused them credit, after baby Rosetta died, and after Elijah ran off.

Ruby sat silent and dry-eyed in the shack for hours. When Truth came to check on her, she said, "I wanted Mama to understand, Miss Truth. I didn't want to hurt her."

"Yes, child, I know you didn't mean no harm," Truth said. "Just cause I'm blind don't mean I can't see."

***

The family took Isabella to the closest doctor, Frederick T. Madison, who practiced in his home a mile away. Dr. Madison sometimes risked his professional reputation in the Brownsville community to hang out with JC on Peters Street, mainly at the lunchroom owned by Fat, who liked and trusted him. As the family crowded around Isabella following the doctor's examination, he explained that a major stroke had affected her ability to move her limbs. "She might not recover," he said. "In fact, it's entirely possible that she'll have another stroke if she doesn't have peace and quiet. A woman her age, in her late fifties, cannot tolerate a lot of stress." The doctor's grave expression said he knew more than he was letting on about their complicated family.

"Fifty-seven's not old. Plenty of people live to seventy," said Mary Alice, who was holding Isabella's limp hand.

"What about her speech?" Beatrice asked.

"She can talk if she wants to," replied the doctor. "She said, 'Forgive me,' while I was examining her. Do you know what she meant?"

"Mama, what's he talking about?" Beatrice asked.

Isabella's tongue stayed still in a body that had assumed the stiffness of a corpse, although she was alive.

"Say something, Mama. This is making me crazy," Beatrice said.

"Leave her alone," Mary Alice said, stroking Isabella's hair.

"See? That's what I mean," Dr. Madison said to Fat, who was on the verge of crying and not caring who saw. "Aggravation is not good for your mother."

"I have a right to talk to my own mother," Beatrice said.

"Shut up, Bea," Fat said. "Think about Mama, for a change. You ain't the boss of this family."

The doctor led them to his waiting room. It was nearly nightfall, and the girl who ran his front desk had gone home. "Let Mrs. Redmond rest," he said. "She'll talk when she's ready. Trying to force her won't do any good. Fat, you're the man of the family, right?"

"That's right," Fat said, although no one else in the family had bestowed the title on him, certainly not Beatrice, who looked as if she wanted to tap dance on his head.

"Then I'm sure you'll see that your mother's not disturbed."

***

They sent word to Ruby; Isabella was in stable condition and expected to survive. After saying a prayer of thanksgiving, Ruby put

Lovelee to bed and sat in her shack with Isabella's Bible. "But they that wait upon the Lord shall renew their strength; they shall mount up with wings as eagles; they shall run, and not be weary; and they shall walk and not faint." The words seemed to have been written for her, and she read the whole Book of Isaiah in search of solace.

It was time to leave Atlanta, time for the country mouse to go home. Didn't the Lord say: "In returning and rest shall ye be saved; in quietness and in confidence shall be your strength…?" The words girded her with new courage. With the passage of the years, Ruby's memories of Soperton had turned idyllic and persuaded her that going back might work. Their old cabin was unoccupied, so she had heard, and she still knew how to sharecrop. She counted her money from the ring—twenty-two dollars and change; she needed to borrow five dollars from Fat to retrieve the ring from the pawn shop and return it to Mrs. Beale with an apology. Fat loved his sisters, especially her, the baby of the family, and she was sure he'd lend her more to get set up in Soperton. Callahan would probably take her back. People who had the means were leaving sharecropping for cities, mostly in the North, and the old man might need help. Life would be hard, but at least she wouldn't have to explain Lovelee. People down home understood such things, which had been ingrained in their lives for as long as anyone could remember.

Fat could take her down there in his new wagon. Although he wouldn't like it, he'd take her, because she was family. There wasn't anything to keep her in the city if her mother didn't make it. Not Lee, who wanted to kill her; not her relatives, who were ashamed of her; not friends, because Ruby didn't have real friends, only a bunch of good-time people who didn't have the heart for bad times. She didn't even have a job. She couldn't go back to Mrs. Beale's or the lady doctor, whose senile jabbering had almost given her fits.

She smelled Truth's supper of fried catfish and walked over for a plate. Outside on the steps, Carol and Charlie jumped apart when she walked up. Ruby stepped between them and went inside. "Hey, Miss Truth, you got enough for one more?"

Truth sat on a rocking chair, fanning with a newspaper. "Help yourself, child," she said, waving Ruby toward the stove. "How's your mama?"

"They say she might be home soon." Ruby smiled as she wrapped a plate in newspaper.

"Now that's what I've been waiting to hear."

"The Lord's really blessing us."

Surprised by Ruby's new-found faith, Truth could think of nothing to say. "Some people, she thought, "need a whole heap of trouble before they find religion."

Ruby took the food home, but after a bite or two, she lost her appetite and put it in the cupboard for the next day. She looked at her sleeping daughter, so innocent and sweet, and vowed to change. Before her husband and Lovelee, she had swung off the trolley after work and into the excitement of people and lights that turned streets into magic. Loose talk, hot liquor, and the hard bodies of men pressed against her were all she had, and she stayed out all night, rather than go home alone. Without Lee, she was free to do as she wanted, but there would be no more nights of roaming bars, searching for a good time. Her daughter was her life.

Chapter Sixteen

Monday, September 17, 1906

When Lee left Ruby's house, he understood Fat's peculiar behavior. The big man had known about the baby. Lee felt betrayed by the whole Redmond family. If Fat had warned him, he might not have gone to Ruby's. He would've bought new clothes and hitched a ride to Chattanooga, perhaps on a wagon driven by a colored farmer going in that direction. From there, he would've continued on to Canada, where the Georgia law couldn't reach him.

Quiet rage tormented every vessel in his body, as he leaned against the back side of a building to plan his next move. He still needed a bath and clean clothes. The sight of him, filthy and bedraggled, would draw too much dangerous attention on the street.

Going into the business district was risky, what with the police probably looking for him, so Lee stuck to the Peters Street area. It was afternoon, too early for the regular crowds, and few people were out and about. The stragglers he saw acted as though they were being chased: hats pulled down over their eyes, faces averted, heads hung low, and trotting close to buildings. He didn't dare ask what they were afraid of. Locked in the brickyard, he had not read the newspaper threats to clean the colored dens out; he did not know how terrified everyone was, but he could tell something was up. Night dragged in, and he walked dark streets, avoiding Fat's lunchroom. How different he felt, and how different things were, from what they had been just hours before. He no longer had a wife, a baby, or a home.

He had asked for the name of the baby's father. Just give him the man's name; that was all he needed. But in time he remembered the position he was in. Years of conditioning by law and custom made him fear not the man but his whiteness, and fear stopped him, in spite of his rage. Lee remembered his cousin, a loud, defiant boy, who disappeared at age seventeen. Some said he was thrown from a bridge into waters that later became known as Murder Lake. "Don't let that be you, boy," Lee's daddy said, planting the first seed of terror in Lee's heart.

As he hustled along, Lee continued to think about Ruby and hated himself for loving her.

When he first saw her, dancing in a juke joint called a "lunchroom," he studied the smooth moves of her hips, the rise of her breasts, and imagined how she would be in bed. He guessed that she was at least twenty and was surprised to learn that she was only sixteen. He caught her as she spun away from her friends, and they danced together, Lee as though he was boxing, pumping his fists in the air and punishing the floor with big brogan-clad feet, thighs straining against thin pants. When the music stopped, Ruby pressed against him without a thread of shame. He imagined how her cinnamon skin would taste, how his body would move over hers. When the light hit right, he saw purple highlights on her lips, deep red on breasts bobbing above the low cut of her blouse, and sclera so white it nearly blinded him. He wanted to bury his face in her breasts, her armpits, and the soft skin on her neck.

Sometime after their second shot of whiskey, they laughed in that guarded way of people who think they might become lovers. They were still talking in Lee's rented room at five the next afternoon. He liked that Ruby was confident, so sure of herself that she didn't play the usual tricks of her gender. She spoke openly about her likes and dislikes, making no excuses for her choices. She seemed a little wild but so what? She didn't look at another man when he was around, although he saw men peeping at her on the sly. He remembered feeling proud that she was his woman.

On an icy, sleety day last February, they married in church. His black suit was a thin, shiny number he bought in a rummage sale for two bucks, and he felt out of place in the congregation of feathered hats and fox stoles. He put the ring on Ruby's finger as wind howled in protest on the other side of stained-glass windows.

He suspected the old woman, Isabella, had known the truth about the baby from the start—the way she grinned at the wedding and kept saying, "Thank you for marrying my daughter." But just hours before, on that day, in the shack, she came at him with a butcher knife, like he couldn't split her clean open if he wanted to. Leaning against a building to catch his breath, he hawked and spat. He would never forget how Ruby lied to him and played him for a fool, all the while saying she loved him. Well, it was over. From now on, the bitch could hide diamonds between her legs, and he wouldn't find them. And he wouldn't lug that baby around for the world to laugh at him.

It seemed that he'd been running his entire life: running through cotton fields to make the daily weight; running from Birmingham cops, who stopped him for minding his own business; and now running for his life.

Lee saw lights coming from Atlanta's ornate, sprawling Terminal Station in the distance and changed his course. The terminal would be too busy. Somebody might stop him.

"Get out of my way, boy," hollered a white man in a tight

waistcoat and straw hat, and Lee jumped off the sidewalk. He lowered his eyes, which seemed to satisfy the man, who went on his way. He caught a glimpse of his torn shirt and bushy hair in a store window and realized he had been lucky so far. The man could have questioned him and called the law. He had to get cleaned up or he wasn't going to make it out of the city, let alone to Canada.

***

Night had fallen and Atlanta's botanical garden of trees provided good hiding places for Lee, who darted behind them as he made his way along. He passed a corner—his corner, where he had collected number slips and sold cough syrup flavored with cocaine. Ruby knew about the numbers but not the business with cocaine. Fat said to keep it under his hat. "Ain't none of her business," he said, laughing and slapping Lee's back. "She's my sister, and I love her, but a wise man doesn't tell his woman certain things. That way, he keeps out of trouble."

The broken-down back street Lee turned on throbbed with people moving like dancers, dipping their shoulders and swaying, as if music played in their heads. Lee kept up a quick, efficient pace— no wasted motion. Deeper into the street, a sharp pain stabbed his side. He'd been injured carrying a load of bricks up a hill at the yard. Guards would let a mule stop to catch its breath but not a man. Distracted by pain, he made the mistake of not paying attention to his surroundings.

"Stop. Police," a voice from behind him shouted.

Lee sprinted away. The block was indigo black, deep in moonshine territory, and very familiar to him. He heard the cop's brogans pounding behind him, and his racing heart nearly tore through his chest. Couples disappeared into dark doorways, as though they had trained all their lives for such moments. Sharp stones cut through Lee's rags-and-strings shoes. He heard huffing and swearing from the cop, who was heavyset and didn't have the physical conditioning of carrying bricks uphill on his back.

"I said stop, or I'll shoot."

Lee was in the wind, running. As he ran with his arms pumping, his lungs fighting to expand and contract, the cop's cursing sounded farther and farther away. Pain was like a knife in his side, and his lungs burned. He wondered when the cop would shoot. He wasn't going back to the brick factory, but neither was he ready to die. He darted down an alley, which was no more than a slip of darkness between identical brick buildings and easy to miss if you didn't know it was there. Lee exploded into it. On the other side was Spring Street and probably more cops. He tried to remember the right door among the half dozen on either side. *Where is it?* He was like a blind man. *Which door is it?* He stopped at one the color of wet soil and rapped.

"Who you?" asked a rumbling voice.

"A hungry man," Lee responded in code, and the door opened.

The big guy at the door jumped away from the bundle of smelly rags that flung itself into the entry room. Holding his nose, he said, "Man, I can't let you in here like that."

"Mr. Eddie here?" Lee asked.

The man uncovered his nose. "You a friend of his?"

"I used to work for him, way before he hired you. He'll want to see me."

The man jerked his head toward a black door in the back.

Eddie's Grill was one of dozens of illegal juke joints in the area that opened at dusk and closed before daybreak. They served boiled pig-ear sandwiches, bowls of black-eyed peas iced with raw onions, mason jars of moonshine, and all the trouble a man or woman could handle. "Dins of sin, mongrels, and miscegenation," the newspapers railed. In an open letter to white newspapers a colored pastor urged the "low-class colored women" in the Peters Street and Decatur dives to have better morals and lift up their race. At least once a month, a preacher stepped into his pulpit and called the wrath of God down on the fornicating, whiskey-drinking, gambling, and dope-taking devils in the city's after-hours joints. "May the good Lord deal with the evil in our midst." In spite of that, or maybe because of it, the dives filled to the brim from one night to the next. White and colored customers enjoyed gin in the same rooms, separated only by curtains—whites in front, blacks in back—fueling the city's dread of interracial sex. When the inevitable raids came, the joints closed for a few days and reopened without much revenue loss. It was a game that played well in a city that wanted a reputation for Christian piety, while it gathered money from wherever dollars would grow.

Lee knew that Eddie's was protected, the law didn't apply, and the cop chasing him was on the underworld payroll. So Lee thought he was safe as long as he stayed there.

Lee walked around tables of card players, past a curtain that had been pushed aside for white men on the other side to see a colored woman in a black dress shimmying on a tabletop. Fumes from whiskey, cigars, and vinegary red pepper sauce choked the air. He tapped the black door. "Mr. Eddie, it's me—Lee."

The door cracked open, and a hammered pink face peeked out before it opened wide enough for Lee to enter. Candles of all shapes and sizes burned on tables and a big desk, where Eddie Baker sat in a silk suit and a bowler hat pushed back on blond curls. The worn chair sank under his broad behind. The furniture was fat upholstered stuff Mr. Eddie brought in after his second wife redecorated their new mansion on Ponce de Leon Avenue. Keeping his eyes on the raggedy visitor, the guy with the hammered face took a seat on a patched sofa near the door. Lee spied a colored guy—about thirty, short, and squeezed into a dark suit—in a chair in front of Eddie's desk. His hand held a stack of dollar bills. He looked at Lee, and one eyebrow rose, as if he had just asked a question and was waiting for an answer. Mr. Eddie waved Lee to the sofa near the door, close to the man who had let him in and a considerable distance from his desk. The man slid over to the farthest cushion after Lee sat down.

"Phew, man. Where you been?" Eddie asked, fanning his hand in front of his nose.

Lee was too embarrassed to open his mouth.

"Well, what are you waiting for—permission to speak?" Eddie said. "You come into my place of business, take up the time of a busy man like me, and then you don't say nothing."

Lee asked for a place to stay, just for a few days until he could straighten out some family problems. He sensed right away that Mr. Eddie, whose eyes didn't meet his, was going to refuse. Lee had seen that hard expression in the past, before Eddie fired a dealer or slapped a whore. But he wasn't a two-bit dealer or a whore. He had a relationship with Eddie, and the big man owed him for bringing in money over the years.

Eddie's lips parted in a stingy smile, and he slammed a desk drawer shut. "Lee, we've known each other for a long time, right? So you know I ain't got but two places to my name—here and home. Now, Miss Rachel, she ain't going for this, so you can't stay at my house. You can't stay here either, cause folks got big mouths. They're already talking about how you busted out of jail." He threw up his hands at Lee's surprised expression. "Don't ask me how they know, but they know."

"How many times have I come in here and laid a thousand on your desk?"

The man counting money on the other side of the desk whistled and turned his head for a long look at Lee.

Lee kept his voice strong, because Eddie didn't like wimps. "Come on, Mr. Eddie, I need to clean up and rest."

"Like I said, ain't nothing I can do." Eddie spread his pink hands helplessly on the desk and squinted at Lee from pig eyes. "I'm not surprised you're in this mess. You always acted funny, like you thought you were as good as anybody. A boy with that attitude's bound to get in trouble."

Lee wanted to punch his doughy face, but the colored man at the desk and the one on the sofa looked like they could handle themselves. Eddie was dead wrong. If you weren't going to help a man who helped you, that was bad enough, but you didn't put him down. So what if he had a tendency to swagger instead of shuffle? So what if he smiled only when it suited him and couldn't keep a job because boss men liked to see teeth, the way they liked to hear cats purr?

He could see that the fat gangster wanted him out of his joint. *Expect nothing and be surprised if you get half of that.* Lee had heard it all his life and so far hadn't seen anything that made him doubt it. Eddie didn't understand what colored people had to go through day in and day out. He could do anything he wanted, have anybody he wanted, and say anything he wanted. Maybe Eddie was the one who had been with Ruby. Lee had seen him look at colored whores like he wanted to gorge himself. He looked at Eddie's hanging jowls and pig eyes and discarded that idea. Ruby was too pretty to be that desperate.

Lee wanted to leave but he smelled and looked too bad to walk the streets. He sat staring at his hands, feeling like a beggar.

"You can stay with me, brother, until you get yourself together," said the chunky colored guy at the desk. He put down the money he was counting and faced Lee. "I needed help once, and somebody stepped up. Ain't that right, Mr. Eddie?"

"What about Annie Ruth?" Mr. Eddie asked.

"In Charleston with her mama. If I'm lucky, she'll stay there."

Lee was suspicious that a man he just met had offered up his home. What was his angle? The guy looked like a preacher or undertaker in his black suit and polished boots, but the red silk handkerchief in his jacket pocket and the diamond chips in his wedding band were the garb of a sporting man. The joker didn't have any hair on his face, which was suspicious. Unconsciously, Lee fingered his own moustache. He was about to say "yes" when he saw Mr. Eddie shake his head. The movement was slight, and Lee would have missed it if he hadn't been trying to figure the other man's angle.

Lee heard the music and laughter out front get louder. Somebody screamed, "Shake that thang, baby." He decided to see what was up with the joker at the desk and walked over to him. "Uh, I appreciate the offer, but I don't even know your name."

"Daniel Scott Franklin Moss. But just Danny to everybody," the man said, thrusting out his hand, which was the size of a salad plate.

Lee didn't like the feel of his hand. A man didn't have no business with a hand that soft, like he'd never worked from can't-see to can't-see, like he didn't know how to fashion bricks from mud and haul them like a mule up a hill. Danny wasn't a teacher or preacher, a doctor or lawyer, who deserved cottony hands. He made his living in the rackets, a dangerous thing. A hard thing. A man's hands should say something about the type of work he did. As he let go of Danny's hand, Lee looked quickly for old knife wounds or missing fingers and saw none of that.

Danny pushed the stack of money on his side of the desk to Eddie, who pulled off a couple twenties and handed them back.

"See you later, Mr. Eddie," Danny said, standing up on stout legs.

Maybe the guy didn't have an angle. Lee decided to stop being suspicious. He had to trust him or it was back to the brickyard. "Uh, listen, man," Lee said. "I'll take you up on that offer. Thanks."

Danny's face was cloudy. "It sure is hard to help some people."

"Naw, man. It ain't like that," Lee said. "I can see you're for real, and I appreciate the offer, I really do."

"Well then, let's get going. My wagon's around the corner."

"See you boys later," Eddie said.

As Danny led the way out, Lee looked back at Eddie, who was smirking.

Chapter Seventeen

Friday, September 21, 1906

Isabella stayed in Dr. Madison's clinic for several days—an "observation period" that the doctor said was crucial—before her children carried her to Beatrice's house, which they decided was the best for recovery. Fat had noisy young boys at home, and Ruby's house was not considered. They arranged for Zenobia, to care for Isabella during working hours. "I'll watch the baby, too," Zenobia said, throwing that in to persuade Ruby to go along.

Beatrice lit her large stove while Mary Alice made Isabella comfortable in the front bedroom. A good cook who usually took great care with meals, Beatrice let the cubed steaks and biscuits burn while she ran back and forth to check on Isabella. She criticized Mary Alice for bathing their mother with water that was too cold and giving her drinking water that was too warm. She kept up her sharp complaints until her sister threatened to leave.

Although Dr. Madison said Isabella's speech wasn't affected by the stroke, she lay mute on the bed. Why had she asked for forgiveness? Beatrice wondered out loud in the kitchen with Mary Alice.

"She's probably sorry for playing favorites with Ruby," Mary

Alice said. "It's ruined that girl, made her selfish. She's done what she wants her whole life, with no thought to consequences. That's why she told Mama that rape story. She should've known it would give her a stroke. She's got what they call a 'narcissistic personality.'"

"A what kind of personality?"

"A bad one." Mary Alice blushed. She'd heard Reuben use the phrase and wasn't really sure about its meaning.

Beatrice understood what it meant; her question had been sardonic. She thought Mary Alice had a lot of nerve talking about narcissism and selfishness, having put herself first from the day she left Atlanta. A loving daughter would have kept in touch her family, especially her mother. If anyone had given Isabella reason to worry, it was Mary Alice.

And she wasn't pregnant anymore. She'd confessed that in an off-hand manner that shocked Beatrice, who hadn't believed she would really have an abortion. Mary Alice looked the same—slender, hair like fire, eyes like ice, and showing no sign of remorse. How could she have killed her own flesh and blood and not have remorse? It was unnatural, against everything that was sacred. Didn't the Bible say so? The reverend at Best Baptist certainly did. Beatrice looked at her from across the table and thought, "She's the one who should ask for forgiveness, not Mama." Worst of all, Mary Alice had begun to talk about Gwyneth Forester as though they were *sisters*. It was Miss Gwyneth this and Miss Gwyneth that. She suspected that Gwyneth had a hand in the abortion. Whenever Beatrice looked at her sister, she saw something unclean that pretty clothes and makeup couldn't cover. She already had an adversarial relationship with Ruby, which pained her, and she wanted to get along with Mary Alice. So she was civil to her since the abortion, but they wouldn't be close again.

After dinner, which Beatrice only picked at, she left Mary Alice in the bedroom with Isabella to pack for the move to Ohio. She secretly planned to earn a bachelor's degree at Wesleyan, even though she taught in Atlanta without one. A degree meant the world to her. It would bring one hundred percent acceptance in their social set, where sometimes she felt slighted because she lacked higher education.

She had loaded a box with silver when something occurred to her—she couldn't go to Ohio for three years or even three days. She couldn't leave while her mother was sick. When Elijah deserted them, Isabella cried, but then she dried her tears and went to work like a man in the fields. If there wasn't enough food, she went hungry to let her children eat. She wrapped them in love and pushed them out the door, not only to survive but to prosper. Beatrice stopped blaming Isabella for old Ben long ago. The family had a fortune of two dollars when Ben proposed, and Beatrice admitted that she, too, had seen marrying him as the only way out of dirt-bowl poverty. The doctor said Isabella would recover, but if something happened while she was away, she wouldn't forgive herself. JC would have to go without her and Phillis.

Staying behind wouldn't be easy. The separation could last months and put an additional wedge in her marriage. After she refused to go to Africa, JC accused her—she believed unfairly—of trying to control his life. She wanted to call all the shots, he said. She was too bossy and headstrong. So she would have to bring up the subject of staying behind with tact and help him see that it was the best thing for their family.

Beatrice put away her packing and looked at the time, which was close to midnight. What was keeping JC? He liked to "unwind" on Friday nights with his friends, drinking and telling outrageous lies, and this was his last night out before Ohio. As long as no women were involved—Beatrice had checked to be sure—she didn't worry, but it was getting late and he was supposed to be home two hours ago.

Purple gases of anxiety bubbled in her stomach, and she went upstairs for kaolin. "Ahh, that's better," she said, after chewing a piece of white dirt. The starchy taste was smooth and soothing as she chewed and swallowed. Her stomach, which had been burning all day, calmed down.

At the sound of JC's footsteps on the stairs just after midnight, she turned over in bed and faced the open door. The plodding, careful way he walked suggested he had drunk too much, which meant he would be depressed. She turned on the bedside lamp, and JC blinked in the doorway. His shirt was untucked, and he looked disappointed, as though he had hoped to undress and go to bed without waking her. She sat up and patted the bed for him to sit. "Just where have you been?" she asked.

"At Claude's," he said, removing his shoes. "I'm not in the mood for jawing tonight, Bea."

"I have a right to ask."

"And I just told you. Now I've got a question. Who's Mary Alice talking to downstairs? I hope she didn't bring a man in here, because this isn't a cat house."

Beatrice drew in a deep breath at his language and smelled bourbon and cigars. "My sister is talking to Mama. We brought her home today."

"Oh, I didn't know she was coming today, not that it matters. Miss Isabella can stay here as long as she wants."

Beatrice massaged his upper back, pressing out knots of tension with her fingers. "I tried to get you at Claude's, but his phone's not working. These new phones, they're not reliable when you need them."

JC didn't reply. Beatrice's complaints sounded trivial after his hellish evening.

"You know Mama didn't have to have that stroke." Beatrice could see that he hadn't been listening, but she talked anyway, hoping to get his attention. "Ruby caused it. She told Mama something bad, and I finally got it out of her. She thinks she can do anything, say anything, because she's pretty. Well, pretty is as pretty does. It's what you do that matters. You think she cares? Heck no. Sometimes I could strangle her with my bare hands."

"Bea, is that fair? We both know Miss Isabella hasn't been doing well for a long time. Ruby's spoiled, not malicious. You're upset about your mother, but don't take it out on your sister."

Beatrice was quiet for a few minutes, as she summoned up the courage to bring up Ohio.

"Honey?" JC pulled her closer.

Ruby fidgeted with her fingers. "Now please don't get mad. Just listen. Uh…I've been thinking, wouldn't it be better for you to go to Ohio and let me and Phillis come later? After Mama's well?" Beatrice felt him tighten up beside her, and his arm dropped from her shoulder.

"For how long?" he finally asked.

"Maybe by Christmas or as soon as she gets better."

"Christmas? What about Ruby and Mary Alice?"

The distance between them felt wide to her, as if they were not in the same bed or even the same house. She thought JC was being difficult. He knew Mary Alice was a live-in maid, and Ruby had a child to take care of. "I can't leave Mama in the hands of my brother and sisters. You know I'm the responsible one in the family."

"Fat isn't irresponsible."

"Fat's a man. He can't take proper care of Mama. And it's a disgrace for Zenobia to do it when Mama has three daughters. People will talk." Beatrice went to the dresser and removed long black pins that held her hair, which fell and blossomed on her shoulders like black flowers. As she brushed, preparing it for brown-paper rollers, her eyes avoided the mirror, which held JC's disapproving reflection.

"I can't leave you here. It's not safe," he said in a tired voice. "As a matter of fact, something happened tonight at Claude's, and if it's an indication of where this town's going, you and Phillis have to come with me. Period." He rubbed his eyes, which burned from cigar smoke and drinks. "I know you say nothing's going to happen. I thought so too…at least I hoped so…but this year has been rough. We used to live in relative peace, and now it looks like all hell's breaking loose. There could be a race riot."

"A race riot in Atlanta?" Beatrice's eyes widened. "Don't be pessimistic; stop poking at things. Nothing's going to happen here."

"It's happened everywhere else, New York, Omaha, and Thibodaux, Louisiana. So many places. That boy, Robert Charles, they killed him and who knows how many colored in New Orleans, probably because he was telling our people to leave for Liberia. Why not Liberia? I'd rather go there than Ohio. Prince Hall, the Freemason, back in slavery, said we should go back to Africa. He had the right idea as far as I'm concerned. Why stay where we're not wanted? White folks are going crazy over these assaults. They're talking about burning our homes and killing us. Any colored man in his right mind ought to leave. We aren't slaves anymore; we *are expendable*."

"I can't go to Ohio or Africa or anywhere, JC. Mama's sick." Beatrice stopped brushing and stood facing him. "It's like I'm in Atlanta and you're in Liberia. Remember that rosebush we had with one rose as big as the palm of my hand? It had a deep red color. I said, 'What a big, beautiful rose,' and you said, 'Only one?' Look on the bright side of things, for a change. Atlanta's our home. We have a few problems, but they'll go away. Things do get better. As a historian, you know that. The press is all about politics, trying to scare people. Nothing's going to happen to me or Phillis. You go on to Ohio, and we'll come as soon as things settle down with Mama. I promise."

"Did you hear what I just said?"

"Was that you or your liquor talking?"

"Don't get smart with me, Bea. If I don't talk about that dirt you eat, don't talk about what I drink."

Beatrice peered in the mirror and hurriedly wiped Kaolin from her mouth. Although JC knew about her habit, she always cleaned up afterward but somehow missed those specks.

JC shook his head. "We have to leave, and that's all there is to it."

She looked at his slumped shoulders and the misery in his eyes, and her heart softened. It was more than depression, which she had gotten accustomed to. He looked as though he had seen the end of the world. "What is it, JC?"

"Come here. I want to feel you close to me," he said, lying down.

Suddenly afraid, Beatrice slid between the sheets and put her head on his shoulder.

JC talked somberly about his evening at Claude's. And for once in their marriage, she listened without interrupting.

Four of them, friends for years, sat at the kitchen table with a bottle Claude had bought in his honor. JC was smoking a cigar and thinking about calling it a night, because the liquor had run out.

"You can't go, prof, not before we toast you," Claude said.

JC held up the bottle, which had only a corner left.

"That's all you got, man?" slurred David, the mortician.

They agreed that a toast was in order to send JC off right. So Claude left to borrow a bottle from a neighbor on the edge of Brownsville, just before a field of weeds and stunted trees but only minutes away by wagon.

An hour passed, and Claude had not returned. JC suggested that they look for him. The other guys said Claude was a grown man and didn't need a posse to take care of business. JC opened the front door and looked out, hoping to see his friend. Without streetlights or a moon, the night was a black sheet that covered everything. He closed the door softly because he didn't want to rouse Claude's wife and children, who were asleep in the back bedrooms. He shrugged when the men looked at him.

"Maybe he went to that gin house downtown," David said.

"All the way over there in the middle of the night?" said Claude's cousin, Doyle, a grocer in Brownsville. "My cousin ain't no fool."

The men laughed and sat back to wait and talk about inconsequential things in the manner of nervous people. They knew how dangerous it was to gallivant alone in the dark, although they thought Brownsville was far safer than downtown.

"Somebody should've gone with him," JC said after a few minutes.

"Aw, man, he was just going down the street," David said.

Then why wasn't he back? They all wondered but wouldn't say.

Just when they were on the verge of going to look for Claude, the front door banged opened and a bundle of bloody rags fell inside. When it stood up, Claude's bass voice said, "They tried to kill me."

JC heard a scream behind him and turned around as Claude's wife, Vivian, sank to the floor.

"Hush, Viv," Claude said. "You'll wake the kids. I don't want them to see me like this." She crawled to him and wiped his face with the edge of her robe.

"Who did this, man?" JC said.

"White boys," Claude said.

"Damn," JC muttered, though he wasn't surprised, considering the ugly mood in the city.

The men all talked at once. Cussing and threatening to kill the attackers, they carried on before Vivian helped her husband to his feet and led him to their bathroom.

They had to squeeze in the small space, which, like all Brownsville toilets, didn't have plumbing or a sewage system and was more decorative than functional. JC, David, and Doyle watched in grim silence from the doorway as Vivian bathed Claude's face with water from a bucket. He didn't flinch when she poured stinging iodine into wounds on his back and arms. A blood clot, like a slice of liver, fell from his battered nose and floated in the water. "Those bastards tried to kill you," Vivian said.

JC thought he wouldn't ever forget the despair in her voice and the dullness in her eyes, like an old mirror. He stood quietly but agitated inside as the truth sank in. If they weren't safe in Brownsville, they weren't safe in their own homes.

After Vivian finished cleaning her husband up, they talked in the parlor.

"You should've taken one of us with you," David said.

"For what? So they could beat the hell outta both of us?" Claude said. The bruises on his yellow skin were turning brownish red. "They came out of that field like ghosts, white hoods and sheets, clubs, and I don't know what all. About six of them. They surrounded me before I could run." He didn't look at Vivian, who sat next to him with clenched hands in her lap.

"But why?" she asked.

"They hate us because they hate us," said David, now stone sober.

"No kidding?" Cousin Doyle's lips cracked in a mocking smile. "Hey, David, don't you have guns? It's time for something they understand."

David shook his head. "Don't ask me about no guns. I ain't got no guns, and I don't know where to get none."

They knew he smuggled guns in coffins. They didn't know who was buying or where the guns came from, but the undertaker had a good side business going.

JC thought it was a mistake to ask David out in the open like that, because he would lie for sure. Selling guns to colored people was against the law. Beatrice wanted to buy a gun like the one Elijah had used to shoot rabbits, and JC said it was too dangerous to have one in the house because of Phillis.

David and Doyle went home, and JC found himself seated across from Claude and Vivian, who clung to each other as if they were drowning. A short, compact woman with small features to match, she looked lost in Claude's big embrace. JC heard her sniffling and Claude's deep breathing, and knew their moment was too intimate for a third person, yet he felt stuck in the chair, paralyzed by despair. He looked at his hands, which were large, veined, and rough from cutting cane in his youth. They had lifted loads heavier than the average man and had broken the necks of goats. They now looked powerless.

He recalled reading the words of Absalom Jones, the great abolitionist and preacher, "…throw off that servile fear, that habit of oppression and bondage…." So fitting for the night he was having.

"This is the beginning of some bad shit," Claude said. "Our lives are at stake, and we better get ready."

Our lives are at stake. JC decided to ask David, when he could catch him alone, to sell him a gun. "I better get on home. Beatrice and Phillis are there alone." Claude's obvious relief at his good-bye made him wish he had left earlier.

Beatrice threw her arms around him in bed. "Thank God, you're safe. Maybe things could blow up, but I can't leave Mama, not now."

"Well, leaving you and Phillis in Atlanta," JC said, "is out of the question. I won't go to Wesleyan." He sounded firm, even as doubt rumbled in his bowels.

"Let's talk about it tomorrow, JC. It's late and we're tired." She thought her husband's threat was empty. That thing at Claude's was probably isolated—exaggerated by a man who'd had too much to drink, although the white sheets detail scared her. She guessed they would discover which of them was right sooner or later.

Chapter Eighteen

Saturday, September 22, 1906

Ruby went to see Isabella in Brownsville after the rest of the family cut her off. Beatrice accused her of almost killing their mother with a selfish, deplorable attempt to get sympathy. Ruby hadn't seen Mary Alice or Fat in days, but she figured they felt the same way, and it broke her in ways she couldn't describe. She only knew that getting up each day was difficult, and she felt abandoned. Isabella's love had been her rock, and now that she was finally home, Ruby crawled from bed for the journey to Brownsville.

Her sisters were having coffee in the kitchen when she walked in. Beatrice glanced up and went back to her coffee. Ruby had come expecting rebuke, so a whispery smile playing on Mary Alice's lips surprised her. She grinned. "Good to see you, Mary Alice. I thought you had a live-in job."

"I'm taking the day off," Mary Alice said and reached for Lovelee. She nuzzled the baby's sweet body, and a wave of remorse washed over her. "Oh, I wish I…" she said and stopped. There was no sense in crying. Flushed away, her child would never be. She tried to forget that she had almost been a mother, but the sight of Lovelee or any infant brought gales of regrets.

Ruby headed to Isabella's bedroom.

Beatrice jumped up and blocked the door. "Don't upset Mama. I'm warning you."

Ruby pushed her way into Isabella's bedroom. "Oh, Mama," she murmured and knelt on a rag rug Isabella had given Beatrice for a wedding present. Her mother's skin had turned darker, her eyes were like old pennies, and her mouth was open, emitting breaths that mixed with generous scents of talcum powder and rubbing alcohol in the room. Ruby raised her mother's limp hand to her lips for a kiss. She spoke slowly, as if to someone hard of hearing, apologizing but saying nothing about Greenfield or the assault. She gazed into Isabella's eyes for signs that she heard. "Sorry, Mama," she said for the fifth time. "I tried to be the daughter you want, but I ain't good like you. I made too many mistakes."

Isabella's eyes closed. "Go get the others," she said in a raspy voice.

Stunned for a few seconds, Ruby didn't move until Isabella repeated it, and then she ran to the kitchen with the good news.

"This better not be more of your foolishness," Beatrice said, running to the bedroom with Mary Alice.

The sisters gathered around their mother's bed. "Mama, they're here," Ruby said.

Isabella stayed mute, and Beatrice scoffed and turned to leave.

"Wait, child. I got something to say," Isabella said, softly gasping. "I can't take this to my grave."

"Don't say that, Mama. Ain't nobody dying." Ruby took her baby from Mary Alice and slumped into a chair at the foot of the bed. She tried to quiet her pounding heart with a hand on her chest and silently prayed for God to help her mother.

"Go get your father," Isabella said between deep breaths. "Bring him home."

Her daughters shook their heads. Despite their differences, they were as one when it came to despising Elijah.

"Bring him home? For what?" Beatrice slapped her palms together as if ridding them of dirt.

"Not me," said Ruby, who thought the stroke had affected Isabella's mind. "He ain't done nothing for me, and I don't owe him a thing."

"Hush, child. You want people to forgive you, but you don't have forgiveness in your heart," Isabella said. "Y'all turned out to be some pretty hateful women, and that's my fault. May God have mercy on me."

Ruby exchanged miserable glances with Mary Alice and hung her head.

"Sorry, Mama," Mary Alice said. "We're glad you're talking, but I can't see going all the way to Chattanooga for Daddy when he made it plain long time ago—he doesn't want to come home. He's through with us."

Isabella coughed, a raggedy noise that sounded like death. "I have to make things right cause your poor daddy's might need you after I'm gone," she said. "He didn't leave y'all, he left me." Between long silences, where she appeared to be searching for the right words, Isabella told her daughters that the conception of their sister Rosetta had been an accident, that the baby was born when they were penniless and hungry.

"One night I couldn't take her crying no more. I didn't have no milk, just watery stuff seeping out. I didn't have no money and no way to get none. Your father was gone, gallivanting off somewhere since before Rosetta was born. Something went crazy in my head. I forgot there is God, who sits high and looks low. I forgot He gives us no more than we can take. It was the hardest thing I ever did, but I shut my eyes and rolled over in bed. I laid on top of her till she stopped moving. Poor little baby. Look at the terrible mama she had." Isabella stopped, and tears rolled to her pillow. "She didn't cry no more. She blew out a tiny breath and was gone, like she left something undone on the other side. Your daddy saw me from the door and run in, mad. He slapped me, put his hands around my neck and squeezed, but I begged and he let go. He said I weren't worth killing. He called me names, and I didn't say nothing cause I was all them things.

"He went under our bed and pulled out this little box, and we put Rosetta to rest in the yard. It was a awful, awful sin, and when I die I got to face my poor baby and give account of my iniquities. I'm gon tell her how sorry I am and hope she'll forgive me. I hope y'all forgive me. Wasn't none of it your daddy's fault. It was mine."

Isabella's daughters were too astounded to speak.

"Please say something," Isabella said.

Beatrice had witnessed the burial while her sisters slept, and she thought Rosetta died from starvation or an infant sickness. She'd heard that infanticide wasn't uncommon in poor cabins in Soperton, but not her mother. Not Isabella, who was a good Christian woman. "Mama, that's your stroke talking, not you," she said after several minutes of silence. "This is exactly what Dr. Madison told us to expect. Confusion. Crazy talk. Why you wouldn't hurt a fly...But if word gets out, it'll bring in the law and you'll be in trouble. Let Rosetta rest in peace." She threw open the window next to the bed. "Goodness, it's hot in here." Beatrice patted Isabella's tears with a towel. "It's enough to make anybody talk crazy."

Numb with shock, Ruby stared at her mother. She had lost weight and was like a ghost of herself under the white sheets. Her big blinking eyes were soaked with tears. Ruby tried to think back. How old had she been when Rosetta died—six maybe? She hardly remembered the baby, except for endless crying. She knew the infant, so little that she wasn't allowed to hold her, was hungry. She was, too. The crying must have been unbearable to Isabella, trying to force milk from empty breasts. Rolling over wasn't something Ruby could've done. She would sell herself on the street before she'd hurt Lovelee. Her mother's circumstances, though, had been desperate, and a woman couldn't really know what she would do.

Isabella said she drove Elijah away; Ruby thought she was wrong. The old man left because he wanted to. He had been in and out of their lives for years, and Rosetta's death gave him an excuse to finally abandon his responsibilities. "It's all right, Mama," she said. "You did the best you could."

Isabella blinked and more tears slid to her pillow.

"I'm going to call the doctor," Beatrice said, heading for the telephone in the living room, "and ask him to examine Mama."

Mary Alice had slumped speechless against the bedroom wall. She was amazed to know her mother had carried her secret for so long. Physically Mary Alice had recovered from the abortion with Gwyneth's help, but mentally she wasn't at peace. She couldn't stop thinking about the baby. She turned her circumstances over in her head. What if she had kept her child? It was difficult to look back, because avenues she thought were closed now seemed to have been open. She had been afraid of facing Isabella, but how could a woman who rolled over on her child judge her? If she had only known, she would've have kept the pregnancy. Beatrice had tried to persuade her; she wished she had listened.

She saw Isabella's eyes on her. "She wants forgiveness, which I don't have to give," Mary Alice thought. "I better get out of here before I lose my mind."

Miss Gwyneth had sent for her, and at first she didn't plan to go, but Isabella's confession changed her mind. She brushed her mother's damp cheek with her lips, and the old lady's face relaxed. "You're still Mama. You took care of us when nobody else would. I should ask you for forgiveness, not the other way around. So let's leave the past where it belongs—in the past. Hmm? Rest and I'll be back as soon as I can." Mary Alice fished a note from her skirt pocket. "I've got to go. Miss Gwyneth wants me. She's got some kind of emergency."

"With Mama like this?" Ruby said.

"You know I wouldn't leave if I had a choice, so don't try to make me feel guilty." Mary Alice was already at the door. "Mama's fine. She's talking, aren't you, Mama? I'll leave a number on the kitchen table and be back as soon as I can."

"You sure do love Miss Gwyneth. Just let her beckon and there you go." Ruby said.

"That's not fair," Mary Alice said over her shoulder as she started down the hall. "Miss Gwyneth's been good to me."

And Mama hasn't? Mary Alice was running away again. Ruby could see it in the look in her eyes, like she was already on a train or boat to God-only-knew where. Her so-called emergency had come too suddenly and conveniently. The girl wasn't reliable, never had been, because she wanted to be somebody she wasn't.

Ruby sat back to nurse her baby. The infant's warm gums and contented suckling soothed her frazzled nerves, and a sudden, fresh breeze from the window cooled the air.

She wondered what Beatrice really thought about Isabella's confession. Her eldest sister was an expert at hiding behind pretty manners. Nobody could put on a show for the public better than Beatrice, whose personal image was her number one priority. "What will people say?" She could imagine her crying into JC's chest. Not that Ruby cared what people thought, because their opinions didn't feed her or pay her rent. She was going to stick by her mother and let her talk her heart out about anything she wanted. Whenever she wasn't working and as many times as Beatrice would let her in the house, she was going to nurse Isabella. Their mother had taken care of four children all by herself, and now the four of them couldn't take care of her? Ridiculous.

She held Lovelee up and looked into her eyes, which were serious, as though she understood. Who could tell what a baby was thinking? Isabella said Lovelee was born with a veil over her face and was bound to see things beyond her years. Ruby wouldn't be surprised if she did.

Beatrice called Ruby into the living room, away from Isabella. "I finally got Dr. Madison on the phone. He won't come. I tried to talk him into it for the longest time. He said Mama's condition really hasn't changed. He said there's trouble, and it's liable to come this way." She put her hand on Ruby's shoulder. "Did you see anything when you came through town?"

Ruby shook her head. She had noticed crowds of boys roaming the streets that morning. Although some chanted "Teach those black devils a lesson," she hadn't thought much about it, because she'd seen worse in *Atlanta Georgian* and *Atlanta Evening News* headlines. Crowds downtown for Saturday shopping—nothing unusual about that. Add to it thousands who had come that weekend to hear William Jennings Bryant, the old cross of gold man, and another thousand attending a dental convention, there were bound to be a lot of people out and about. Uneasy in the beginning, Ruby had decided it was nothing by the time she reached Brownsville.

"There probably won't be any trouble," Beatrice said. "But to be on the safe side, I think you should stay here tonight. Didn't I see Mary Alice go past me like greased lightning? Where's she going?"

"Miss Gwyneth has some sort of emergency." Ruby began to gather her baby and purse into her arms. "I got plenty of time to get home before dark." She didn't want to stay with Beatrice, who would likely accuse her—again—of causing Isabella's stroke. Probably nothing would happen before nightfall and she would be safe at home by then.

While Ruby wrapped her daughter in a light blanket and stuck a six-inch hatpin that she carried, just in case, in its fold, Beatrice went upstairs to talk to JC. Ruby could hear them moving around above her head and imagined that her sister was burning up his ears.

Instead of walking to the trolley, Ruby rented a carriage to save time. The air was still and heavy, and artificial brightness covered everything, as though a tornado was threatening. She looked up, expecting to see a black funnel in the distance, and was relieved to see lacy clouds stitched across a silky-blue sky. She settled back in the taxi, thinking the world had to be at peace on such a beautiful afternoon.

***

Ruby didn't know a riot had begun in downtown Atlanta, just blocks from Lydell Alley. A roaring mob of ten thousand white men carrying torches, bricks, bats, heavy chains, guns, and knives had burst onto Five Points and spread out in all directions. They first attacked establishments on Decatur Street: tearing them apart, looting them of money and liquor, stripping pictures of near-naked white women from the walls, beating patrons and owners (of both races), and leaving blocks of smoldering buildings and shacks. During the afternoon, they looted colored businesses on Peachtree, Pryor, Whitehall, and Central Avenue, burning whatever goods they could not carry away. They pulled down trolley lines to immobilize cars and beat passengers, some of them to death. They hanged men from lamp poles and shot them so full of holes their clothing fell off their bodies in shreds. They raped women and burned homes, all the while daring anyone—including the city's feckless sheriff—to stop them.

Frantic calls to the sheriff's home went unanswered. His maid later told the governor's maid that everyone in the house had been ordered to let the phone ring. Officially, the sheriff said he had slept through the ringing.

On Houston Street, a mob scattered when a man fired his pistol, but they otherwise murdered and pillaged communities in a manner rivaling the Vandals. They paraded severed ears, fingers, and toes through the streets, and hung the hats of lynched bodies on lamp poles. Rough red midnight stormed in and painted the city with blood and fire. As word about the riot spread, colored men and women hid in their homes or stayed at work, protected by their white employers. But the news hadn't reached the trolley carrying Ruby and her baby, and so she rode home on a route that would take her through the city's core.

***

Mary Alice went through the motions of sweeping clean floors and dusting spotless furniture at the Forester house. She wondered why Gwyneth Forester had sent for her. She was only supposed to work a half day on Saturdays and had asked for the day off to take care of Isabella. When she arrived, the house was as pristine as she had left it the night before. It seemed Miss Gwyneth was inventing work for her—work that usually was done for Christmas and New Year parties.

Usually serene Gwyneth Forester was in a timorous state, stabbing out half-smoked cigarettes and swallowing cups of straight black coffee, which only increased her agitation. She occasionally broke the silence with deep, alarming sighs. Mary Alice watched from the corner of her eye. The feeling that something was wrong stayed with her as she beat dust from a Persian rug, polished silver, and ironed a basket of linen and Mr. Forester's shirts. At nightfall, she shook smoldering coals from the iron into the kitchen sink, and drenched them with water. Miss Forester, who had said nothing all afternoon, flipped a cigarette into an overflowing ashtray and told her not to leave.

"I want to talk to you," she said.

Talks with Gwyneth left Mary Alice feeling unsettled, and she dreaded hearing her usual lamentations about Mr. Forester's domineering behavior.

"I suppose you've heard about the assaults," Miss Forester said, pining Mary Alice to the kitchen sink with sharp eyes.

Mary Alice nodded. She had read the newspapers and wondered what Negro was crazy enough to attack white women in their homes in broad daylight. She hadn't said a word at work, because you didn't discuss assaults with your employer, especially one as high class and proper as Gwyneth Ann Forester. Gwyneth and the rest of polite society, including the newspaper editors, preferred the euphemism, "assault," to the more exact word—rape. To Mary Alice, it was confusing, because assault could be anything from accidentally touching a white woman to looking at her in an insolent way—if the man were colored.

Miss Forester continued, "I heard my brother talking to his friends this morning, and something's going to happen. People are angry. My brother was ranting and raving, saying all sorts of impolite things. Anyway, they said somebody's got to pay, starting today. Not that they'll do it themselves—my brother's not like that. We're quality people."

Mary Alice couldn't speak. She could hardly breathe, so great was the weight pressing on her chest. This was the reason she had left the South. This was why she tried to pass. This meant she would have to scurry home like an insect running for cover. She remembered her sick mother and grabbed her purse from the kitchen counter. "I'd better go, Miss Gwyneth, and get ahead of things. My mother needs me."

"Don't go out there, unless you want to get hurt, maybe killed. Mr. Forester said they're going after your people. It'll be shoot first, ask questions later. Stay here until it's safe. This house is big, and my brother won't know you're here...if he comes home, which he probably won't, not on a Saturday night."

Mary Alice blushed. "But they won't know I'm colored."

"My brother does, not that I'm saying he'll be with them. I think...I pray to God...he has more sense. Just stay put and don't argue with me. I'm offering you a safe place. You better take it."

Mary Alice had seen the Forester brother a few times—mixed gray hair, tall and sleek in a fine wool waistcoat, and a voice overflowing with contempt. He wouldn't waste time on empty threats. She stayed out of his way, which was easy, because he came home late, if at all. She heard he frequented lunchrooms and whore houses, all the while bullying his sister about maintaining her good reputation. Unlike New York, Atlanta was a small city, where everybody knew you or knew somebody who did, and she might be identified as colored. Gwyneth Forester was a good woman, who had helped her before and was offering help again. Gathering up her purse and apron, she took them to her little room under the stairs.

She made a supper of grilled cheese and tomatoes with sweet iced tea, which Gwyneth ate alone at the dining room table. Mary Alice didn't eat, and she slept very little throughout a long, hard night.

Chapter Nineteen

During breakfast in Danny's second-floor apartment on Courtland Avenue, where Lee had been hiding for several days, he read about himself on the back page of a newspaper: "Wanted for escaping from a prison detail, an extremely dangerous Negro with tight, kinky hair, a black-and-white moustache, skin like coal, short in stature, strong, and belligerent." A fifty-dollar reward was offered for information leading to his capture. Lee had stayed at Danny's longer than he intended to give the coast a chance to clear. He now saw that was a mistake, because it gave the cops a chance to spread the news of his escape. Lee sat at the kitchen table, slowly running his forefinger across the paper and absorbing the fact that the story was about him. With a sixth-grade education, he had trouble with one of the words and it rolled around in his mind. What did *belligerent* mean? Danny probably didn't know either, and Lee had too much pride to ask. It was bad enough knowing the whole city was looking for him. Only Mr. Eddie and Danny knew where he was. As for the reward, well, those two wouldn't care about it—chicken money compared to their loot from the rackets.

Danny had done his best to make Lee feel at home. He spread sheets on the sofa for him to sleep and found clothes that fit him. He cooked dinners of neck bones and rice, greens, ham, and fish, which they ate with pints of shine. That morning, Danny was working on a second pint with their breakfast of fatback and cathead biscuits.

The newspaper unnerved Lee, who feared being sent back to the brickyard—a death sentence as certain as a hanging. A savvy hustler, Danny read the paper and seemed unconcerned that the escaped convict was very likely the man having coffee in his kitchen. Lee concluded that he was a good guy, although a bit too friendly with slaps across his back and penetrating stares. As Danny bragged that he actually ran the juke joint, and Mr. Eddie only provided a front for big men downtown, Lee quietly let him ramble from one drunken boast to another.

Danny said Lee could stay as long as he wanted. He waved his hand around the small kitchen, slash living room, and declared there was plenty of room for two. Lee wondered when his wife would return and turn him in to the police.

Near the end of the day, Lee figured it was time to go. He guessed that the streets had emptied of farm families on their way back home. Country people, their eyes blinded by city lights, wouldn't notice him anyway. Just the same, a wanted man shouldn't loiter as much as he had. With the newspapers calling for his capture, he decided to catch a freight train going north instead of hitching a ride. The new terminal wasn't far. He would hop on a train to DC and then Canada. "I gotta go," he said, just before dark.

Danny's big hands caressed the rim of his glass of shine. In a white robe since morning, he sat across from Lee at the table. Red veins crisscrossed in his eyes and highlighted dark pupils. "I ain't pushing you out, man. Annie Ruth won't be back for a week, *if* she comes back."

"You saw the paper. If I stay, they gon find me. These crackers is getting crazier and crazier about race mixing, like they ain't doing it, like they don't know about backdoor babies. I definitely ain't for no mixing myself, but they don't know that. Next thing you know, they gon have my balls swinging from a tree. Naw, I got to catch the next thing smoking."

"But you said your wife just had a baby. She going with you?"

"I ain't got no wife, no baby neither. I said the bitch I *used* to be with had a baby. It ain't mine."

"I understand, man. Don't get mad at me." Danny put down his glass. "She must've hurt you real bad. Stay and I'll help you get over it." Danny gently touched Lee's shoulder. Though fleeting, it was an obvious caress, and his first unmistakable pass.

"Whoa, wait a minute. I ain't funny. I don't truck with that." Lee pulled away. Danny smiled as if nothing had happened and as he shifted his body, the robe fell away from his naked thighs.

"Aw, naw," Lee said. *What the hell is this fool thinking? Everybody knows I'm all man—no ifs, ands, or buts about it. What the hell?*

"You don't have to pretend, Lee. I know that's why you stayed so long. It's just us. Nobody will know." Danny stood and swayed.

Lee had looked at women the way Danny was looking at him. He cocked his fist. "I said hell naw. I ain't funny. I don't want nothing to do with no sissy. I'm getting outta here. Move your funny ass out my way." He felt like a fool for not guessing the truth in the first place.

"Get the hell out, then. I don't see nobody stopping you. Cats like you pretend they don't know when they know exactly what the deal is. Get out of my house, and if you know like I know, you'll put that fist back where it belongs. Hit me and see if I don't tell them cops. Hit me and see."

Lee thought his voice sounded higher pitched and more dramatic than before. They both knew Danny was bluffing about the police, who were likely to arrest him, too, for being a homosexual.

"Get outta my house," Danny ordered.

Lee shrugged and slipped his bare feet into Danny's castoff shoes. They fit. "Thank goodness for big feet," Lee said and saluted Danny before walking out.

As he opened the downstairs door, he smelled smoke and heard a noise like yowling animals. He poked his head out and stretched his neck down the empty street toward downtown to the north and Auburn Avenue to the south, trying to see where the commotion was coming from. It seemed to be everywhere at once and nowhere in particular. His first thought was to run for it. A posse must be after him, and fear crept across the back of his neck. He considered going back inside before realizing it didn't make sense. A sheriff's posse wouldn't set fires, and there were definitely fires nearby. An image of himself with Danny popped into his head, and he jumped out on the sidewalk. Whatever it was, he would take his chances.

He set out north for the train station. The streetlights, what few there were, had not come on, and everything was in a hazy, smoky netherworld. Walking toward the center of town, he maneuvered around broken glass and blood on the sidewalks.

Six blocks away from Danny's place, Lee heard a sudden roar of rebel yells—"Whoo, whoooo, owww, owww"—and dropped into a doorway that led to a shopping arcade. He ran through the arcade to the other side, and there he saw them, a gang of young white men armed with long rifles, ax handles, and chains headed toward Spring Street, torches blazing over their heads. He turned and doubled back. A man on a box a block away waved pictures and yelled, "Look at these here pictures of white women. They was hanging in a nigger place on Decatur. Are we gonna let them niggers do this to our women?" The crowd around him hollered and stomped their feet. Lee could smell their gin and sweaty anger from the recessed doorway.

"There's one now," a man yelled, pointing to a young boy with a twisted foot and a shoeshine box, who was limping away from a barbershop.

"Get him," another voice shouted.

Lee started forward to help, and common sense stopped him. As the gang pounced on the boy to beat his head in with pipes, Lee shot away in the opposite direction. The boy's pitiful moans of "Oh, oh," and the gang's curses followed him as he ran.

Lee eased back into the arcade. His heart felt as though it would leap from his chest as he wondered which way to go. If he chose Peachtree Street, he would surely run into another mob. Spring Street wasn't safe either. Lee waited until the crippled boy's cries ceased and his attackers could be heard storming away. He tiptoed out of hiding to the street that was now empty except for the boy's broken body. Lee walked to him and looked at his sightless eyes. Where had he seen him before? Lydell Alley? He couldn't be sure and it wasn't safe to ponder for long. The boy was dead, and there wasn't a thing he could do. Lee ran on. The station was still a fifteen minutes away on a normal day. God help him if he didn't reach it.

He zipped along in the gloomy shadows of buildings, on the lookout for the mob. He saw a streetcar that would have taken him within a block of the train station but dared not board it. Stepping into the doorway of a meat market, Lee pulled his cap down over his eyes and waited for the car to pass before moving on.

The rioters spotted him sprinting toward the train station. He heard their jeers and taunts, their footsteps pounding, and the chains they dragged and whipped in the air. He glanced over his shoulder. There they were—two blocks away and gaining—a mob of torches, blanched faces, and white hats gleaming in the night. It would have been bad enough if they were cops, instead of killers heading straight for him. With his heart pounding hard enough to break through his chest, Lee looked ahead at the faraway lights of the station and realized he wouldn't make it.

"Niggah," someone yelled. "Get him. Protect our women."

If Lee had run into a dark alley that snaked behind the street before the station, perhaps he would have lost them and come out alive. Or if he had hidden in a gigantic ash can under the viaduct, he might have survived and continued on his way to DC and Canada. Instead, he took the straight path, and they caught up to him and pounced. Some kicked. Others punched and spit tobacco juice and sour beer that made him vomit, even as he begged for his life. Before he blacked out, he thought it was strange—they were beating him without uttering a word.

******

His gait was unmistakably rhythmic, rolling back on his heels, moving faster than Ruby could remember, in a hurry to be somewhere. Regardless of the low-riding cap, she recognized him before he melted into the shadows of a doorway. Rising a bit from her seat, she almost called out to him. "Lee, baby. Let's go home." Then again, what would be the point? Before he left their house, he said, "I'll see you in your grave." So Ruby gazed out of the window as the streetcar rolled past the doorway where he had ducked, and she silently wished him well. Darkness had descended, and shards of broken streetlights and windows littered the streets like fallen stars. She could see that something was definitely wrong, as Beatrice warned, but hopefully the worst of it was over, and she would reach home safely. As the streetcar passed where Charlie was killed, Ruby's attention was on Lee, not on the opposite sidewalk where the boy's body lay.

The car rumbled under her hips, and her snoring infant's breath, as clean as snow flurries, caressed her face. Still not fully aware of the riot, Ruby wet her fingertip and smoothed down Lovelee's soft eyebrows.

At Marietta Street, she heard a roar. *Lions? Other wild animals? It couldn't be; not in Atlanta.* The roar got closer, and she could distinguish angry voices. She saw a bright flush on the trolley driver's neck as he yelled at a passenger, an old man, "Don't take all day. If you getting on, goddamn it, get on and let's go."

The old man hustled through the back door and sat down on the seat across from Ruby. His eyes reached out to her. "It's bad out there, miss."

She nodded nervously. "What's going on?" she asked, hoping it was only some country boys kicking up their heels on Saturday night.

"White folks gone crazy," the old man whispered, leaning toward her, his breath reeking of onions. "They's burning and robbing everywhere. Killing, too. The police play like they trying to catch them and ain't stopped nothing. I seen them stand aside, and let those boys run from place to place doing what they want. Streetcars done mostly stopped running. They pulled down the lines. I ran as best I could to catch this one. No telling when it's gonna be stopped, too." He rubbed his arthritic knees. "Lord, have mercy."

Ruby clutched her baby closer. "What's it about? The assaults?" Her voice was low, intended only for the old man, not the driver or other colored passengers—three laborers and a large young woman sitting on the edges of their seats, listening. The front seats, though usually packed with white riders, were empty.

The old man nodded and folded his body up close to the window, clearly not wanting to talk any more.

The car clacked along to Five Points and stopped at the Fourth National Bank corner, where gangs of hoodlums bunched up— Dublin, Newnan, and Buford boys with a few quarters in their pockets and moonshine in their heads. Their enraged roars billowed below a sky wiped clean of stars. Terrorized, Ruby huddled in her seat. Another mob seemed to be a distance away, maybe on Broad Street. Or on the southern side of Peachtree, near the new hotel.

Should she take a chance and hop off? She decided it was safer to stay on. As the trolley came closer, she saw dozens of blazing torchlights and heard a man order everyone to go home and let the law handle things. The crowd responded with whooping, "Get the Niggaaaahs."

The exit door was a few feet in front of her. If the mob attacked the streetcar, she would be caged in. She could run, but the streets were like a fiery pit. Ruby felt the hand of death on her shoulder and shuddered. Whatever happened, she would not let them harm Lovelee. She would fight for her baby, even if it meant she had to kill somebody.

"Y'all shush now," the driver said, though the car was as quiet as a tomb, and jerked his fare pouch from under the seat. He stopped the trolley in front of a crowd that blocked the track. Hordes of men rumbled and tumbled in from all directions, screaming as though trying to scatter animals across a savanna. They pulled down the streetcar cables and the car went dark. The driver escaped through the open door. Metal scored against metal, vandalized trolley cables coiled on the streets like gigantic black snakes. Ruby hung onto her seat, as men with venom in their veins rocked the car from side to side. "Woooh, woooh," they howled.

Ruby gasped when six men with sticks climbed aboard. The old man, the young woman, and laborers huddled in the dark on back seats. The mob leader, a burly, blustering guy about her age charged down the car, with his cohorts close behind. They banged seats with metal pipes. "There's niggers on this here streetcar," snickered the leader. "We can't see em in the dark, but we smell em. Right, boys?"

Ruby pressed her body against the window. Her fingers closed around the hatpin in Lovelee's blanket.

In torchlight on the street, she saw the old man slither out the open back door and fall. Two boys grabbed him up and tossed him back and forth like a ball. Pleading with them, the old man tried to protect his head with his hands. "Please. Let me go. I ain't done nothing," he repeated over and over. His shirt rose and exposed his naked abdomen, which they punched until he buckled and collapsed. Ruby turned away.

Meanwhile, the heavy-set young woman tiptoed to the back door, waving an umbrella with an icepick point. The burly boy thrust forward to jump her. "Watch me deck this fat heifer," he said over his shoulder to his friends, who were following. The woman stabbed in the dark. "Jesuuus, help me," she screamed, and they jumped back, tumbling over seats. She plunged through the door and ran outside, jabbing at a rioter, who tried to stop her. Fighting as though she had lost every sense except the smell of blood, she poked one in the eye and then another. Ruby watched in amazement as the woman escaped while men tried to help their bleeding buddies.

The trolley gang advanced. When they reached the back, a sandy-haired boy, enraged by the woman with the umbrella, slashed a laborer, who sat bug-eyed with fear. The knife blade opened up his cheek; blood gushed out, and two gangsters fell upon him, striking with sticks and their bare hands until his body was still. When the leader tried to block the other laborers from escaping, a muscular and crazed ditch digger punched and pounded his way to the street. At the sight of the man's ferocious expression and his cocked fists, the swarm on the street fell out of his way. Inside the car they jumped on the third laborer, who struck back with his metal lunch bucket. Ruby's eyes had adjusted to the dark and she could see a little. "He hit a white man," the leader shouted and she heard the thud of sticks on the man's body on the floor. When the terrorists stopped, his cries had been silenced forever, and his hand still clenched his lunch bucket. They kicked his body out the door and jumped off the car, screaming for souvenir ears and fingers.

Their leader turned to Ruby. Huddled in a dark corner and trying to track the bedlam around her, Ruby hadn't noticed that Lovelee's light blanket had fallen away from her face. The burly leader stared down at her daughter.

"Gal, where'd you get that white baby?" he demanded.

"She's mine."

"Gimme that baby. I bet you stole her." He smacked Ruby's mouth and reached for Lovelee.

Ruby whipped out the hatpin and, and in one swift motion, embedded it deep below his waist. She almost felt sorry for him as he clutched his crotch and slumped down in the aisle at her feet. His head pitched forward, his eyes rolled back with agony, and his mouth opened with cries she had heard from pigs her father used to slaughter.

She felt dizzy for a moment, and then she leaped off the car with Lovelee. The street gang saw the white baby in her arms and hesitated long enough for her to hit her stride. Sticking the hatpin in hands that tried to stop her, she fled south. She turned away from a juke joint, where a naked colored woman wailed as a trio shoved bottles between her legs. A horse-drawn wagon sped by, and the driver used a whip to keep drunks from climbing on board. Behind Ruby footsteps hammered the ground, and she imagined hands around her throat. They were getting closer, and she was almost out of breath. She turned a corner, saw a door a few feet away, and darted inside. Hands grabbed her. "Over here," said a man's voice in the darkness. She heard the door slam and lock and the mob raced on.

"I saw you coming with that baby," the man said. "What you doing out there?"

He lit a small candle and Ruby saw that he had cropped hair and skin like copper. "Thanks for saving me, mister," she said, looking around at the shelves of fabric, cans, flour, and sugar. "I thought I was a goner. This your shop?"

The man said his name was Ethan Middlebrooks and the shop belonged to his boss, Mr. Ahmed, who had gone home and left him to protect his property. Ethan went behind the counter and lined up a mean-looking pistol, scissors, and a sword with a vicious-looking curved blade that he said was a scimitar.

"And Mr. Ahmed let you have that gun? A white man? You fooling me," Ruby said.

"He's white and then he ain't…I mean he comes from cross the water. A place called Lebanon. I been working for him fifteen years, so he knows I can handle myself. He's too old to fight." Ethan's thin fingers rubbed the pistol as he eyed her with an appreciative grin. "Who am I talking to, if you don't mind my asking?"

"Ruby Norris."

"I take it you're married. How come your husband didn't keep you at home?"

"Used to be married." She noticed he didn't ask about her baby. During the rest of the night, they huddled in the store and talked, and not once did he seem curious about Lovelee.

Although she could hear the city raging outside, Ruby felt safe. Ethan gave her water and cold biscuits. He made a bed from a cardboard box and soft fabric for Lovelee, who snored as if she were at home. Ruby didn't sleep and neither did Ethan. The sound of glass breaking in a shop across the street sent him running to the front with the gun. He stood there until the rioters moved on. When somebody shook the door's handle and went away, he shushed her and pointed to the window. "I bet they saw Mr. Ahmed's sign," he whispered with satisfaction. "It says this is a white-owned establishment."

She discovered that Ethan liked to talk. While they sat on the floor in the rear of the store, he told her stories about growing up in Atlanta before the building boom, before people starting migrating in by the thousands from nearby towns and even from the Middle East and Asia. He lived with his parents and twin brother in a house on Randolph Street. They wanted him to leave Ahmed, who was working him to death, or so they thought. But Ethan stayed, because Ahmed was a good man and promised to sell him the business after he retired. "I've been saving for that day and I think it's just around the corner after this. Mr. Ahmed doesn't like trouble," he said. Ruby sensed he was trying to impress her.

Somewhere a bell rang ten times. Ruby's body froze until the last knell. "What's that for?" she asked.

"Probably the riot." Ethan said and patted her shoulder. "Don't worry. You're with me."

He'd been talking for hours when she heard thunder and rain hit the roof. The low rumble of rioters quieted after a while, and she guessed the storm had driven them inside. She dozed a minute and awoke to Ethan's lips on hers. She pulled away and shoved him.

"I'm sorry. You're so pretty I couldn't help it."

"Try that again and I'm leaving."

"Don't worry. I see you're not that kind of a girl."

They both knew she had to stay until things outside calmed down. Ethan kept his word, though, and left her alone for the rest of the night.

Chapter Twenty

Sunday, September 23, 1906

Before daybreak, Ruby fell asleep with her head on her chest. Hungry cries from Lovelee woke her and she put the baby to her breast and covered them with a cloth Ethan provided.

He opened the door and peeked out. "Clear," he said, "except for some boys on the corner. They look like military."

"Thank God, the heathens are gone," Ruby said, peering over his shoulder at the quiet street.

She waited an hour before setting out to see whether her house in Lydell was still standing. Everything she owned was there. "Thanks, Ethan," she said and kissed his cheek.

"If you wait till dark, and I'll close up and go with you."

"It's OK. I still have my hatpin." It was supposed to be a joke but neither of them laughed.

Ethan stepped out ahead of her and looked around. "It's clear."

A militia man stopped her before she had gone a block. He was a boy—really—and looked almost as afraid as Ruby. "Where you going with that white baby?" he asked and signaled his friends, two boys patrolling in the center of the street. They trotted over, bayonets drawn.

Ruby bristled. "This is *my* baby."

The boy laughed and looked knowingly at his grinning friends. One of them poked Ruby in her arm with the tip of his bayonet. She yelped and jumped out of reach. "Please. Don't hurt my baby," she said, as blood trickled down her forearm.

The boy who had stopped her turned poppy red; his eyes flashed a warning to the others. "OK, gal. I'm letting you go," the boy said. "And if anybody stops you, tell them Corporal Ross Moore, Georgia State Militia, said to let you pass on my authority. You got that?"

Ruby nodded and walked on with weak knees.

She used alleys she knew as well as her name. They covered the city like strings in a net. Anyone who didn't live in the area could pass the houses on the main thoroughfare without being aware of the alleys, where much of the community lived. It was considered a slur to be called an alley bat, but that day, Ruby would have worn the epithet like a crown. If her luck continued, Lydell Alley would be untouched.

Jackson Way looked like a tornado had touched down. Doors and windows were stripped from houses. Showers of glass covered porches. An empty jewelry box lay open on the muddy path in front of Ruby. Clothes littered porches and steps. A fire had burned a two-story white house, which was still smoldering, even after the rain. Jack's Candy Shack on the corner was gone; only the foundation remained. In a neighborhood where Sunday morning meant dressing up with Bibles in hand for a march to church, not a soul was in sight. Ruby stopped and surveyed the street, amazed at the destruction.

From the entrance, the alley looked untouched. "The looters missed it," Ruby thought, "or figured it wasn't worth the trouble." The alley didn't have houses with porches and gardens, polished furniture or china to destroy out of envy. No jewelry boxes to empty. She walked past doors standing ajar and didn't see any of her neighbors. Everything was as quiet as a church on Monday morning—no cussing, crying babies, or loud music. She didn't stop until she and Lovelee were home. "Thank you, God," she whispered, finding her things intact. "You protected what little I have."

While bandaging her wounded arm with a clean diaper, Ruby wanted to see Truth. She took her baby and went to her friend's shack. The door was open and the blind woman and her daughter were gone. A full coffee pot was on the stove, and two plates of bread and beans were laid out on the table, as if they were going to return in a minute. Ruby went next door to Charlie's house. A black bow hung by a string on the door. She wondered who had died—the boy or his mother? Where were the Browns and Johnny Guitar? Where was everybody?

Too tired to trek back to Beatrice's house, Ruby went home, fell across her bed, and slept. Waking up that night with her breast in Lovelee's mouth, the only thing she felt though the length of her body was despair. She thought about her family in Brownsville and Lee's body downtown, and she burst into tears. Lovelee stopped nursing at the sound of her mother's crying. *"Oh mother," she wanted to say, "don't cry. We are alive. Therefore, we have hope."*

***

Torrents of rain in the early morning hours cooled tempers and stopped pillaging, at least for a while. The governor had called out the state militia, which couldn't control the mob as well as the old-fashioned Georgia rainstorm. Water fell in gales, turning unpaved streets into thick gravy. It sizzled on steamy, red faces, cooling them off. Thin pine trees whipped in the wind. Blinded by the rain, a young tough from Covington smashed the head of his friend, mistaking him for a light-skinned colored boy. After rejecting the mayor's appeal to clear the streets, the rowdy crowds finally sought shelter in homes, hotels, and churches until the storm passed. Some, of course, went home to Decatur, Griffin, LaGrange and other towns, where cotton fields and mules needed attention.

The lull was particularly fortunate for the people of Brownsville, who usually left their homes for Sunday school. This Sunday they made it no farther than lower Whitehall, where warnings whispered from doorways and windows and the sight of boarded-up shops, blood, and broken glass in deserted streets turned them around.

Fat's family did not leave home, because the white man who owned the whorehouse next door to his lunchroom phoned with a warning: "Come to work at your own risk."

"There's only one thing they understand—a pistol." Fat's voice boomed as he sought his audience's attention in the cloistered backroom of a tailor's shop. It was a meeting of Best Baptist elders and leaders from other churches, who'd gathered in a hurry to work out a defensive plan for Brownsville, just in case. They were community leaders with college degrees, business licenses, and teaching certificates, and they dressed in ties and ascots, white barber jackets, cutaway coats, grocer aprons, and ordinary overalls. There wasn't a scalawag or do-nothing in the bunch. Many had sent their wives and children to the safety of a nearby college and a seminary.

Fat had the floor and intended to keep it. "Now I just heard from people who say they done burned down Decatur and Peters Street. My restaurant, the only business I had, is gone. They say I was doing illegal things, but I say they the ones who illegal now. They done strung up some brothers and stuffed they private parts in they mouths. The fella who told me said he saw people's fingers in jars. Real live fingers, man, some with rings on em."

"Barbaric," said a man near the locked door. "Why do they hate us so?"

"It's this." JC's friend, the young newspaper editor, tapped a long finger on his deeply pigmented wrist. "My paper's been following racial animosity in this city for a while, and even though they say it's a rebellion against the influx of foreigner workers from overseas, it's clearly racial. And above all it's, sexual. Put that in all capital letters. Miscegenation or so they call it.

"Things are, in reality, much worse than you said, Mr. Redmond. They shot a fourteen-year-old girl through her heart. One of my reporters said they splayed a brother across that statue of Henry Grady down on Marietta. The brother's fingers, toes, ears, and clothes are missing, taken as souvenirs. He's still down there, swelling up like a balloon, about to burst in this heat. White folks won't move him; colored scared to. Leaving a man lying dead in the streets for hours like that takes away his humanity. It means he's lower than a dog. And you know the city's so-called civic leaders and big shots wouldn't treat their precious dogs like that."

"You think they're behind this thing?" asked a loud voice.

Fat snorted. "Is water wet? Everybody knows they don't give a damn about the colored man. Who can we go to for help? The police? They're friends of the white hats. The mayor? They say he was downtown yelling his head off and it didn't do a damn bit of good. 'Stop,' he said. 'Now go on home, boys.' And they kept right on killing us."

Nobody in the windowless backroom said anything for several minutes. They needed time to comprehend the horrors. As they soaked it in, they became so angry they couldn't think straight. Fat stood wide-legged in front of them, breathing in air heavy with dust, bits of thread and rage. He was too furious to speak.

The owner of a barbershop broke the silence by loudly clearing his throat.

Fat took that as an opening to move the meeting forward. "How many of y'all got guns?"

A dozen hands went up. Another dozen or so men kept their hands in their pockets.

"How many ready to use them?"

This produced heavy silence.

The professor stood, cane in hand. "You fellows must realize if we don't rise up now, they'll be rolling over us a hundred years from today. I was in Alabama when this abomination began and had to race back to protect my family. And just so everybody knows, I have no intention of running around like a squirrel in a cage. I mean business." He pounded the cane's brass tip on the floor, and every head turned in his direction. "We are less than nothing without our women, the backbone of the race, and I, for one, will not let any man have his way in my house, with my woman, not as long as I have old Nellie here." He patted a large square pocket on his jacket, where his pistol resided. "And I have a shotgun at home to protect me and mine."

"Now, Professor, not so fast," said Brother Albert Johnson, who claimed to have laid his church's cornerstone. "The reverend wouldn't be pleased to hear such talk. Christians are peaceful people."

JC pulled up on his long legs. "Not during the crusades they weren't. I'm as peaceful as anybody, but I promise you I'll kill the first one who lays his hands on my wife or daughter. You can take that to the bank."

"Pastor said if colored people would be responsible and turn in the criminals among us, wouldn't be no trouble. Some of us ain't got no morals at all." Brother Johnson squinted at JC from behind thick glasses. "Are you a member of our church? Your face doesn't look familiar. Maybe you attend another house of worship."

"If you look around, you'll see you ain't in church," Fat said, waving Johnson back to his seat. "His wife, my sister, is a member of

Best Baptist, and like I told y'all, this meeting is open to every able-bodied colored man in Brownsville. It ain't about church or denomination. It ain't about who has what. And it sho ain't about light skin and good hair, things that don't do nothing but divide us. It's about sticking together. Now let's get back to business, or do y'all plan to sit around like a bunch of chicken-livered women while these peckerwoods kill us, while they assault our wives and daughters and burn our homes? Let me see the hands of the men with guns again." When two dozen hands went up, Fat reared back on his substantial legs and grinned. "Now that's what I'm talking about."

"With all due respect, Brother Redmond, I ain't running and I sho ain't chicken-livered," said a bank porter, whose back was curved from years of mopping floors. "I'm sick and tired, and I'm ready. I don't need no gun." He held up fists like bricks. "I'll put these up against any man, white or colored."

"We can use a good pair of fists," Fat said, "but we need this, too. This here's the equalizer." He held his gun high for the others to see.

Brother Johnson rolled his eyes upward. "Lord, help us. Deacon Redmond done brought a gun in here."

"That's right, Fat." JC said, patting his brother-in-law's back. "We won't start a fight, but we'll end it."

"I say let every man worth his salt bring his gun," Fat said. "If we see anything that shouldn't be, let bullets from Mr. Colt do the talking. See, there's one thing I done found out in my twenty-eight years—all men is flesh and blood. They bleed the same."

The porter pushed up his sleeves. "I'm with you, Deacon."

"I'm tired of talking. We need action," Fat said.

"Don't we need a leader, too?" asked Thomas, also a deacon and a friend of Brother Johnson. "*Somebody with education and experience?*"

"Looks like we got a leader already," said JC, who was losing patience. Such querulous, vacuous meetings kept him away from churches.

"Waal," drawled Brother Johnson, "he's not educated, and I hear tell he's having relations outside his marriage. I think that makes him unqualified."

"Johnson, why you all in my business?" Fat asked. He had broken up with Harriet, who left town, and as far as he could tell, Zenobia knew nothing about his affair. The way he saw it, nobody had been hurt.

JC cut in. "We always want to know if somebody's 'qualified.' I bet we would've asked Abraham Lincoln, a man with only three years of formal schooling, yet a brilliant leader and an autodidact, if he was qualified."

"Enough talk! Let's rise up," said the professor. "All this talk makes me think somebody's scared."

"Scared?" Fat said. "I ain't scared of nothing, except this jawing." He hoped they couldn't hear the hysterical beating of his heart. He wasn't sure they could stop the armed mob that was probably on its way to Brownsville. Deacon Johnson talked earlier about phoning the sheriff for protection and locking themselves in their houses. Fat said he wasn't going to let his family see him "shaking like a leaf on a tree." He went to the meeting, which was called by word of mouth, determined to do something, even if he lost his life. Somehow, while the others sat on their hands and talked, he wound up standing in the front of the room.

After a more minutes of posturing from Brother Johnson and his friend, the men elected Fat as their leader, and he assigned teams to spread the word to meet at the top of the road leading into Brownsville with guns, knives, canes—whatever weapons they could muster. The men quietly filed out the door. As they drove wagons back to their homes, cinders from burning buildings in the central city blew into their eyes.

"It won't be long now," Fat thought. "They killed a man in East Point this morning, strung him up in a tree like he was an animal. Brownsville's not that far away." He heard the police had joined the rioters. Who would protect the people? When the newspapers railed about the assaults on white women, the sheriff promised to kill every "coon" in Atlanta. They had to have guns and fight or perish. They had to straighten their backs or be damned. Isabella and Elijah had told him how it was back in the old days. And as far as he could see, that was how it still was. A colored man took his whippings or died. His ability to endure the lash was his only strength. Well, things were going to change if he had anything to say about it. He wasn't going to run away like his father and leave his family to fend for themselves.

When Fat arrived at his house, Zenobia was in the front room with the boys, who sat on either side of her as she read aloud from the Bible. Her brown eyes looked up from reading. "Fat, Beatrice called and she said some people got hurt. She said we better——"

"Beatrice talks too much. It was just a little trouble," Fat said. "We'll take care of it." He said nothing about the meeting. As a woman, Zenobia couldn't do much, and telling her about bodies rotting on Atlanta's streets, men hanging from lampposts, rapes, fires, and hate stinking like sulfur would upset her. He couldn't stand a crying female. Besides, it was his duty to protect her.

He told her the trouble was miles away. He was being careful, that was all. He supposed she didn't believe him, but Zenobia was an easy woman who didn't like to argue. She was happy with their life. He had recently asked her to slow down her catering business, because her hands would be full with taking care of his mother. Not much later, he overheard her bragging to friends that she had been "set down" at home and didn't have to work—a dream—usually unrealized—of many colored women. She didn't ask about his financial affairs and appeared satisfied when he said her main duty was making a home for his children and his was earning a living.

"Just to be careful," he said, pulling her away from their sons. "Take the boys to our room and lock the door."

"What about you?"

"Don't worry about me. I can take care of myself."

Their oldest boy, Elijah III, sensed trouble and wailed in a thin, frighten voice.

"Shut up, boy. Be a man," Fat barked, and the child hushed, fearing the back of his father's hand. Fat grabbed his sons and carried them to the bedroom. As he expected, Zenobia followed. He checked the lock on the only window in the bedroom and placed a stout stick across it. Even after Zenobia turned the key in the front door behind him, he rattled the knob to be sure it was locked.

Chapter Twenty-One

Monday, September 24

Word circulated that the sheriff and a band of vigilantes were going to "rid the city of unruly, uppity negroes in Brownsville." Men from there and surrounding areas met at the entrance to the main road, which was really a dirt path into a community without paved streets. They wouldn't start trouble, Fat had vowed, but would stop any man, who tried to attack them. He cheered when the president of a colored seminary and other top men in the community pledged their support.

On his way to the entrance, Fat stopped to pick up JC, who persuaded him not to come in and check on Isabella. "No time for that," JC said. "Everybody's fine and they're with Beatrice. She can be as tough as any man. She'll take care of your mama and sisters." So Fat joined the Brownsville posse without knowing that his mother had rolled over on his baby sister, a story Beatrice and her sisters would bury forever. He didn't know Mary Alice had not returned from Gwyneth Forester's or that Ruby had set out alone with her baby. JC didn't want him to know those things, because a distracted Fat would not be useful in the coming confrontation.

They joined hundreds of nervous men packed together near

Lakewood. The road was clear of its usual Monday traffic: vegetable and fruit vendors, schoolchildren, handymen looking for work, and old men out to stretch their legs. The Brownsville Men, a name they chose, waited in a silent, tight knot, ready for and dreading a fight. As Fat took a position on the frontline and JC walked to the rear, the men tipped their hats and mumbled solemn greetings.

Facing them, Fat shouted, "Now we ain't hogs for slaughter and we sho ain't rapists or criminals. We're men with hearts and brains. So let's act like it."

Hands shielded eyes from the glare of the sun as necks craned to see. "We ready, brother," they replied.

Fat stood with his feet wide apart, looking over the volunteers. He knew many of the men from church, his lunchroom, or the neighborhood. They weren't soldiers, just ordinary men, like him, determined to protect their homes and families. The rioters had terrorized the city, and except for a few brave hearts, nobody stood up. Brownsville would be different. Maybe no one would write stories about how they protected their homes. Maybe their dead might go uncounted. Maybe liars would say the colored people of Brownsville, Summerhill, and Buttermilk Bottom caused the violence. But if he didn't die that day, he would sit on his back doorsteps and tell his grandchildren the truth, and they would know their grandfather was a man.

Let them come like men, and we will meet them that way.

He fingered the gun in his pocket and strutted across the front line, meeting the eyes of each man. He returned to his spot, toed the ground with his boot, and swore under his breath. *Where in the hell are they?* He knew they were coming—the sour smell of hate was in the damp air. His fist clamped around the handle of his pistol, and his finger searched for the trigger. He didn't *want* to kill anybody— God knew he didn't—but he would if driven to it.

As the Brownsville Men waited, white, porous clouds drifted across the dismal expanse of sky, and the voices of nature were mute. Birds stopped singing, barking dogs lost their voices, and the men had run out of threats, boasts, and banter. They clutched the handles of pistols and clubs, and the smell of their cheap cigars was like burning trash.

"Look yonder," a man yelled. A reddish cloud of dust appeared on a low hill north of them and rolled forward.

Fat saw a phalanx of men, a few walking and banging cans, but most riding horses or wagons and howling for blood. Builders, grocers, bank tellers and postal clerks in white hoods rolled together like nefarious avengers. Behind them tagged the faded overalls, raggedy shirts, and cloth hats of the rabble that hung out on Decatur and Peters. And all around, darting in and out of their paths, feral-looking dogs bayed, as if they had sighted a gang of wild turkeys.

"Aw, hell. Look at that," Fat said when he saw the sheriff leading the gang.

Deacon Johnson cheered. "Hallelujah! I knew they'd come. I told the sheriff we needed protection."

"You a fool, Johnson. That's not protection you seeing," Fat said. "They coming to get our asses."

A deputy's badge glinted high on the shirt of a husky man riding beside the sheriff. His horse's flanks had a blanket of white lather and the poor animal looked close to collapsing under its hefty rider, who threw back his head and yelled, "Protect white women."

This put more steam in the riders and they charged forward, dragging the sour smell of hate with them.

"Show no fear, men," Fat shouted, although his bowels churned with it. "Don't let these peckerwoods scare you."

"Let's burn er down, boys," yelled another man with the sheriff.

As the riders advanced, Fat and his men scattered, weapons in hand, to strategic positions on either side, as they had planned. Fat felt the sharp teeth of a hound dog in his leg. He jerked his leg away and brought his heavy foot down on the animal's head, spewing brains and blood. A rider with crazed eyes raced toward him. Later Fat tried to recall who fired the first shot—the sheriff or his posse or a Brownsville man. He did remember seeing a uniformed deputy fall off his horse. A red stain ran across the deputy's shirt, blood trickled from his lips. Fat and men on both sides were firing, stabbing and bludgeoning, but the sheriff's men had more guns, ammunition, and accuracy. Their bullets struck several Brownsville men, who lay on the ground in a mess of blood and flesh. A heavy stick struck like a hammer on Fat's head, and he went down on his knees before another blow knocked him unconscious. When he woke up, he and more than two hundred colored men were under arrest, shackled together chain-gang style waiting for transportation to jail. Blood from a head wound painted Fat's grim face red. His right arm felt broken, and his gun was missing.

Wagons soon arrived, and the prisoners dragged themselves aboard, amid blows and curses from their captors. Three shotgun-carrying deputies accompanied the first wagons of dejected captives to town. At the jail, Fat heard that a deputy and an unidentified Brownsville man were dead. He thought somebody would pay for the deputy's death, and perhaps he would be the one.

***

The four men, who invaded Beatrice's home, hid behind white hoods. As they cussed and broke both locks on the front door, she screamed and sent Phillis upstairs to lock herself in a bedroom. They dragged Beatrice from her hiding place behind the curtain of a living room closet.

"Where's your man?" One of them held her arm behind her back.

"He isn't home." She made up a grayish lie about JC whereabouts.

The invader twisted her arm. "Where's the money? And don't tell me you ain't got none."

"What money?" Beatrice thought he would twist her arm off. Screaming would frighten Phillis, and she would do anything as long as they didn't hurt her daughter.

"Then I got to get me some of this tail. I can't leave with nothing."

A thug with thick hands and mean eyes yelled, "Whoo hoo. Get ready for some real men, gal." He grabbed his crotch and laughed.

Beatrice froze, thinking she would be assaulted and maybe killed. She would always thank God for directing the eyes of the tallest thug to moving boxes behind her sofa and a silver candle stick that she had laid on one of them. "Look at the loot," he hollered, and his friend dropped her on the floor. They all fell on the boxes in a thieving frenzy. Cowering against a chair, Beatrice could only silently pray for them to leave her home.

"Where'd they get this silver?" a tall one asked no one in particular.

"Stole it," said mean eyes as he stuffed a gunnysack with a large platter, candlesticks, and cutlery.

"We worked for it," Beatrice snapped, and an iron hand slammed against her face. She covered her painful, fiery eye. "Oh, you've put my eye out."

"Shut up, you ugly bitch," said a short, skinny fellow with blond eyebrows poking from under his hood. "Open your mouth again and I'll cut your throat." He punched her head and she fell backward.

Although a hood muffled his voice, she recognized the man who delivered their milk.

She stayed on the floor, pretending to be unconscious while they ransacked the downstairs rooms, whooping and busting up furniture. She heard them running toward Isabella's room and then a deep groan, which wrenched her soul, but she kept her head down. In a minute, footsteps raced out the front door, which was wide open, and from the corner of her eye, she spied their gunny sacks of loot— her things—as they disappeared forever. Beatrice waited a while longer to be sure they were gone before she rose and bolted upstairs to check on Phillis. She wanted to dance with joy after seeing her daughter asleep on the bed with a thumb in her mouth. Nothing mattered more to her. Nothing.

Beatrice closed the bedroom door and scrambled downstairs to Isabella's room, where she found her mother's body on the bed, sightless eyes staring above a twisted mouth. "Oh, no, no," she breathed, realizing that Isabella had suffered a third and fatal stroke, brought on by rioters in white hoods storming her room. She fell weeping beside the bed and lifted her mother's hand, which was still warm. The copper wedding ring she had worn for thirty years was missing and wounds covered her finger.

"You didn't deserve this, Mama," she said, closing Isabella's eyes. "I'm so, so sorry."

JC was among the few Brownsville men, who escaped. He walked into his house, covered in dirt and blood from a cut on his face, and shouted for his wife and daughter. Beatrice answered from Isabella's bedroom.

"Jesus," JC breathed when he saw his mother-in-law's body. "What the hell happened?"

Beatrice fell against him and laid her head on his chest. "The white hats. They broke in here and scared Mama to death. It had to be them…Oh, God… because she was fine when I last checked." She waved a listless hand at the torn curtain and an overturned dresser. "The bastards took her ring and ransacked everything." She touched the wound on his face. "But you're cut…I've been so worried."

"It's nothing." JC brushed her hand away. "Where's Phillis?"

"Sleeping in her room. I locked her in, and they didn't see her."

He rushed out and bounded up the stairs, and Beatrice followed. He opened the door to his daughter's bedroom. Phillis was still asleep. "Look at her, my princess," JC said and grinned. "I knew she'd be sucking that thumb."

He closed the door and they went to the downstairs sofa, the only furniture that hadn't been demolished. Broken furniture and glass, shredded clothing, and paper littered the rug. Garbage filled the fireplace and feathers from ripped pillows covered the sofa. What the thieves couldn't carry, they destroyed. Staring at the trashed room, a symbol of murder and malicious destruction, Beatrice began to cry.

JC put his arm around her shoulder and touched her eye, which had begun to swell. "Did they....?" he said, unable to articulate the awful question, but he had to know. "They didn't..."

"They started to and God saved us. They wanted you, but I told them you were out of town." She wiped fresh drops of blood from his face with her hands.

He took a white stocking from the floor and pressed it to his wound to arrest the bleeding. "Just look at your eye. While I was hiding, they were beating my wife." JC slammed a fist into his palm. "Goddamn the bastards. I could kill them. I could—"

"If you had been here, they would've killed you. Four men against one."

JC went to the kitchen, which had tar on the walls, smashed dishes on the floor, and glass from the broken window sparkling like water in the sink. Tobacco spittle stained the torn curtains. They had stolen the door to the icebox and most of the food. What could they do with only the door or did they take it for spite? JC wondered, as he stood cracking his knuckles in the middle of the room.

He took pieces from a bowl of melting ice, wrapped them in a handkerchief, and took them to Beatrice. He sat on the arm of the sofa and held the ice against her swollen eye. If he had been home, his gun would've stopped her attackers. Or maybe that wasn't true. He had a chance to kill one in the battle of Brownsville and failed. After a vigilante on horseback struck him across his shoulders with a club, he fired his gun, missed, and the man kicked the gun from his hand. It landed in the midst of churning crimson earth, lost to him forever. JC escaped through the confusion and dust stirred up by hundreds of fighting men. Far away from the battle, he hid in a woodshed under a pile of junk until everything was quiet. Instead of hiding, he should've come home with the hammer he found in the shed and beat the hell out of the men in his house.

"I'm sorry, darling," he said.

"You and the other men did what you could; you let them know we're not going to sit back and be slaughtered anymore. My eye will heal and we can buy new things. But poor Mama." Tears flowed down Beatrice's face. "They scared her to death, JC. She was an elderly lady and they didn't care. Those belly crawlers didn't give a damn."

"It's over. They've gone back to whatever holes they came from."

Whenever Beatrice thought her tears would stop and she had gotten control of herself, they started again. Life hadn't been fair to her mother. She never had a chance with money or marriage, so who could blame her for the desperate thing she did? If those beasts hadn't broken in, she might've lived longer. She might've seen her husband again and maybe reconciled with him. But they owned the world, those white men, and people like Isabella only existed in it.

"We have to do the burial soon," JC said after the sun had set and a solitary candle burned on the mantel.

"Call David. Let his funeral home pick Mama up."

JC's rubbed his forehead and carefully chose his words. "I'm sorry, honey. He can't come here and we can't go there. It's too dangerous."

"What are you saying?" Beatrice searched his face.

"I know this is hard, but we have to bury her ourselves...in the back yard."

"Absolutely not. I won't do it. Mama was a Christian and she's got to have a proper *church* service. She can't be thrown in the ground like a heathen. People will think we don't care about her."

"I'll take care of everything. I promise."

"Without a preacher?"

"Beatrice, please."

It took a while, but Beatrice finally agreed to a backyard burial. She admitted to herself that the Atlanta she knew was gone. Freedom and opportunity hadn't been great but, comparatively speaking, the city was better than Jackson, New Orleans, or Birmingham—so she'd thought. Now bodies were in the street, JC said, unclaimed by terrorized loved ones. Houses were burning and people didn't know what the end was going to be. Nothing was the same; everything was upside down. From the jumble on the floor, Beatrice collected Phillis's rag doll and a smashed picture frame and sat quietly with them in her lap.

They heard crying and raced upstairs. Their daughter sat on the side of her bed. "Mama, I'm hungry," she said.

"Is that all, honey child?" Beatrice said. "Mama will bring you something to eat." She went to the kitchen and prepared a dinner of cheese, bread, and water—the only food left—and took it upstairs.

While Phillis ate, she asked about the bad men, who broke into their house. JC promised they wouldn't return and to distract her, he told stories about talking animals and fairy godmothers. "Parents are like godmothers, because we keep you safe," he said, tucking her into bed. He and Beatrice stayed with her until she was asleep again.

Beatrice decided not to tell her about Isabella until morning.

Downstairs, JC put his arm around Beatrice's shoulders. "You know, this riot made me think twice about going to Africa," he said.

"Oh?" Beatrice sucked in her breath and waited.

"It seemed like a good idea at first. Even Lincoln thought the solution to the race problem was to send us back. But I think he might've realized it was a foolish idea. Imagine shipping two million people, mostly born here, to a strange land. Deport them. Drop them down in the middle of foreign languages and cultures, without compensation for years of labor. I read the other day that most Africans say we can't come home; we've been away too long. The reverend didn't write me about that." He snickered. "They took the door to the icebox, which told me that they want to drive us from our nice homes and businesses. Going back to Africa would play right into their hands, because they'd take what little property we have."

Beatrice nodded and let him talk.

"The white hats, politicians, and rabble can't stand to see us prosper. They don't want us to survive." His eyes turned hard. "Well, we will survive. I'm going to stand like a man and prosper in spite of them. I'm going to stay in this country, where I was born and bred, and have what's mine, because I helped build it. That way, twenty years from now, maybe Phillis won't have to deal with this crap."

"Only twenty years, huh? Sounds really optimistic but I hope you're right." Beatrice was pleased but trying not to show it. "I used to be like that, but this taught me something, too. I said they wouldn't come to Brownsville, because decent, responsible colored people live here. Like a fool, I blamed the nasty juke joints and people's bad behavior. Not anymore. Enough is enough. When we get to Ohio, I want to stay."

"We'll see," JC said. "I feel lucky that you and Phillis are OK. They say Lena Walton, was assaulted. Six men ran "a train" on her and she hemorrhaged. She didn't make it. A man over on Delaney Street was wounded. He was hiding in his bed, and they shot him in front of his wife and children. So things are still hot."

"You're scaring me, JC. My brother and sisters are out there."

"Sorry, babe." JC kissed her forehead and plodded upstairs. He returned in a clean shirt and pants. "I think I'll check on Fat and your sisters. Rumors are flying; somebody might know something."

Beatrice was anxious, her mind was in a jumble about her family, and she couldn't think straight. They could be dead, though she prayed it wasn't true.

JC asked the operator to get Fat's house for him. Zenobia said she hadn't seen her husband. She sounded as if she had been crying. "Bad news," JC thought and hung up. He took the paper with Miss Forester's number from Beatrice and asked the operator to connect him. She did and there wasn't an answer. "Let me see what I can find out," he said to Beatrice. "I'll be back."

Watching JC walk from the house with hunched shoulders, Beatrice asked God to bring him back.

Chapter Twenty-Two

Tuesday, September 25, 1906

JC returned the night before with no news about her sisters and a strange reluctance to say anything about Fat. Beatrice felt something was wrong, though she was afraid to go and see for herself.

"I don't know where my family is," she said in despair, "and I don't want you to get killed looking for them. If they're alive—and by the grace of God they are—they'll come to see Mama, because they don't know she's gone. If they're dead, I don't want to know about it—not now. I can't take any more."

JC responded by going to the grave he was preparing for Isabella.

Beatrice paced and worried all morning. By noon, still no word. Her mother's body was decomposing in the bedroom and would have to be buried that day or conditions in the house would be unbearable. She closed the bedroom door, but the image of Isabella lying lifeless on the bed haunted her.

JC came inside after he finished digging. "There's some news I've been wanting to tell you and didn't know how. They got Fat."

"Who? Where? I'm telling you, JC, I can't take anymore."

"Some people, friends of mine, said they locked him up. They got hundreds of us in the Tower." The Tower was the city's notorious jail and courthouse.

Beatrice breathed in deeply. At least Fat was alive. She had been sure he was dead. The neighborhood was broiling with news about the dead cop and a score of colored men, who were killed in retaliation. The sheriff and vigilantes had returned to Brownsville and fired into homes. JC said he had seen them shoot the janitor from their organizing meeting. The old cat decided his iron fists weren't enough and was killed carrying a rusty musket that hadn't been fired since the Civil War.

"Bea, I swear I feel like killing that son-of-a bitch sheriff," JC said.

"If you do, six more like him will spring up."

JC said he saw bodies in the streets. Only a few people were brave enough to transport their slaughtered loved ones to a funeral home during daylight. Move a body and be arrested or shot. So corpses lay rotting in the hot sun. The newspapers reported twelve dead, including a white policeman and an old white woman who suffered a heart attack during the riot.

"They didn't count Mama," Beatrice said.

JC said he personally knew of thirty deaths, including Charlie, the crippled boy from Lydell Alley. His friend, the newspaper editor, a courageous but hunted man, said there was good reason to believe the correct number was forty, all but two of them colored.

Just before nightfall, Zenobia came over with her sons. The boys and Phillis kept a din going upstairs while their parents talked downstairs.

"We need to break Fat out before they kill him," Zenobia said. Her once pampered hair hadn't seen a comb in days, and dark circles surrounded her eyes.

"It's better to see how things shake out," JC said. "No sense in everybody going to jail."

He said he heard about trials for rioters. The judge had already sentenced several colored men to years in prison—no bail, no parole, no probation, no defense lawyers, and no evidence. The Brownsville men charged with the policeman's death were jailed without bond. There was talk about lynching. To white rioters, he delivered fines, lighter sentences, and lectures about drinking and carousing. A lone white man, accused of disobeying a policeman, received a sentence of six months, which was promptly suspended. From the bench, the judge announced that he couldn't send young white boys to jail, because "it would mean their complete ruin."

"He's a corrupt old bastard," JC said and drank deep from a glass of whiskey.

"We've survived worse than this," Beatrice said, "Mama used to say you can't hold somebody down without staying down yourself. If you get up, that person will get up. And Atlanta's too proud to stay on the ground… I know this town…not while the whole world is watching. It's going to be all right."

"That's easy for you to say, Beatrice. Your family, including your daughter's daddy, is at home," said Zenobia, curled up on the rug with a scowl. "I ain't worried for myself. It's my children. Their daddy's in jail, and ain't no telling when they gon let him go. You know they always want men for their chain gangs."

Beatrice patted Zenobia's shoulder. "Don't ever think I don't care about Fat; he's my brother."

JC said he would get Fat from the Tower the next morning.

"Don't play with me, JC," Zenobia said. "How can you do that?"

JC stood, stretched and was careful to sound confident. "I've got the colored press and a bunch of preachers working on it. They're meeting downtown right now with James English and the other big cheeses. English is probably running the meeting like he runs everything else, but that can't be helped. Imagine those folks asking to sit down with us at the colored YMCA on Butler Street. Now that would be something to see. They want this whole thing done with. Wipe the riot from the history books, and don't talk about it. And if you have to talk, polish it up a bit; make it pretty if you can. Say it was about illegal immigrants taking jobs from folks, something like that.

"They're having a fit because it was in the Paris press. Thirty or forty dead? That's fine. But having the whole mess in foreign newspapers is strictly unacceptable. This New South thing is like gold to this city. So you better believe they'll release Fat, a deacon at Best Baptist, as an example of white southern largesse." JC kissed Zenobia's cheek. "You and the boys sleep here tonight. I guarantee you Fat is coming home tomorrow."

From her chair at the living room window after dinner, Beatrice looked out on a gloomy night covering the damage she had seen in daylight: fire-gutted homes and once-neat lawns strewn with garbage. She heard overloaded wagons and carriages lumbering on dark streets as families fled for good with their possessions piled high and their children held close. Many probably didn't know where they would end up, yet they were going. If things went according to plans, her family would join the exodus one day soon.

The coffee and bacon Zenobia was preparing in the kitchen didn't stir Beatrice's appetite. She couldn't eat until she knew where her sisters were. She watched the white-stone path to her house, hoping to see them walk up.

Fat was in jail awaiting a trial, so she knew he was alive. *Ruby and her baby and Mary Alice, where are they? If only I could see Ruby one more time, I'd stop criticizing and let her know I love her. God, let me see her and make amends before it's too late.*

Her rift with Ruby— nurtured by small grievances and insults— now seemed petty. As Beatrice looked back, she saw that it was her fault, because she was almost grown and should have known better.

Ruby was only six the day they began to despise each other.

After picking blueberries on another farm near their cabin down home, Beatrice returned with her basket and stopped near an open window of the house, because she heard her father's voice and he sounded angry. "She's sixteen, going on seventeen and grown enough. Why can't she marry him? This might be her last chance, cause she ain't light skinned like Mary Alice or pretty like baby girl. A plain gal like that can't be picky."

He was talking about a rough country boy who had asked for her hand. Beatrice thought the boy was dull and entirely unsuitable.

Her mother's reply was gentle. "She's smart, Elijah. Plenty folks say so. She say she gonna be a teacher."

"Too proud for her own good, that's what she is."

Beatrice dropped the berries and ran through pine trees to a stream that separated their farm from another sharecropper's. She sat on a boulder and brooded.

Ruby, who had heard the conversation, too, came outside and found her. "Daddy say you ugly, you ugly thing."

"I might not be pretty to you or Daddy, but my behind will make either one of you a Sunday face." Beatrice smacked her sister's back and burst out crying.

Not sure about the meaning of the words but knowing that Beatrice's tone was hateful, Ruby wailed and ran home to report it to Elijah. When Beatrice showed up for supper, her father slapped her so hard she thought her head would separate from her neck. Her father's words, though, hurt more than the slap. But hatred missed the road, as sometimes happens, and she transferred it to Ruby, whose smooth skin, perfect lips, and large eyes were a constant reminder that she was the pretty one. Her junior sister had ridiculed her, and nothing could erase it.

The riot changed Beatrice's mind after she saw death all around;

men, women, and children perished in seconds. Some didn't even have time to say goodbye. She wanted to see her sisters and reconcile with Ruby before it was too late. Beatrice had been tired of their feud for years, but too proud and stubborn to do anything about it. Many times she wanted to tell Ruby, "I love you", and some little spat stopped her. But it wasn't too late—she hoped. The Bible said put away childish things, and if Ruby wasn't dead, she would make peace. As far as she was concerned, their war had seen its last battle.

She listened for the sound of footsteps outside. *Where are those crazy girls? They should be here if they're coming. Where are they?*

***

Ruby came upon the body—soggy with rainwater and face up—on her way to Brownsville. She stared at the face, which was human and somehow wasn't. Bloody gashes replaced the ears, and the lips were pulled back in a grimace that testified about the final moments of life. His fly was open, and when Ruby saw what was missing, her breakfast crept to the top of her throat. She covered her mouth and prepared to step around the victim, but something familiar in the misshapen face stopped her, compelled her to come closer, which she did and leaned in. By some miracle, the nose had not been broken, and it rose regal and bloody with a slightly hooked tip. Ruby had admired that nose while Lee hovered over her naked in bed. She stared at the moustache, ruby red with blood, except for a drop of white hair in a corner. Her shattered mind screamed, *It's Lee. Jesus, have mercy.*

After vomiting into the bed of a charred carriage, Ruby removed Lovelee's blanket and spread it over Lee's face. It would have to do until she could phone the undertaker. She waved a horde of blue flies away from his body and steadied herself against the carriage. It was time to make haste; the demons who killed her husband might still be around. In a few minutes, she had recovered enough to be on her way. She would later wonder where her energy for the journey to Brownsville had come from. Along the miles through alleys and side streets, she wept for Lee. They had lost too much, too soon. It was not unheard of for a couple like them to put things aside and go on. Now it was too late. Worst still, nobody would pay for his murder. She knew how things worked. "Escaped Convict Killed by Persons Unknown," the headlines would say while the murderers would go on with their lives as if nothing had happened.

At the end of an alley, she walked past a horse barn, where the animals munched peacefully on buckets of feed, undisturbed by the riot. A scrawny boy in a militia uniform, carrying a rifle, locked eyes with her. He looked to be no more than fifteen and uncertain about what to do next. Ruby lowered her eyes and held her breath while the boy shuffled from one foot to the next. When he waved her on, she exhaled.

In the middle of Marietta Street, the ten-foot-tall statue of Henry Grady had become a funeral bier. Ruby smelled the body before she saw it, thrown like a sack of old clothes at the base. With maggots breeding in every orifice, it released a deathly stench that nearly spun her around. Which of the ten victims reported by the newspapers was he? At his birth, surely his mother had cried in pain and his father with joy. Had a woman loved him as much as she loved Lee? Was that woman now grieving so hard she couldn't stand? Had she gone on anyway, because she had a baby like Lovelee to take care of?

Ruby approached a range of tall buildings and spied a cluster of men on a corner. One carried a torch, which lit his ruddy face. Up to their eyebrows in hot talk, they didn't notice her. For all she knew, they might have been the ones who killed Lee. She inched away from the corner, and took a side street.

Chapter Twenty-Three

After early autumn winds bathed the city, its leaders dressed it in righteous absolution. A newspaper declared the end of the riot but predicted a "war of extermination" next time; the mayor blamed irresponsible newspapers for inciting young toughs; colored ministers called for better comportment from low-class elements, who had created riot conditions in illegal juke joints; businessmen following the leadership of James English wrote with an eye to repairing the city's damaged national and international image: "White and black have realized their mistake and all have returned to work with a determination to right matters." Banks were open, the brickyards were producing again with convict labor buttressed by new arrests, cotton sales boomed, Coca-Cola consumption was at previous high levels, and trains and streetcars with armed militia on board ran on time.

The state militia had restored tenuous order to Atlanta's broken neighborhoods, yet many people of both races were afraid to leave their homes. Alarming stories emerged of men parading a murdered man's fingers and toes through the streets and the deadly stoning of a Western Union messenger at the Forsyth Street Bridge. The president of Gammon Seminary was beaten with a rifle butt, proving that any colored man, regardless of his social status and education, could be brutalized. Likewise, any colored woman could be assaulted, and her attacker would not be punished.

The mayor issued an open statement to the press: "As long as black brutes attempt rape upon our white women, just so long will they be unceremoniously dealt with."

**

In this atmosphere, Gwyneth opened her front door for the morning newspapers and scanned them nervously:

Negroes shot a police officer in Brownsville and burned down their own homes.

Eight black rioters and an elderly white woman, who was rightly terrified of being assaulted, paid the ultimate price.

Law and order have not yet returned; a committee of upstanding citizens meets to save our beloved city.

Responsible Negroes ordered to stay in their homes after dark or risk being shot on sight.

White women captive in their homes, forced to cook and do heavy laundry without help.

The men who fought to save white southern womanhood commended for their bravery.

Gwyneth folded the newspapers away in her desk drawer.

She remembered seeing blood on her brother's clothes the night before and guessed he had done more than "keep the boys straight." Knowing his natural tendencies, she imagined him instigating violence and salivating over cruelty. Powerful and wealthy, his friends owned the newspapers, ran white-hat gangs, controlled politics and money, and even had a hand in the distribution of illicit liquor. When it came to boosting the city, they had no equals. In their Atlanta, the sun was brighter, the water wetter, and riches were more abundant than anywhere else in the world. "The devil's in all of them," Gwyneth thought. Of course she didn't say this to her brother, because he was not to be challenged.

Saturday through Monday, while large portions of the city were being destroyed, Forester would leave at nightfall and return early the next morning. He'd march upstairs and down, ranting in tirades that turned the air in the house foul.

Fortunately for Mary Alice, he did not go near the little room under the stairs where she hid. She put a pillow over her head to muffle the sound of his voice. She did her business in a slop jar Gwyneth provided and ate late at night, alone in the kitchen; Gwyneth had her meals at the dining room table. From the sound of Forester's voice, Mary Alice gathered that the city was being consumed by murderous rage, instigated by men like him. She yearned to go somewhere far away.

Mr. Forester raged all Tuesday morning about lazy, trifling niggers

Gwyneth said, "Now, brother, it won't do any good to talk like trash. Remember, you're a gentleman."

"Damn right. If it wasn't for civic leaders like me," Forester shouted from the upstairs hallway to the dining room, where his sister had retreated, "they'd take over, and decent white women won't be able to leave their homes. It'll never happen as long as I'm alive. You hear me? You should be glad I'm looking out for you, because without a husband, you'd be at the mercy of black rapists."

Gwyneth lowered her eyes and wished the day would come when she could be free. It wouldn't be long if she could find the courage to take the final step. She opened a drawer in the breakfront and slammed it shut. The rope was still there, waiting for her.

Her brother continued. "Every white woman in this city should be grateful to me and the boys. Damn niggers. I'll hang every one of em."

To Gwyneth's relief, he soon went to bed with a glass of bourbon.

His loud snores traveled to the dining room where she sat with folded hands, waiting for him to be gone again.

Hours later, he appeared downstairs in a clean shirt and suit. "I've got some business with the boys downtown," he said and dropped the names of the mayor, a soft drink bottler, and a newspaper editor, which Gwyneth doubted he really knew. He adjusted the bowler hat on his head and smiled. "They invited me to a meeting, you know. Guess I'm a pretty important man in this town."

Gwyneth nodded. Wherever he was going, whatever he planned to do, she was glad to see him leave, for the sake of peace. She scuttled to Mary Alice's room. "You better leave before he gets back," she said in an urgent voice. "The trouble is over."

"I heard," Mary Alice said, rising from her narrow bed. *What does she think? I'm not deaf, even though I've be afraid to say anything about her stupid brother. He's been ranting and raving, loud enough to raise the roof off this house. And she's been coming down here but hasn't said a mumbling word about it. Not even when she caught me crying. It's like I don't have feelings. Like she thinks I'm not human like her, but I don't think that's true, because she saved my life. It's because she's afraid of that man and she should be. He's a monster. If she had a backbone, she'd leave, too. I hope she does, because I'm afraid for her.*

Gwyneth continued. "It was worse than I thought—much worse. May God have mercy all of us. My brother's gone now, so go before he gets back."

"Thank you, Miss Gwyneth." It was all Mary Alice, who was stiff with fright, could manage. Instead of a refuge, the house had become a horror and a prison, and she wanted to leave.

******

The odor of smoke was pungent as Mary Alice left the house and walked toward downtown. In a white dress and wide-brimmed hat borrowed from Gwyneth, it was as if she were a spirit, moving airily on deserted streets before silent houses. She wore a fancy pair of Gwyneth's oxfords with leather laces, shoes she had been able to afford only in New York. The shoes and the way Gwyneth pinned her hair under the hat to cover up frizzes supported Mary Alice's persona—a courageous lady out to handle urgent household business. She wore gloves, so if stopped, she could say that her sick husband was at home with their children, and the absence of a ring on her finger would not be suspicious.

Gwyneth said she wanted to offer her car, but the driver hadn't come to work, and neither of them knew how to drive. Mary Alice glided past the car parked on the street and thought she was better off. The driver was a nosy old man, who might have asked dangerous questions.

She was careful to stay away from the main streets, where she imagined gangs still roamed. Even so, she was jumpy. Overripe, late-season, peaches fell with thumps from a tree behind her. Startled by the noise, she hugged her small leather bag of clothing closer and feared rough hands might drag her away. She heard a cough and hid behind the trunk of an oak tree in somebody's yard, until she was sure it was nothing.

Gwyneth had saved her from death twice, at times when she was too foolish to ask for help. In fact she had resisted, which made the woman's open hands even more mystifying. Unlike other women who did favors for their help and then overworked them as payback, Gwyneth hadn't asked for anything in return, except perhaps companionship.

When Mary Alice said she wanted to leave town, Gwyneth suggested San Francisco. In a soft, longing voice, she painted pictures of streetcars on undulating, hilly streets. "People out there are from all over—nobody cares exactly where." Gwyneth had only read about

San Francisco in magazines, but talked as though she knew it firsthand. "The earthquake hit the city hard," she said, "but it'll bounce back, I'm sure, as good as ever. This is an exciting time to go. Everything's being rebuilt, new people popping in." With lowered eyes, she said that a man she knew as a young woman had relocated to San Francisco. When she recovered from a major illness—the nature of which she didn't say—he invited her out for a visit. Her brother forbade her to go and that was the end of it. Only loose women followed men they were not married to Mr. Forester said.

"I wish I'd been stronger," Gwyneth said. "Every now and then I still receive letters from my friend. He hasn't written lately, but that's OK. I'll hear something soon." She caught her breath. "If he's alive..."

Mary Alice blew softly through her lips. What a corseted life Gwyneth was leading. Someone else was directing every move she made, and she was still being punished for a decision she made many years ago. *Why doesn't she leave? What's keeping her in this dark house with her hell-raising brother?* Mary Alice could never live like that. Her life belonged to her, and she was going to live it the way she wanted. At the last stop on her journey above ground, when it was all over, she would have to leave the train alone. She had family who loved her and she loved them, but they couldn't dictate the terms of her life. One day soon, she hoped Gwyneth would think the same way.

As far as Gwyneth knew, Mary Alice wanted to leave town because of the riot. She was too smart to say she wanted to be as free as a white woman, and San Francisco offered the same anonymity as New York, much more than Atlanta. She looked white and had learned in New York to think and act white, so who in California could say she wasn't? Her plan took shape in her head as she hid from Mr. Forester and packed some of Gwyneth's castoffs. This time, she would admit to being from the South—the white South—new to the city and looking for work as a waitress. San Francisco was far enough away that nobody would guess she wasn't who she appeared to be.

"Like I said, the only problem is the earthquake, which isn't active now, so it's safe." Gwyneth had sat in a kitchen chair smoking a cigarette, while Mary Alice finished up in the room under the stairs. "Here's another blouse," Gwyneth said, coming to the door. "It needs a little fixing."

Mary Alice took the blouse, stuck her pinky finger through holes where buttons had been, and shrugged. "You know I can fix anything, Miss Gwyneth."

She regretted leaving without seeing her family, especially Isabella. But she had to go and leave no trail. She didn't dare send word, not even from San Francisco, because this move required a clean break. She didn't want risky letters or phone calls. No family photos. Most likely, they would think she was killed in the riot, which would be painful for them, especially her mother, but it just couldn't be helped. Miss Gwyneth promised to keep her secret when they inquired. "Tell them I left before the trouble started," Mary Alice said, after making up a story about a violent argument and a family split, "and you haven't heard from me since."

Without thinking about rejection, she extended her hand and Gwyneth took it. "Thank you, my friend," Mary Alice said.

She walked toward the train terminal, which had resumed operations. Daylight wasn't far away, but it might as well have been midnight from the appearance of the empty streets. The teeth of broken bulbs hung from light poles. The normal crowds of businessmen, families, and military boys had vanished. Even the stray dogs and pigs that usually prowled around the terminal had gone into hiding. The absence of life worried Mary Alice. Perhaps there wouldn't be a train. Just as she bought her ticket from a polite agent, who addressed her as miss, she heard it coming. Until then, she hadn't realized how frantic she was.

"Need help with your bag, ma'am?" asked a porter, whose friendly face reminded her of JC. She handed her small valise over, and like a woman used to having things done for her, followed him into the first-class car marked "Whites Only", and settled down for her long journey. She looked around at empty seats and figured the car would fill up when it reached Chattanooga. *This time, things will be different. In San Francisco, I might marry and have children, two or maybe three, and nobody will ever know the truth.*

Chapter Twenty-Four

While Mary Alice settled back in her comfortable seat on the train and dreamed about a new life in San Francisco, Ruby rapped hard on Beatrice's door. JC opened it, grabbed her by the hand, and pulled her inside. "Get in here, woman. Where have you been?" JC said. "You're making people nervous."

Ruby tried to make fun of his nervousness to calm herself. "Well, ain't you glad to see me?"

"Stop talking off-the-wall stuff. Bea's been going crazy, looking for you. Bea," he shouted up the stairs, where she was napping with the children, "your sister's down here."

"Which one?" Beatrice bounded down the steps. "Ruby, honey" she said when she saw her. "I've been so worried."

JC wiped sweat from his brow with his hand. "If y'all need me, I'll be in the kitchen having myself a stiff drink."

"Baby girl, baby girl." Beatrice kissed her sister and Lovelee. "All this time, we thought the worst and here you are, alive and as pretty as ever."

"Is that you talking, Beatrice?" Ruby leaned back, eyes stretched in disbelief. "Oh, you must mean the baby."

"Of course I mean you—both of you. Can't you accept a compliment?"

"It sounds funny, coming from you."

Zenobia walked in from the kitchen. "Ruby, give me that baby. She needs a bath and some rest," she said and took Lovelee upstairs.

Before Beatrice could stop her, Ruby sprinted toward Isabella's room, calling, "Mama, it's me."

A few feet from Isabella's door, Beatrice grabbed her sister's arm. "Wait. Don't go in yet."

But her sister pulled away and pushed open the door. Isabella's body lay washed and wrapped in a white shroud, as Beatrice and Zenobia had prepared it. Screaming, Ruby fell against the wall. Beatrice tried to pull her away, but the girl sank down, hugged her knees, and wouldn't rise.

"You saw her, Beatrice. She was talking and everything," Ruby said, as tears washed her face. "What happened to my mama?"

Beatrice knelt and hugged her. "The white hats came here. They scared her, we think."

"Oh, my God—Mama." Ruby's eyes burned into Beatrice's face, searching for reassurance. "Tell me she didn't suffer."

"She didn't." Beatrice finally convinced Ruby to stand and guided her to a chair at the kitchen table. She dropped into a chair across from her.

"Nobody saved her. She just died like that." Ruby said.

"Don't cry, Ruby. You're going to make me break down if you don't stop."

Ruby was silent. She stared at Beatrice and slowly realized that her sister had been helpless against white hats. Maybe if she had stayed, instead of going back to the alley, the two of them might've have protected their mother. She had fought her way off a trolley with only a hat pin, and she could've stopped her mother's killers. But she left, because she thought Beatrice was mean to her.

"She went fast. They didn't assault her." Beatrice said. "I'm sure of that."

Ruby heart warmed with gratitude for that news. She had been attacked and beaten, and the thought of her mother enduring an assault would have been too much. Ruby drank sweet mint tea with Beatrice, the first liquid she'd had all afternoon, and they didn't speak for a long time. She looked around at the damaged kitchen and thought least she hadn't had pretty things in her shack to lose.

They began to talk about their mother's faith and devotion, though neither daughter mentioned her confession about Rosetta. The less said about it, Ruby thought, the better. On her third cup of tea, Ruby told Beatrice how their mother had fooled old man Callahan for months before they ran away from Soperton. "She put on a big-time shucking and jiving act for the old fool, and he sopped it up like a biscuit on a plate of gravy. He said we were loyal, the best tenants he ever had."

They burst out laughing together, which lightened their sorrow. Two deaths in one day left Ruby wanting to fold up inside and grieve, but she pressed on in spite of her heavy heart. Isabella would want her to be strong for Lovelee's sake.

Through the broken kitchen window, Ruby saw JC arranging a handful of chairs outside in the light of a lantern. "What's JC doing?"

Beatrice told her about the backyard- service they were going to have for Isabella.

"That's like throwing Mama away," Ruby said and fresh tears welled in her eyes. Nothing was going right; the world wasn't showing her family any mercy.

Beatrice explained the state of things when it came to funerals. "At least she's being buried, and this yard is ours. It'll stay in our family." Even if they didn't return from Ohio, the house couldn't be sold, she decided, not with Isabella buried in the back yard.

Ruby accepted it, figuring she had no choice. She didn't even know when or where she would lay Lee to rest. Suddenly exhausted, she laid her head on her folded arms.

Beatrice touched her sister's head. "I want to say something if it's OK."

Wondering what more trouble there could be, Ruby raised her head and gazed at Beatrice.

"Let's hang up our gloves, Ruby. We've wasted precious time fighting."

"But—"

"No. Please let me finish. It was my fault more than yours. I was jealous because Papa made a fuss over you. When it looked like something had happened to you today, a lot of thoughts went through my head. I wanted to tell you I love you."

"I love you, too," Ruby said, thinking again that they could've saved Isabella if they had been together.

"This is our second chance and we have to take it. The blood in your veins runs in mine. Whether we like it or not, we share memories that connect us, and when we're old, God willing, we'll laugh together like we did tonight."

Ruby squeezed her sister's hand. "I really hated fighting with you. I used to cry about it when I was little. To tell the truth, I did bad things, because I knew you wouldn't like it. And you ain't never disappointed me in that department."

Beatrice smiled. "Now this doesn't mean we won't have little spats, but when we do, we'll let them go. Right?"

Ruby nodded.

Zenobia walked in with Lovelee in her arms. "Ruby, you know Fat's in jail," she blurted.

Ruby's head jerked up. "What the hell for?"

"He's getting out first thing tomorrow, so don't worry about it," JC said, coming through the back door just in time.

"I ain't necessarily in no hurry, but his sons keep asking about him," Zenobia said and screwed up her lips.

"And where's Mary Alice?" Ruby asked.

"We think she's with that Forester woman, but we can't get them on the phone. None of us want to go sashaying in a white neighborhood to look for her," Beatrice said. "She'll probably show up like you did."

"She might and she might not." JC said.

"That girl. I love her but I wouldn't be surprised," Ruby said. "You know she likes to pass."

"What?" said Zenobia. "I didn't know she was one of those."

Ruby cut her eyes at Zenobia, whose new attitude was curious. She'd always been easy and quiet to a fault. So what was going on? Zenobia was family, but she wasn't blood and she needed to watch her mouth. Ruby wanted to set her straight, but she left her sister-in-law alone; things were already bad enough.

"I think she might be in New York again," Beatrice said. "I just hope she's OK."

"Everybody ain't able to run around by herself during a riot, right Ruby?" JC laughed.

"Please stop playing, JC. We're worried," Beatrice said.

"Y'all gon bury Miss Isabella without Fat?" Zenobia said. "Humph. I guess it serves him right."

"We don't have ice," JC said, "and it's hot as hell in here. It has to be tonight."

Let Zenobia keep running her mouth, Ruby thought, and I'm a punch her out. "He'll be upset, but my brother's strong. He'll be all right."

Zenobia grunted. "I guess so since his whore left town."

It was as though a firecracker had gone off in the room. JC's mouth dropped open. Beatrice and Ruby exchanged shocked glances.

"You know about Harriet?" said Beatrice, who recovered first.

"I'm not a fool. Fat might think so, but I know he's been tipping out on me. What's done in the dark *will* come to light. And shame on y'all for keeping his whore a secret. Well, I guess that's family for you."

"You knew it and took it. That was your decision," Ruby said.

"I loved him, but I ain't taking nothing no more. I found out loving a man more than yourself ain't natural. Especially when he's two-timing you."

JC slapped his knee and chuckled. "Still waters run deep, don't they, Zenobia?"

Zenobia rolled her eyes, but kept her mouth closed.

"Well, I'll be damn," he said to Beatrice while getting dressed for the funeral in their bedroom. "I think your brother's got a surprise coming. The woman he left behind isn't the woman he's coming home to."

***

JC's brief eulogy praised Queen Isabella Redmond for living a difficult life the best she could and for being a Christian woman, whose legacy would live on in her progeny. He prayed for her soul and said nothing about baby Rosetta, for which Beatrice and Ruby were grateful.

Beatrice walked to the red gash in the earth and dropped in a single rose from her garden. "This earth holds only my mother's body," she said. "But her beautiful soul has flown away. I'll always remember you, Mama. I'll always love you."

He asked Ruby, who was weeping, if she wanted to speak.

"My heart's too full," she said, having no way to describe the pain of losing her loving mother, her best friend.

After JC covered Isabella's grave, the family gathered in the house—Zenobia and Ruby in kitchen chairs and Beatrice intertwined in JC's arms on the broken sofa. The children played subdued at their feet. Ruby could feel her mother's presence in the house. She saw it in Beatrice, who settled their feud. Nothing could have brought that miracle about, except Isabella's forgiving spirit. Surely she was smiling down on them, including Mary Alice, wherever she was.

"Is the trouble over?" Ruby asked JC. They had begun referring to the riot as "the trouble," a euphemism that would survive in the family for a century.

"I think so. From everything I've heard, the city is pulling herself together. People want to forget and get on with making money."

"I mean for us, JC. Colored folks."

Beatrice cut in. "I don't think JC or anybody else can answer that. JC's been out and about asking around, but only time will tell."

"Wait a minute, Bea," JC said. "They have a so-called Committee of Ten that supposed to fix things, and they want colored leaders on it. Now that's a start. The rest is up to all of us. I'm writing an editorial about it."

"Good for you." Ruby thought about Lee and her mother—both dead because of the trouble. *To hell with the Committee of Ten.* "But when will it really end?"

"Never." Zenobia sniffed.

""Nothing lasts forever," Beatrice said. "Right, JC?"

"You're the one talking." JC carried the children, who had crumpled on the floor like sleepy marionettes, upstairs to bed.

Beatrice watched Ruby nursing Lovelee, and the peaceful scene encouraged her. This was not the end of her family, only the beginning. Mary Alice might be in New York, or she might come waltzing home alive, as she had before. She thought how fitting it was that Ruby said she'd decided not to return to Soperton. Ruby—who bragged about fighting off an attack on a trolley and strutting past state militia—had become a capable woman with a pretty face that masked her courage. She would flourish, no matter what. And Fat would be released the next day. How lucky he was to be alive. The riot had beaten them down, but the children of Isabella Redmond were strong and would prosper, not matter what.

"What do you think about letting Ruby stay here?" Beatrice asked JC before going to bed. "She can take care of the house and Mama's grave."

JC reminded her that they had interviewed a young university couple, who would make suitable tenants while they were in Ohio.

Beatrice shook her head. "My sister's a widow with an infant, and she can't go back to Lydell Alley. She needs a decent place to live, and you're refusing? That's not the JC I know."

"Look, Bea. It's late and I'm tired. If you want your sister to stay here, she can. Just don't make a big thing out of it, and stop pushing me."

Too agitated for real sleep, the family dozed off and on, until morning when smoke from smoldering house fires crept inside and peppered their eyes open.

Chapter Twenty-Five

Wednesday, September 26, 1906

The family left Brownsville for the downtown courthouse the next morning. They chose to wear black with touches of white in a lace collar or pocket handkerchief. Beatrice said it was important to look like good, decent people if they wanted due consideration from the authorities, especially the judge. She lent Ruby a dress, and Zenobia, who was two sizes larger, wore the shapeless frock she slept in, apparently to be defiant. Beatrice sniffed at her rumpled appearance and kept her distance. They left for court after dropping the children off with a neighbor.

JC had the money—two hundred dollars taken from a stash Fat buried in his backyard—for whatever arrangements. The sight of JC digging in her yard for secret money incensed Zenobia. First Fat had an outside woman and now hidden money. What would be next?

At the courtroom housed in the Tower on Decatur Street, colored men packed onto benches like bowling pins set up to be knocked down. In leg and wrist chains, Fat shuffled in with a long line of prisoners in sweat-stained shirts. His freckles were like dried specks of blood across his cheeks. Ruby thought his clenched jaw and burning eyes marked him out as defiant, which might kill his chances with the judge. Many of the other prisoners appeared to be afraid, and their eyes darted here and there. She counted fifty of them—young, middle-aged, and old—facing hearings that day. The prosecutor was the only lawyer present; defense attorneys were not allowed, even for the few who could afford them.

The courtroom reminded Ruby of the day Lee was convicted, which seemed like an eternity ago. Scared and pregnant, she had sat beside Isabella and cried. Lee kept a brave face on, but she knew him well and thought he was devastated inside.

The trial for Fat and the other prisoners moved as fast as one of those new automobile assembly lines, and Ruby's eyes focused on the stern-faced judge, who sometimes handed down sentences without looking up. Rob Branhan, a dark man, was brought trembling to the bench for assaulting two white women, given another court date, and dragged away. Will Mobley was fined ten dollars for insulting a white boy. Alonzo Humphries was ordered to pay five dollars for refusing a white man's orders to move on. Leon "Cat Man" Robinson was convicted of insolence. It was a court for misdemeanors and several men, charged with robbery, assault and attempted murder—all felonies—were ordered to another court for prosecution. The line of accused men appeared to be endless, and Ruby waited anxiously for Fat's turn.

She watched with suppressed rage as a bailiff led in a muscular white man, who sat alone on a bench behind the other prisoners. She recognized the white man as the brute she stabbed with her hatpin. He walked with a marked limp and appeared to be in pain, which she was glad to see. He was next, and he stood while the prosecutor charged him with vandalizing trolley cars. "A soft crime," Ruby thought, "nothing like the killing the bastard's really guilty of." The judge levied a seventy-five dollar fine and sentenced him to six months of probation. With a smirk that infuriated Ruby, the trolley guy limped out of the courtroom.

At midday Fat had not been called, and Ruby went out to feed her baby. She leaned against a wall in the restroom while Lovelee nursed. In spite of grieving for her mother and husband and worrying about Fat, she had held herself together all morning, but in the depressing toilet with no witnesses, tears poured out of her. Lovelee stopped feeding and wailed in sympathy with her mother. As Ruby wiped at her eyes with a cloth and hushed her baby, a young woman came in dressed in a head tie like a washerwoman. She raked her eyes over the contrasting complexions of the mother and baby and sucked air through her teeth before going behind a curtain to pee.

Ruby went hot. "Me and my baby ain't none of your damn business," she hollered and slammed out of the toilet.

Back in courtroom, she took a seat between Beatrice and JC. Zenobia sat two seats away. The frown on her sister-in-law's face told Ruby all she needed to know about the woman's prickly disposition.

"Everything OK?" Beatrice whispered, and Ruby nodded.

Fat was finally called, and he scrambled up from the bench. After he said that he was Elijah Redmond, Jr., of Brownsville, a court prosecutor stepped up and stated the charges: rioting, arson, assaulting a deputy, and resisting arrest. From the corner of her eye, Ruby saw with amazement that Zenobia's face had not lost its calm composure, and JC sat with his arm thrown nonchalantly across Beatrice's shoulders. *Look at these people, acting like they're at a recital. They must know something I don't.* After the prosecutor's statement of charges, the judge asked for a plea from Fat, who said he was not guilty. The only evidence against him was a cop's statement that the prosecutor read. The cop wrote that Fat had been the ring leader of the Brownsville rioters. He incited them to destroy property and attack the deputies, resulting in the death of an officer. Ruby held onto her seat, as Fat's knees buckled a bit and he hoisted himself straight.

Just when Ruby was sure a good outcome was impossible, a short red-faced man in a brown suit tiptoed to the front with a note for the prosecutor, who read it and passed it to the judge. As the judge read the note, his face fractured and turned crimson. He looked up and said nothing for what seemed like forever to Ruby. "This is bad," she whispered to Beatrice, who looked unruffled. After several minutes that included another consultation with the prosecutor, the judge sentenced Fat to a two-hundred-dollar fine and two years' probation. Ruby had to pinch her arm to keep from shouting with joy.

Still in chains, Fat looked relieved as he followed the bailiff out of the courtroom. Ruby caught his eye and thought she saw him wink.

It was only when JC paid the fine at the bursar's window, counting out two-hundred soiled dollars, that Ruby became suspicious. How did JC happen to have the exact amount of the fine? She figured it was better not to ask. He had connections with people who knew influential people, and she guessed he had worked it out that way. "I hope you're proud of JC," she whispered to Beatrice.

"Always," Beatrice replied and grinned.

Fat was free. They brought him to a small, littered anteroom, where his family waited. Zenobia stood with folded arms and kept her distance from her husband.

"What's wrong, baby?" he said. "I'm free."

Zenobia eye-balled him with a murderous expression and didn't answer.

"I'll talk to you later," Fat snapped.

On the street outside the jail, Ruby and Beatrice pasted kisses on Fat's broad face. Ruby kept touching his shoulder to be sure he really was free. JC shook his hand, pumping it up and down and beaming.

"Where's Mama and Mary Alice?" Fat asked, looking around.

"Wait till we're home," Beatrice said. "You've been through enough already."

Fat stopped walking to the wagon parked a half block from the tower and faced her. "What does that mean? I ask about Mama and Mary Alice, and you start hemming and hawing. Somebody better tell me something right now."

"We've got bad news," Beatrice said and told him that Isabella died during the trouble.

Fat's face turned as tight as a fist. "They killed her?"

"She had a stroke when they scared her," Beatrice said. "There wasn't a thing we could do."

"And Mary Alice?"

"We don't know where she is," JC said. "She might be with Miss Gwyneth or she's run away again. We don't believe she's hurt." He placed his hand on Fat's upper arm. "Nobody's seen her since the trouble; we're still looking."

Fat sank into quiet thought. Although jail was rough, hearing about his mother was far worse. He wanted to cry, but pride made him hold it in. His large body felt deflated, as he dragged himself to the wagon and climbed on.

As Ruby watched her brother, a hand touched her shoulder, and she turned to face Ethan from the dry goods store.

"You're a hard lady to find," he said, smiling. "I've looked high and low since the other night."

JC cleared his throat and threw an amused glance at Ruby, who screwed up her face. He and Beatrice then looked at Ethan with obvious curiosity.

"Oh, I forgot my manners," Ruby said and introduced Ethan as the "angel," who rescued her.

They shook hands all around, except for Fat and Zenobia, who sat on the wagon seat with a mile between them and took no notice of Ethan.

Ruby pulled her friend aside. "What you doing here?"

"I came to pick up papers for the shop. Mr. Ahmed's ready to sell. He said he saw enough war in his country to last the rest of his life, and the riot was too much." Ethan's eyes flickered with excitement. "Anyway he's moving on. He didn't say where. Since they say you shouldn't look a gift horse in the mouth, I didn't press him."

Ruby's heart warmed as she listened, but she wasn't ready for a relationship so soon after Lee's death. Although she saw that Ethan was friendly, the way a man is when he's interested, she might never want another man as much as Lee. She looked away from his copper skin glowing in the sunlight like a beacon. It was time to bury her husband and make a home for her baby. If Ethan was willing to wait until she was ready, then something good might happen. But not now.

She shifted Lovelee from one arm to the other. "Well it's nice seeing you again," she said, preparing to move on. "It's time for us to go."

"I don't see anybody rushing but you," JC said, laughing and looking at the others. "Y'all in a hurry?"

"Stop it, JC," Beatrice said, even though she sounded amused. "You play too much."

"I'm ready to go." Fat's voice was harsh.

"In a minute," Ruby said.

"Hold your horse, man," JC said. "Can't you see your sister is taking care of business?"

Ethan asked for Ruby's address and phone number. He offered to hold Lovelee to free her hands, and she let him take her. Her new address—Beatrice's house—thankfully was not in an alley and she scribbled it on a paper for him.

Watching Ethan walk back to the courthouse, she had renewed hope. "We'll see," she thought. "God willing, we will see." She climbed into the wagon with her nursing baby and the rest of her family for the ride to Brownsville.

On the way, the wagon struck a rock in the road, which jostled them, and Ruby's nipple slipped from Lovelee's lips. Before Ruby guided it back in place, a *celestial finger pressed the baby's philtrum, the indentation in her upper lip that served as a reminder to keep the things she'd heard on the other side to herself. The trouble is over, little one, a voice said. Now you must run on and see what the end will be.*

Chapter Twenty-Six

Sunday, September 30, 1906

Fat and Zenobia had battled each other all night, and they were still at it when the sun rose and church bells called the faithful. He had taken up his war station in the back bedroom and she was at hers in the kitchen. Across the house, they fired recriminations. They had been fighting, off and on, since he left jail, and neither was willing to give in or call a truce.

The fight, of course, was about his outside woman—Harriett. Zenobia's attitude was incomprehensible to Fat, who didn't understand how a woman could know about her husband's affair, say nothing for years, and then explode after the other woman left town. He couldn't say what had set Zenobia off, where she had gotten the balls to get in his face and cuss him out, as she had several times over the past week. Back-door man, two-timing punk, and lying, double crossing bastard, were among nasty things she called him. Who was the crazy woman sharing his bed and who poured bitch into her? She wasn't acting as a wife should. Everything a woman could want in food, clothing, and shelter, he had provided and there she was, with her ungrateful self, threatening to leave him. And take his children. Hell no, he thundered, his children were not going anywhere, and if she tried to take them, he would track her to the edge of the world. He knew it was dramatic, but he hoped she understood this wasn't a show, and he wasn't selling wolf tickets..

As for having an affair, Fat admitted nothing. Only a foolish man would do such a thing, and he wasn't anybody's fool.

But he was coming undone and knew it. Friday night in the kitchen, he raised his hand after Zenobia refused to cook his dinner. "Lay your hands on me and this will be the sorriest day of your sorry life," she said and darted to the stove for her cast-iron skillet. Of course, he didn't hit her; he never had and never would, even though the woman was trying his patience. He only wanted to scare her, but the new Zenobia wouldn't scare. She demanded a promise of fidelity, and when he promised, she said, "I don't believe your lying ass."

Funny, how a man could lie and juggle a woman and a wife for years, and then when he told the truth, his wife refused to believe him. What was he supposed to do with that?

"Ten years, ten long years," she kept saying. "I gave you everything, and you didn't give me nothing but a long way to go and a short time to get there."

The day of his release from the Tower, he ran to their bedroom and cried himself dry about Isabella, while Zenobia put the boys to bed. She let him cry alone, which was the way he wanted it at first, but later when they were in bed, he noticed how frigid she was and asked a question that triggered the first shot in their war: "What's wrong with you?" He shuddered, remembering her response. He hadn't known she knew how to cuss. What the hell was wrong with the woman; didn't she know Harriet was long gone? Didn't she realize he wasn't in love with Harriet, that he loved her?

Shaving for church, he examined his face in the mirror. He was still a young man with a face that was a bit too serious, but that helped in his business. In a way, he was lucky, because he still had his wife and children. Thinking about them sustained him while he was in jail. Now if only Zenobia would talk sense, but she was as much a puzzle as the other women in his life.

***

His mother died loving his father, who treated her as his footstool, and Fat never understood her devotion to a man like that. Thoughts of Eli rankled his blood, but as the man of the family, he had to honor his mother's last wish and bring the old man home. Beatrice relayed Isabella's surprising request and seemed to know more than she would tell. She was another one, a real mystery sometimes, with her tight-lipped, bossy self. The old man would have to live with him, because Ruby, who had plenty of room in Beatrice's house, said she didn't care what Isabella wanted; she couldn't live with Satan.

He didn't know Mary Alice's whereabouts. He phoned Miss Forester a few days back, and she said his sister left her house alive and well, but she didn't know her whereabouts. "If she contacts you, please let her know Mama passed away," he said, only half believing Forester's story. The woman and Mary Alice were friends, and she probably knew a lot more. Mary Alice was another one, who was hard to figure out, running off whenever she felt like it. With problems of his own, he gave up trying to find her.

He phoned Florette's house his first night out of jail and spoke to the old man, who sounded truly sad when he told him Isabella was gone. Fat asked, but again Eli wouldn't say why he left home in the first place. In a week, Fat would take the train to Chattanooga, his first trip there in ten years, and collect his father. He asked Zenobia what she thought about Eli.

"I don't care," she said.

She had changed too much. Two days in jail and he came home to a hell raiser, to a woman who was edgier than Beatrice if that was possible.

Ruby wanted to bury Lee before Beatrice left for Ohio. JC was too worn out to go for the body, so Fat went and found it near the train station, where she said it would be. Angered by the body's condition—lying in congealed blood and body fluids, swollen to bursting and covered with flies—Fat swore under his breath. He wondered why a man like Lee, a standup guy in anybody's book, had to die and fester in the street like an animal. He spread a tarp on the ground and called a drunk from the street to help. Somehow, they rolled the body into the tarp and he drove it to Brownsville. He stood with Ruby and the rest of his family at the backyard-gravesite. At her request, he read from Psalm 121: "The Lord shall preserve thee from all evil; he shall preserve thy soul." After praying for Lee's soul, Fat covered the grave, and led his distraught sister back to the house. "Her tears will dry up," he thought. "She's strong and a mother now, and she'll go on just like Mama did."

But as for Zenobia, who stood on the far side of the yard with her hands on her hips, Fat thought he'd never understand that she-devil.

After the burial, Beatrice said they wouldn't be back. Atlanta wasn't right for them, especially their daughter, who was still afraid of bad men breaking into their house again. JC stood mute beside his wife as she spoke for their family.

Fat wondered how JC could stand it. Beatrice was his sister, and he loved her, but what did she mean saying things like that and calling the shots all by herself? Although JC told him it was a "joint decision," it didn't sound that way. Fat shook his head to clear it. The man had a good teaching job, and when things settled down, there would be promotions for him at the university, yet he was willing to throw it away, because a woman said so. Trying to figure JC's angle, Fat invited him for farewell drinks at a joint in the Decatur woods. At the end of their all-night celebration, his brother-in-law seemed content, maybe even happy, but Fat didn't understand him any better. .

The next afternoon, Fat took Beatrice's family to Terminal Station for the train to Ohio. On the way, he tried to talk some sense into JC's head.

"Man, I know what you're trying to say, but my goal is to make my wife happy," JC said. "And she tries to make me happy. We're a team, regardless of how it looks to somebody peeping in."

It didn't make sense to Fat, who believed a man was either the boss in his house or a mouse.

"Fat, you better mind your own business," Beatrice said. "You have your hands full with Zenobia."

"Watch out brother, Bea's fired up." JC chuckled.

Fat helped them take their bags to the side door of the station, the one for colored passengers. Wondering when he would see them again, he kissed his sister and niece. After shaking JC's hand, he left them on the platform waiting for their train. He was sure they would return, because his Bible didn't say Ohio was the Promised Land. One day, wayfarers in the north might smell trouble in the air and come home again.

***

A church bell rang somewhere, and Fat hurried into his clothes and out to the kitchen where Zenobia was having coffee. Half-eaten pancakes soaked up syrup on the boys' plates, and Fat could hear them playing in their bedroom.

"Why ain't you dressed for church?" he asked.

Zenobia pulled her yellow chenille robe together. "I ain't going. I'm tired of watching you play deacon when you ain't nothing but a cheating devil."

"Suit yourself." Fat felt coiled inside but calmly poured a cup of coffee. He tasted the coffee, which was cold, and emptied the cup in the sink.

As he started for the door, Zenobia said, "I won't be here when you get back."

"I said suit yourself." Fat's heart was thumping hard enough to break his ribcage. He hadn't thought that she would leave. He loved her; she couldn't leave.

"I didn't know all along about you and that girl," she said. "I lied, because I felt foolish not knowing what was going on in my own house. Somebody from church told me right before the trouble."

"Somebody from church—who?"

"You sound surprised. Everybody knew about it."

"Somebody told you a lie to break the peace in your home. What's her name?"

"*His* name, Fat. It was a man—one of those guys in that meeting—and we both know he wasn't lying."

Fat's mind raced through the names of men at the meeting and settled on Deacon Johnson, who hadn't wanted him to be the leader. Yes, he had to be the one, not that Fat could do anything about it. As a deacon, he couldn't knock the hell out of the old fool, but he would give him a piece of his mind.

Maybe if he told Zenobia that he didn't love Harriet, it might work. She was only somebody to play with. The girl had wheels in her hips, lust on her lips, like the old song went, and she fooled him. But if he said that, Zenobia might knock his brains out with her skillet. He had to keep denying the affair. Right now his wife was bluffing, but she might really leave if he admitted it.

"The man was lying, Zenobia. He's jealous of us. You know people get jealous when they see something good. Come on, baby, you know I love you."

"Don't try to fool me, Fat." Zenobia's lower lip trembled, because she wanted to believe him. She loved him, and leaving wouldn't make her happy, but she couldn't let him keep taking advantage of her. He had to give her a reason to stay.

Fat saw tears in her eyes and hoped he had broken through. If he came home every night, like he was supposed to, and showed her how much he loved her, she might give him another chance. "I love you, Zenobia. I know you're hurting, and maybe I caused it, but all I can do is love you and nobody else." He brushed a tear from her cheek with his fingers.

Zenobia jerk her head away. "Go straight to hell, Fat."

Fat drove to church through streets that had returned to normal Sunday morning activity. Families rode in wagons and carriages or strolled to church in their best clothes. A boy throwing newspapers on front porches waved at him. As he parked his wagon, he heard the choir firing up a spiritual. "Go Down Moses."

When Israel was in Egypt land
Let my people go
Oppressed so hard they could not stand
Let my people go.

With heavy footsteps, he took his place in the line of dark-suited deacons marching in. Faces he had seen every Sunday morning for a decade were missing. Gone to jail, Chicago, New York, or to the grave, the deacon behind him said, and Fat's walk slowed. Brooding, he took a seat on a front pew and half-listened to the preacher's fantastical sermon about not inviting racial animosity with bad behavior.

Afterwards, he walked to his wagon, and a deacon, Brother Royal Adams, hailed him. Fat had known the man for years and respected him as an elder. He slowed down and doffed his hat. "Brother Adams."

"Glad to see you, boy, glad to see you," said Adams, who had a habit of repeating himself. When he hadn't shown up at the meeting before the trouble, Fat was relieved, because anything Brother Adams had to say would take twice as long as it should. "Glad to see you're alive and well. It's a sin and a shame what happened here, a sin and a shame."

In no mood to waste time discussing the trouble, Fat wanted to hurry back to Zenobia—if she hadn't left him. He figured he would know as soon as he opened the door and dinner wasn't on the stove. Zenobia always prepared Sunday dinner the night before—a feast of ham, baked chicken, garden vegetables, cake, and rolls. Since she hadn't gone to church, she should be cooking right then. He walked to his wagon and patted his horse's rump. "Glad to see you, too, deacon," he said, grabbing the reins from the hitching post. "I'm in a bit of a hurry…"

"This won't take but a minute, just a minute," Adams said. "I heard you had some trouble with your place of business that burned down, burned clean to the ground."

His lunchroom was destroyed in the trouble, and he was looking for somewhere to reopen. The Committee had turned Peters, Decatur, and other streets into white-only areas, where a colored man couldn't own a shoe-shine stand. The two hundred JC used to bail him out left him with a fortune of fifty bucks. He was in a panic to find a place and fast.

"Sure did," Fat said, thinking about ways to escape. He had business at home to take care of, and Adams was in the way.

"Well, seeing as how you're a family man, and all, I thought you might be interested in relocating, relocating on Auburn Avenue. That's where the smart cats are going, and I've got a place to rent. I'm too old to work it, too darn old."

Fat's face brightened. He knew Auburn, where several colored men had good businesses, and it was far enough away from Peters Street and the downtown business district. "How much you want for rent?"

"Why don't you take a look? Just look at it first."

Fat agreed to ride to Auburn in the deacon's carriage and come back for his wagon. Within minutes they arrived at the storefront and Fat followed Adams inside. The place was dusty, needed painting, and had a plate-size hole in the back wall. But being a man who was always open to possibilities, Fat allowed the deacon to show him how a lunch counter and chairs would fit perfectly. He showed him a shed in back that could serve as a kitchen for ribs, chicken, whatever menu he wanted. "Everything has to be legit, though, totally legit," he said. "No numbers or whiskey. None of that stuff."

Fat looked at him with innocent eyes. "You don't have to worry about that with me," he said, which was the truth, because he was on probation and couldn't risk it.

The deacon's first figure was three times more than Fat could pay, so they haggled on the ride back to the church. Fat had made enough deals with tough moonshiners to know when his opponent was weakening, and seeing that the deacon wasn't dealing from a position of strength, he held his ground.

"OK. Ten dollars a month and it's a deal. How's that for a deal?" the deacon said. He extended his hand, which Fat shook and jumped on his wagon.

He arrived on his street in time to see a wagon pull away from Ruby's house and remembered that it belonged to Ethan. He promised himself to talk to his sister about the scandalous nature of such a visit, however innocent it might be, so soon after burying her husband.

Wasting no time, he drove on to his house. Zenobia could be halfway to her mother's and he had things to say, apologies to make. He sat on the wagon seat for a minute, looking at the drawn shades. His ears strained but didn't hear a sound. "It's over. She's gone," he thought. "And I bet she took my children. Damn." He climbed down and opened the door. The aroma of frying chicken rushed out, and curled into his nostrils like oxygen. Happiness spread across his face, and he went to the kitchen, lifted Zenobia up and whispered an apology into her ear. After dinner, they talked for a long time. "My job is to make you happy," he said, not realizing he had borrowed the loving words from JC.

Chapter Twenty-Seven

Friday, October 5, 1906

In San Francisco, Mary Alice had finished her shift as a waitress in a tea room and was at dinner with a young gentleman she met her first day on the job. He was a businessman, in the city for a month to manage his properties, which were damaged in the earthquake. Under an invented name that was nothing like her real one, she had been out with him every night since then. They preferred quiet dinners in elegant restaurants, which were rare in a city that was rebuilding.

In the middle of their conversation about growing Cymbidium orchids on his estate in San Diego, Mary Alice's eyes filled with tears. Her companion covered her hand with soft, pink fingers and spoke in a polished manner he acquired in a New England prep school.

His touch and soft gray eyes were reassuring. "Tell me what's wrong, my little southern belle." Her accent had attracted him from the beginning, and he never tired of hearing it.

"Oh, honey child, I received a letter. A dear friend passed away," Mary Alice drawled. She had to be careful; she'd told him her family was dead.

Although pictures of sick Isabella haunted Mary Alice and she worried beyond measure about her mother, she hadn't contacted anybody in Atlanta since arriving in the city. So in a state of depression the night before, she phoned Gwyneth Forester.

"I'm sorry, Mary Alice, your brother phoned and there's terrible news. Dear…your mother passed away," Gwyneth said.

Although Gwyneth said she didn't know how Isabella died, Mary Alice thought the riot must have been the reason. The San Francisco newspapers had been full of gruesome details about Atlanta. She leaned against the wall in the hallway of her rooming house and wept. When Gwyneth asked for her phone number, she said she was using a kind acquaintance's phone—a one-time deal.

Her dinner companion squeezed her hand. "You must've been very close to your friend. I'm so sorry."

Blinking back tears, she nodded and signaled for a refill of wine, a Chardonnay that cost as much as her weekly tips. When the waitress, a bronze woman, thick in the waist, sauntered over with a knowing smile, Mary Alice recognized the look, having seen it many times in New York. And she responded with cool eyes that denied everything.

Author's Note

The author enjoys book clubs and describes them as "priceless to me as a writer." To schedule the author for book clubs or other discussion groups, free of charge, please contact her: asinshakespeare@gmail.com.

96374092R00176

Made in the USA
Columbia, SC
29 May 2018